C000050723

CHRISTOPH

THE CASE OF THE
THREE-RING PUZZLE

CHRISTOPHER BUSH was born Charlie Christmas Bush in Norfolk in 1885. His father was a farm labourer and his mother a milliner. In the early years of his childhood he lived with his aunt and uncle in London before returning to Norfolk aged seven, later winning a scholarship to Thetford Grammar School.

As an adult, Bush worked as a schoolmaster for 27 years, pausing only to fight in World War One, until retiring aged 46 in 1931 to be a full-time novelist. His first novel featuring the eccentric Ludovic Travers was published in 1926, and was followed by 62 additional Travers mysteries. These are all to be republished by Dean Street Press.

Christopher Bush fought again in World War Two, and was elected a member of the prestigious Detection Club.

He died in 1973.

CHRISTOPHER BUSH

THE CASE OF THE THREE-RING PUZZLE

With an introduction
by Curtis Evans

DEAN STREET PRESS

INTRODUCTION

Rosalind. If it be true that good wine needs no bush [i.e., advertising], 'tis true that a good play needs no epilogue. Yet to good wine, they do use good bushes, and good plays prove the better by the help of good epilogues.

—SHAKESPEARE, Epilogue, *As You Like It*

THE decade of the 1960s saw the sun finally begin to set on that storied generation which between the First and Second World Wars gave us detective fiction's Golden Age. Taking account of both deaths and retirements, by the late Sixties only a bare half-dozen pre-World War Two members of the Detection Club were still plying their deliciously deceptive craft: Agatha Christie, Anthony Gilbert (Lucy Beatrice Malleson), Gladys Mitchell, John Dickson Carr, Nicholas Blake and Christopher Bush, the subject of this introduction. Bush himself would pass away, at the age of eighty-seven, in 1973, having published, at the age of eighty-two, his sixty-third Ludovic Travers detective novel, *The Case of the Prodigal Daughter*, in the United Kingdom in the spring of 1968.

In the United States Bush's final detective novel did not appear until late November 1969, about four months after the horrific Manson murders in the tarnished Golden State of California. Implicating the triple terrors of sex, drugs and rock and roll (not to mention almost inconceivably bestial violence), the Manson slayings could not have strayed farther from the whimsically escapist "death as a game" aesthetic of Golden Age of detective fiction. Increasingly in the decade capable of producing psyche-delic psychopaths like Charles Manson and his "family," the few remaining survivors of the Golden Age of detective fiction increasingly deemed themselves men and women far out of time. In his detective fiction John Dickson Carr, an incurable roman-tic, prudently beat a retreat from the present into the pleasanter pages of the past, setting his tales in bygone historical eras where he felt vastly more at home. With varying success Agatha Christie made a brave effort to stay abreast of the times (*Third Girl*, *Endless Night*), but ultimately her strivings to understand what was going on around her collapsed into the utter incoherence of *Passenger to Frankfurt* and *Postern of Fate*, by general consensus the worst mystery novels that Dame Agatha ever put down on paper.

In his detective fiction Christopher Bush, who was not quite two years older than Christie, managed rather better than the Queen of Crime to keep up with all the unsettling goings-on around him, while never forswearing the Golden Age article of faith that the primary purpose of a crime writer is pleasingly to puzzle his/her readers. And, in contrast with Christie and Carr, Bush knew when it was time to lay down his pen (or turn off his dictation machine, as the case may be), thereby allowing him to make his exit from the stage on a comparatively high note. Indeed, Christopher Bush's concluding baker's dozen of detective novels, which he published between 1957 and 1968 (and which have now been reprinted, after more than a half-century, by Dean Street Press), makes a generally fine epilogue, or coda, to the author's impressive corpus of crime fiction, which first began to see the light of day way back in the jubilant Jazz Age. These are, readers will find, "good bushes" (to punningly borrow from Shakespeare), providing them with ample intelligent detective entertainment as Bush's longtime series sleuth Ludovic Travers, in the luminous twilight of his career, makes his final forays into ingenious criminal investigation.

*

In the last thirteen Ludovic Travers mystery novels, Travers' *entrée* to his cases continues to come through his ownership of the Broad Street Detective Agency. Besides Travers we also regularly encounter his elegant wife, Bernice (although sometimes his independent-minded spouse is away on excursions of her own), his proverbially loyal secretary, Bertha Munney, his top Broad Street op, Hallows (another one named French, presumably inspired by Bush's late Detection Club colleague Freeman Wills Crofts, pops up occasionally), John Hill of the United Assurance

Agency, who brings Travers many of his cases, and Scotland Yard's Inspector Jewle and Sergeant Matthews, who after the first of these final novels, *The Case of the Treble Twist* (in the U.S. *Triple Twist*), are promoted, respectively, to Superintendent and Inspector. (The Yard's ex-Superintendent George Wharton, now firmly retired from any form of investigative work whatsoever, is mentioned just once by Ludo, when, in *The Case of the Dead Man Gone,* he passingly imparts that he and Wharton recently had lunch together.)

For all practical purposes Travers, who during the Golden Age was a classic gentleman amateur snooper like Philo Vance and Lord Peter Wimsey, now functions fully as a professional private eye—although one, to be sure, who is rather posher than the rest. While some reviewers referred to Travers as England's Philip Marlowe, in fact he little resembles the general run of love and leave 'em/hate and beat 'em brand of brutish American P.I.'s, favoring a nice cup of coffee (a post-war change from tea), a good pipe and the occasional spot of sherry to the frequent snatches of liquor and cigarettes favored by most of his American brethren and remaining faithful to his spouse despite encountering a succession of sexy women, not all of them, shall we say, virtuously inclined.

This was a formula which throughout the period maintained a devoted audience on both sides of the Atlantic consisting, one surmises, of readers (including crime writers Anthony Berkeley, Nicholas Blake and the late Alan Hunter, creator of Inspector George Gently) who preferred their detectives something less than hard-boiled. Travers himself sneers at the hugely popular (and psychotically violent) postwar American private eye Mike Hammer, commenting of an American couple in *The Case of the Treble Twist*: "She was a woman of considerable culture; his ran about as far as Mickey Spillane" [a withering reference to Mike Hammer's creator]. Yet despite his manifest disdain for Mike Hammer, an ugly American if ever there were one, Christopher Bush and his wife Florence in the spring of 1957 had traveled to New York aboard the RMS *Queen Elizabeth*, and references by him to both the United States and Canada became more frequent in the books which followed this trip.

Certainly *The Case of the Treble Twist* (1957) features tough customers and an exceptionally cruel murder, yet it is also one of Bush's most ingeniously contrived cases from the Fifties, full of charm, treacherous deception and, yes, plenty of twists, including one that is a real sockaroo (to borrow, as Bush occasionally did, from American idiom). Similarly clever is *The Case of the Running Man* (1958), which draws, as several earlier Bush books had, on the author's profound love and knowledge of antiques. By this time Bush and his wife, their coffers having burgeoned from the proceeds of his successful mysteries, resided in the quaint medieval market town of Lavenham, Suffolk at the Great House, a splendidly decorated fourteenth-century structure with an elegant Georgian-era façade which he and Florence purchased in 1953 and resided in until their deaths. The dashing author, whom in 1967 *Chicago Tribune* mystery reviewer Alice Crombie swooningly dubbed "one of the handsomest mystery writers on either side of the Channel or Atlantic," also drove a Jaguar, beloved by James Bond films of late, well into his eighties.

The Case of the Running Man includes that Golden Age detective fiction staple, a family tree, but more originally the novel features as a major character a black American man, Sam, the devoted chauffeur of the wealthy murder victim. Sam, who reminds Ludovic Travers of Rochester, "Jack Benny's factotum of television and radio," is an interesting and sincerely treated individual, although as Anthony Boucher amusingly pronounced at the time in the *New York Times Book Review*, he speaks "a dialect never heard by mortal ear"—an odd compounding of "American Negro" and London cockney.

The Case of the Careless Thief (1959) takes Ludo to Sandbeach, "the Blackpool of the South Coast," as the American jacket blurb puts it, with "a dozen hotels, a race track, a dog track, a music hall and two enormous dance halls." Anthony Boucher deemed this hard-hitting, tricky tale, which draws to strong effect on contemporary events in England, "one of Ludovic Travers' best cases."

Likewise hard-hitting are *The Case of the Sapphire Brooch* (1960) and *The Case of the Extra Grave* (1961), complex tales of murderous mésalliances with memorably grim conclusions. The plot of *The Case of the Dead Man Gone* (1961) topically involves refugee relief groups, while *The Case of the Heavenly Twin* (1963) opens with a case of a creative criminal couple forging American Express Travelers Checks, concerning which Americans of a certain age will recall actor Karl Malden sternly enjoining, in a long-running television advertising campaign: "Don't leave home without them." In contrast with many of his crime writing contemporaries (judging from the tone of their work), Bush actually learned to watch and enjoy television, although in *The Case of The Three-Ring Puzzle*, a tale of violently escalating intrigue, Travers dryly references Scottish philosopher Thomas Carlyle's famous observation that England's population consisted of "mostly fools" when he comments: "I guess he wasn't too far out at that. But rather remarkable an estimate perhaps, considering that in his day there were no television commercials."

Of Bush's final five Ludovic Travers detective novels, published between 1964 and 1968, when the Western World, in the eyes of many, was going from whimsically mod to utterly mad, the best are, in my estimation, the cases of *The Jumbo Sandwich* (1965), *The Good Employer* (1966) and *The Prodigal Daughter* (1968). In *Sandwich* a crisp case of a defrauded (and jilted) gentry lady friend of Ludo's metamorphoses into a smorgasbord of, as the American book jacket puts it, "blackmail, black magic, a black sheep, and murder." It all culminates in a confrontation on a lonely Riviera beach in France, setting of some of Ludovic Travers' earliest cases, between Ludo and a desperate killer, in which Bernice plays an unexpectedly active part. Ludo again travels to France in the highly classic *Employer*, which draws most engagingly on the sleuth's (and the author's) dabbling in the world of art and is dedicated to his distinguished Lavenham artist friends, the couple Reginald and Rosalie Brill, who resided next door to Bush and his wife at the fourteenth-century Little Hall, then an art student hostel for which the Brills served as guardians. In *The Guardian* Francis Iles (aka Golden Age crime writer Anthony Berkeley) pronounced that *Employer* represented Bush "at his most ingenious."

Finally, in *Daughter* Travers finds himself tasked with recovering the absconded teenage offspring of domineering Dora Marport, sober-sided head of the organization Home and Family, which is righteously devoted to "the fostering, so to speak, of family life as the stoutest bulwark against the encroachment of ever-more numerous hostile forces: sex and violence in literature, films and on television; pornography generally, and the erosion of responsibility and the capability for sacrifice by the welfare state." Can Travers, a Great War veteran who made his debut in detective fiction in 1926, bridge the generation gap in late-Sixties London? Ludo may prefer Bach to the Beatles, but in this, the last of his recorded cases, he proves more "with it" than one might have expected. All in all, *Daughter* makes a rewarding finish to one of the longest-running and most noteworthy sleuth series in British detective fiction.

Curtis Evans

1
VANISHED SUITOR

I WOULDN'T go so far as to say I was rocked back on my heels when Bertha Munney buzzed through from her small office just off the reception room and told me that Jedmont wanted to see me. Bertha's been with us at the Broad Street Detective Agency for most of her life and there's almost nothing about the business that she doesn't know, and when she has a certain tone of voice as she announces a possible client, I, and Norris the general manager, have learned to be on the alert. For one thing, that possible client is normally within earshot.

As I said, I wasn't actually staggered to hear that Brian Jedmont wanted to consult us, but I was definitely most surprised. Let me tell you about him and then you'll know why. This call on us, by the way, was on a Monday early in March, 1956.

In our business we have quite a lot of photographic work. You acquire from a client, for instance, a picture of this or that and you need extra copies. Someone—I think it was Hallows, our senior operative—recommended Jedmont to us. That was around 1950 when Jedmont was twenty-six and trying, from a small office not far from us, to build up a business. We found him both reliable and obliging.

I can't say I liked him. About a man who's obviously deter- mined to get on at any cost there's always something that's not exactly engaging. It was that that led to our first skirmish. It came to our notice that he'd had a new business card printed with a list of clients on the back: among them the Agency. That's almost the last way in which we want attention called to ourselves, so I asked him to come and see me. I didn't like his off-hand attitude and his idea that he was doing us a favour, but I insisted that our name be removed.

To announce "Didn't I tell you so?" can be an atom bomb in the matter of personal relationships, and I never publicised the fact that my instinct had been right about Jedmont from the very start. Everyone else, including Bertha, liked him. I thought him ingratiating but she thought he had very nice manners. He was certainly an attractive type: tall, nicely featured, with beautiful teeth and charmingly adjusted hair; just the kind, in fact, to appeal to quite a lot of women. I will say that he knew his job. We've never had better work and we've employed some good men in our time.

This isn't exactly the saga of Brian Jedmont, but it is essential that you know as much about him as I did at the time. The break came some two years later when he was embarrassingly behind on an important job. I went to see him at a new office he'd acquired just off Fleet Street. He'd changed a lot in other ways. What little success he'd had had gone to his head and, though I pride myself on being as suave and tactful as most, he chose to take offence: told me none too politely that I was far from being his only client and, if I wasn't satisfied, there were plenty of other people to whom I could take what in his opinion were trivial jobs. I merely told him that was an excellent idea and left.

A year later he was a press photographer for the *Record* and whether or not he was still doing private work as a side line I didn't know. I think that must have been the case since he was sacked from the *Record* a couple of years later. Hallows was interested and did some ferreting in Fleet Street, but all he could learn was that Jedmont had tried to make a deal with another paper in the matter of some photographic scoop.

So Jedmont went back to free-lancing. He couldn't have been doing very well because after a few months he approached Bertha surreptitiously and suggested that she let me know he'd be glad to do our work again. By then he'd gone back to yet another cubby-hole of an office, this time in one of those small squares off Chancery Lane. I dropped him a polite note saying we'd made other arrangements with which we were perfectly satisfied. Soon afterwards he managed to see Bertha again, and was quite abusive. That was the last I heard of him till that March morning of 1956 when Bertha was telling me he wanted to see me. Me personally, that was: not Norris.

*

I hope I didn't twitch a single belligerent muscle when Bertha showed him in. He hadn't changed too much, except in his attitude, since I'd seen him last: quite presentable, slickly mannered and with a memory conveniently short about the last time we'd met. I got him seated and held my lighter for the cigarette.

"How're things with you these days, Mr. Jedmont?"

"Not too bad," he said. "You knew I'd left the *Record*?"

"I did hear something."

He gave me a quick look at that. "Just knew that you'd left," I added.

"It's just that I don't like taking too many orders from too many people," he told me. Then, somewhat wistfully: "I guess I was always cut out to work on my own. A man's got to be himself, if you know what I mean."

I said I did, then bluntly brought him round to the reason for that morning's call.

"I'd like you to do a job for me," he said. "You're the best in the business. The most trustworthy too, if I may say so."

"You may," I told him. "But don't let the others hear you. Also, there's something else you may not know. We may not be the best but we're definitely the most expensive. Scrupulously trustworthy as you so kindly said, but we're far from cheap."

"I guessed that. But this is quite a short job. Highly important to me or I wouldn't be here."

You could tell from the smooth way he outlined things that he'd done quite a bit of rehearsing. It was definitely not a matter for the police, he said, but a very private enquiry. Later on the police might take a hand but that would be determined by what I discovered. The situation, briefly, was this.

He had an aunt, his late father's widowed sister, a Mrs. Daniel Coome. She'd been left pretty well-off and was spending her time in various hotels. He himself was the only relative. Since the previous November she'd been staying on the South Coast, at the Farina Hotel, Sandford, and from time to time he'd seen her there at weekends. During the last two visits he'd had suspicions about her relationship with another guest at the hotel, a man named

Hubert Courtney. This Courtney was a man of about forty, distinguished looking, very British, but with a slight American accent. He was supposed to have big oil interests in the States, and was ostensibly at the hotel—quite an expensive one, by the way—recuperating after some arduous oil exploration work in Jordan.

"You think he's planning to marry your aunt?" I said. "What's she actually like?"

"The fluffy, doll-headed type," he told me. "Spends half her time in beauty parlours. She's well over fifty, but you wouldn't take her for that. He's not her type. What he's after is her money and she's just the credulous type to let him have it without a trip up the aisle. I'm dead sure of all this, Mr. Travers. I know it from what she's let drop and what she hasn't. You've got to take my word for it. I know she's intending to realise some securities and if she isn't giving the proceeds to him to invest in some non-existent oil company, then you can have every penny in the world I've got. It's the old racket. He's right out of her class, as I said, so why else should he be making himself indispensable? Taking her out here and taking her out there, and never letting her pay a penny. According to the papers, that racket's been worked a lot lately and this Courtney's in it up to the neck, so that's what I'd like you to do. Run your eye over him yourself and form your own opinion."

He gave himself a kind of congratulatory nod. It also announced that now I knew.

"I see. But why wouldn't the police do the job far more efficiently?"

"I'll tell you the absolute truth," he said. "When you get the evidence that Courtney's a crook, I'd like to present it to my aunt as if I'd found it myself. You know, as if I'd had her interests at heart all along and had sacrificed my time and so on. If that doesn't make her grateful, what will?"

"I get the point," I told him.

I stretched out my long legs and gazed contemplatively at the ceiling. A few seconds and I straightened up again.

"I'll be blunt," I told him. "A week should settle things one way or the other. I'll quote you all-in terms: fifty pounds advance and fifty pounds payable Monday next provided we've worked to your satisfaction."

I was almost staggered when he told me promptly that that was fair enough. Even more surprising was his immediate production of the whole hundred, in five-pound notes.

"I'd feel better if you'd hold on to the whole lot," he told me. "If things pan out well and there should be anything to come, I know I can trust you."

I disillusioned him about there being anything to return. We'd be putting in a week's work and his hundred pounds was only a fair payment. We'd consider a repayment only if something miraculous unmasked Courtney in double-quick time, and that wasn't something on which he'd be wise to count. At any rate I had a contract drawn up to his apparent satisfaction, which specified among other things that he wasn't to communicate with his aunt during the next seven days and that if she communicated with him, then he was immediately to inform us. I also agreed verbally to be at the Sandford hotel the following afternoon. A minute or two later I was showing him out.

Immediately after lunch Hallows came in from another job and I outlined the case. If there's a better operative in town I've yet to meet him. For one thing, he likes his work, which is why a man of his education who could have made quite a career in one of the professions has been with the Broad Street Detective Agency almost the whole of his forty working years. I think of him as much as a friend as an employee.

As I said, I told him all I knew about the case. He smiled rather cynically at the idea of Jedmont's using us to ingratiate himself with his aunt. "Wonder where he got the money from?"

"Why?" I said. "Hasn't he got that kind of money?"

"Not from what I've heard lately," he told me. "Still, maybe he's sold one of his cameras."

I'd booked a room at the Farina for myself under the name of Haire. It's my wife's maiden name, not that that matters. Hallows rang and booked himself a room under the name of Hall. We'd make our separate ways in our own cars the next morning. A few minutes' discussion of our different roles and he left. I rang the Yard and was lucky enough to get my old friend, Superintendent Jewle.

Years ago I did a lot of work in conjunction with the Yard, and while I must have made quite a few enemies, I made an awful lot of friends. I worked on many cases with Jewle and, even if we're never the colleagues of old, we trust and like each other. That was why I told him I had a client with a relative likely to be the victim in the wealthy widows racket. I told him what I knew about Courtney.

"Sounds the perfect approach," he told me. "Far as I know there haven't been rises in that kind of racket lately. Those there have been were mostly worked at good hotels. One last autumn at Scarborough might fit in. You can get a photograph of this Courtney?"

"It'll be one of the first things we do," I said.

"Right," he said. "Let us have a copy as soon as you can and we'll see if we can tie this Courtney up with anything else."

I may have a flibberty-gibbet kind of brain but at times it's also a wary one. If I was to keep the police away from Jedmont so as to give him the credit for any exposure of Courtney, then I'd have to slow matters up.

"Don't expect that photograph too soon," I warned Jewle. "You know how things are. He'll have to be set up for it and that may take time. The same with his prints. You'd like them too?"

That was that. The next day I turned up at the Farina in time for lunch. My room was 73, on the first floor. My friend Hall was on the same floor, in 55. He wasn't to turn up till the middle of the afternoon.

It was a first-class hotel and, considering the time of year, there were quite a lot of guests. It wasn't as if the weather was good. Squally showers and near gales had persisted through most of the month, and, in spite of the comparative fineness of my first day, the forecast had been far from good. My waiter at lunch told me there were quite a lot of residents. The Farina, he told me, had never encouraged the tripper trade. Even at the week's pension rate I was paying I didn't think the trippers themselves would even have begun to get what they'd regard as their money's worth.

At least two thirds of those lunching were women, most of them middle-aged or elderly. If Courtney were really a crook, then that hotel was the perfect milieu. Everything, from the discreet bar to the delightful lounges, had the aroma of money. There was the lunch menu, which wasn't of what I'd call the conveyor-belt type. There were few items and what I had was as good as anywhere I'd met in town. The service was unobtrusive and excellent.

It was just twelve-thirty when I went to lunch, and I'd almost finished when a woman came in who, I guessed, was Jedmont's aunt. She answered at least to his description of "fluffy": a short-ish woman, plump and with hair in little ringlets. She had a fluffy sort of scarf round her ample shoulders and there was still more fluffiness at wrists and neck. She went straight to a table a few yards from me and sat facing me.

"That lady who just came in," I said to my waiter, "is she by any chance a Miss Brown?"

He smiled.

"Oh, no, sir. She's a Mrs. Coome: a resident of very long stand-ing, if I may say so, sir."

So there the lady was. I read my paper in the comfortable entrance hall till she emerged from the dining-room, then followed her at a discreet distance into one of the lounges. She took a chair not too far from the glowing fire and produced some knitting from her capacious bag. Another minute and she was engaged in conversation with a couple of women on the chesterfield near by. I could hear every word that was said, but it was all Greek to me: fashions mostly, followed by the royal children and back to fashions again. It gave me no clue as to the lady's mental power, and after a few minutes I went up to my room.

I took a walk round the town and went back to my room. Hallows was due to meet me at three-thirty, but at four o'clock he still hadn't arrived. It was a quarter of an hour later when he did come in. and he had some astounding news. Courtney had left the hotel that very morning!

"You sure?" I said.

"Dead sure. I looked through the register, ostensibly to see if an old friend was staying here, and when I saw Courtney's name I asked if he was some other Courtney—you know the old manoeuvre—and that's how I learned he'd left at about nine o'clock this morning. No forwarding address and no word about coming back. All the desk clerk knew was that he'd left on urgent business and was probably flying to New York tonight. He was here just over three weeks, by the way."

"But why?" I said. "Why leave at this particular time? He couldn't have been scared off."

Hallows didn't know. He'd taken a chance and said the departed Courtney was, after all, the old friend he'd been look-ing for, and from that he learned that Courtney had taken a taxi to the station. The train he was taking was almost certainly the nine twenty-five express to town. Hallows had nipped along to the station and had been lucky enough to find the very taxi. Courtney had left by that train.

I rang for two teas to be sent to my room and then we began a new plan of campaign. Hallows was to get into touch with London Airport and find out if Courtney had really booked a passage or already left for New York. I called the local police and asked for another old friend, a Superintendent Fenward. He was in, and I said I'd be round in ten minutes.

A brief chat about old times and I came to the point. He seemed interested.

"You think this Courtney was a con-man?"

"That was the very well-founded suspicion of my client," I said. "Why he should suddenly leave, and just before we got here, don't ask me. You people didn't by any chance get wind of him and scare him off?"

"Never even heard of him. They've never had any trouble, far as I know, at the Farina."

"Well, there's just one thing you can do," I told him. "I promised Superintendent Jewle at the Yard—you remember Jewle—that I'd get both a picture of this Courtney and his prints. Now there's just a chance that Courtney might come back to the hotel, so couldn't you very discreetly get the management to let you know, and then let me know? I'm only staying on a day or two longer."

He thought he could manage that, so I asked if I could use his telephone. After a short delay I got Jewle at the Yard and put him wise as to what had happened and that, once more, was that.

London Airport—it took till almost dinner time to ascertain it—knew nothing of a Mr. Hubert Courtney. Hallows arranged to call again just before the night plane left, and after that there was nothing for us to do but wait After dinner, when Hallows got into touch again, there was still no news of the wanted man.

"Isn't there just a chance that Jedmont himself might have scared Courtney off when he was down here this last week-end?" Hallows asked me.

I said I'd ring him in the morning and try to find out.

"What you might try to do before bedtime is find out if Courtney had any special contacts here besides Mrs. Coome," I said. "It's just possible he had a confederate. It's standard procedure. Some of those yarns he spun to Mrs. Coome would have had to be backed up."

I was just about to get into bed when Hallows came in. The only person with whom Courtney was particularly friendly—other, of course, than the lady—was a Mr. Manning, and that had been only during the last day or two. Hallows had unearthed a waiter who had taken drinks late on the Saturday night to Manning's room, and Courtney had been there. But Manning, Hallows also learned, rarely frequented the lounges. Most of the time he kept to his own room and the only place he did frequent was the bar.

"You saw him at dinner." Hallows told me. "The middle-aged man with the game leg. You remember: the waiter lent him a hand with his stick."

There seemed nothing in it. After Mrs. Coome had gone to bed that night. Manning might have asked Courtney up to his room. The two must have met. Manning had been at the hotel for a fortnight and Courtney too must have been a frequenter of the bar. I said I'd try to strike up some sort of acquaintanceship with Manning in the morning.

I wasn't in any particular hurry in the morning, and just when I was about to go down to breakfast shortly before nine. Hallows came bursting into my room.

"Manning is leaving! He's just paying his bill!"

We went down to the entrance hall. Manning had paid his bill and was seeing to his couple of bags. He was a tallish, rather shambling man with hair quite grey at the temples. He wore horn-rims almost as large as my own, and he was leaning heavily on his stout ash stick as he walked slowly towards the revolving doors. He had the look of a professional man. But for the fact that he hadn't registered as such, he might have been a doctor.

Manning's taxi left. Hallows and I went to breakfast together. There seemed no point now in keeping apart. The meal didn't take long and then I rang Norris. An operative was to meet the nine twenty-five from Sandford at Charing Cross and follow the man described to wherever he went. It was just a forlorn chance. How Manning could have been a confederate of Courtney we couldn't work out. To do so would have meant another ingratiation with Mrs. Coome, and our information was that Manning had very rarely been seen in any of the lounges.

Hallows went out to get London Airport again and I set about getting hold of Jedmont. I didn't tell him what had happened. All I wanted to know was just what had taken place between him and Courtney, and the answer was nothing whatever. He hadn't got down to the hotel till about dinner-time on the Saturday evening, only to find that his aunt and Courtney had had an early dinner and gone to the theatre. When the two came in just after eleven, his aunt said she was tired and went straight up to bed. She didn't get up till midday and all the afternoon she played bridge with three lady friends in one of the lounges, and it was almost time for dinner when the game finished. He didn't see Courtney at all, except at dinner, and he left the next morning on the nine twenty-five. It was largely from the way his aunt was always raving about Courtney that he formed his opinions of the man; and, of course, from all that talk of travelling abroad and oil wells. I told him on no account to get into touch with me at the hotel and left it at that.

I sat in a handy lounge till a call came for me just before midday. It was Norris, reporting that no one of Manning's description had been on the train when it pulled in at Charing Cross. That was another mystery till I saw it otherwise, and began metaphorically to kick myself. That train had two stops before it reached Charing Cross—London Bridge and Waterloo—and Manning had obviously found it more convenient to get off the train at one of them.

There was no particular point in our staying on at the hotel provided I could manage to have a word with Mrs. Coome before we left. We thought of ways to manipulate it, and at last came up with an idea. The lady was late, as usual, for lunch, and as we passed her table I mentioned Courtney's name. Hallows stopped as arranged.

"I tell you I'm sure Courtney hasn't gone to America! Also he told Smith he was staying in Scotland for the next month or two."

"We'll find him," I said, and moved him on.

I went into the lounge that Mrs. Coome frequented and settled myself with a newspaper in a chair in the far corner. Mrs. Coome came in, and she must have had a very scanty lunch. She stole more than one look at me from her fireside chair, then plucked up courage and came across.

"Excuse me, but I happened to overhear you mentioning Mr. Courtney. Are you a friend of his? My name's Mrs. Coome. Harriet Coome."

"Do sit down, Mrs. Coome. My name's Haire. You were asking about Mr. Courtney?"

"Well, yes," she told me nervously. "We were fellow guests, you know, and really—well, quite good friends."

"You liked him?"

"Oh, a most charming man. And so generous. He was in the oil business, you know. A very great traveller." She tittered slightly. "But if you were a friend of his, you knew all that."

"Maybe," I said, "but let me speak bluntly. What proof have you, beyond his own statements, that he was in oil?"

She reared up indignantly. "He was a gentleman. And I believed him. Besides—"

"Besides, what, Mrs. Coome?"

"Well," she fumbled in her handbag, "he took the trouble before he left yesterday morning to write me a letter. He was called away very suddenly, you know."

"Might I see the letter? Strictly confidentially?"

A moment or two and she gave it to me, her plump face slightly flushed. It was written on hotel paper and the hotel envelope was addressed to Mrs. Coome, Room 26.

Dear Harriet,

I've been suddenly called away. It's to do with that oil company and the matter is so exciting and urgent that it gave me no time to say a personal goodbye. Matters, I am glad to say, are even more promising than I anticipated. I may be in America for some weeks but when I see you again I hope to have even more exciting news for you.

I'm glad for your sake that things have turned out so well. By the way, don't mention this matter to anyone. If a leakage occurred it might influence the price of the shares, and that's something you and I don't want.

Meanwhile, thank you for everything. And every good wish till I see you again.

HUBERT

I gave her the letter back.

"Obviously, Mrs. Coome, you were being asked to invest money—maybe a considerable sum of money—in some new oil company. It's lucky for you that you didn't."

She reared up again, cheeks an angry red. "Are you trying to tell me that Mr. Courtney was a liar?"

"Listen," I said quietly, "I'm an investigator, Mrs. Coome, and the person I came down here to investigate was your friend Courtney, as he now calls himself. Doesn't it now occur to you that he got wind of my arrival and that's why he suddenly left the hotel?"

"I don't believe a word of it!"

"That's your privilege," I told her. "But not a word in the letter is true. He hasn't gone and isn't going to America. And if he ever makes any contact with you again, take my earnest advice and get into touch with the police."

"I suppose you know," she told me icily, "there's such a thing as slander?"

"I do know it," I said. "I also know there're such things as confidence tricksters who prey on credulous women."

I'd got to my feet. "Goodbye, Mrs. Coome. What you do now is your own business. You can't say you haven't been warned."

I didn't see her again; in fact it was to be quite a long, long time before we were to meet. That late afternoon we left the hotel. I offered to pay for the whole week, but the management allowed us a rebate. The following morning Jedmont came to see me at the Agency. I'd rung him overnight.

I told him just as much as was necessary and no more. After I'd given him a cheque for twenty-five pounds, which I thought was a fair rebate, I gave him some advice.

"Your aunt, if I may say so, is a very credulous and stupid woman. If you try to curry favour by telling her you employed an investigator to unmask Courtney, I doubt if in her present mood she'll exactly throw her arms around you. My advice is to wait at least three months. Enquire casually, if you must, about this Courtney, and then, if she admits she hasn't heard from him and you think she's beginning to realise the man was a crook, make a clean breast of your part in it. You agree?"

He agreed. I had my doubts. Jedmont wasn't the type to bide his time, and my guess was that he'd spent a badly needed seventy-five pounds in order to cut himself clean out of an inheritance. Not that it was any business of mine.

He was someone else I wasn't to see again for a long, long time. I didn't hear about him till almost a couple of years later and that was when Hallows showed me a copy of a photographic magazine that had as a special supplement an account of the Berlin Photographic Exhibition. Hallows has two hobbies—chrysanthemums and photography—and he assured me that the Berlin exhibition was the best in Europe. He drew my attention to one particular print: the one that had won second prize. It was a beautiful thing: a bumblebee gorging itself in the crown of a single peony with a butterfly hovering around.

"See the name under it?"

"Monty Jedland," I read, and then I stared. "Don't say it's our old friend Jedmont?"

"That's who it is," he told me. "He's got a posh office now in Lauder Street. At Wingram House. Contributing to all sorts of high-class magazines."

I was going to say something and then I didn't. I said something else and I laughed.

"You and I ought to get a couple of free portraits."

"How do you mean?"

"Well," I said, "it looks pretty obvious. It must be taking quite a big financial backing to be doing what Jedmont's doing, and who's responsible if it isn't you and I? We unmasked Courtney, his aunt saw it our way and Jedmont had the credit. Result, one fat cheque and more when wanted."

Hallows grunted. "If I know Jedmont, it wasn't played that way. I'd say he used that Courtney business to blackmail the old girl. Wouldn't be nice if he spread the yarn round among her girl friends."

"Maybe," I said. "Or Jedmont and Courtney may have been in it together and it's Courtney who knew his goose was cooked as regards the oil swindle and decided to put the screws on instead. Maybe he holds an incriminating billet doux or two from the lady."

All of which poses the old question of how stupid can you get, and I'm not referring to Harriet Coome. When I think back after five years, I know that five years ago we ought to have arrived at something like the truth. It wasn't an easy bit of deduction, and yet it was something we ought to have taken into account, and that's one of those things that sometimes make me wonder why I have the effrontery to call myself a detective. Still, there is one small consolation. I'm not alone in idiocy. Thomas Carlyle once remarked that the population of these islands consisted chiefly of fools. I guess he wasn't too far out at that. But rather remarkable an estimate perhaps, considering that in his day there were no television commercials.

2
ROADSIDE LIFT

ON A Monday morning at the beginning of November, 1961, Hallows and I drove to Petcham, some fifty miles north-west of town, to confer on behalf of United Assurance with the local fire authorities in the matter of a factory which had been practically destroyed. We finished our business early on the Tuesday morning and left at about half-past eleven.

Our direct route home was on the A 41, but there were various reasons why I didn't take it. For one thing, that route means a lot of heavy traffic, some too fast and some, more dangerous, far too slow. Then again, we were in no special hurry and I'd remembered making that trip a year or two back and coming to a detour on account of floods. The detour had taken me through quiet, lovely country and I'd also had lunch in a nice little pub in a village named Davenant Parva. Add one other thing: you can get some lovely weather at the beginning of November, and that morning was better than quite a few we'd had all summer. It invited one to stand and stare.

So we turned right, off the main road, and as soon as we'd passed Dansbury Jail and the last of the bungalows, there we were in virtually unspoilt countryside. This isn't a travel guide to rural England, so all I'll say is that soon after midday we reached the village and pulled up outside the Peace and Plenty. We had a preliminary drink while waiting for the landlord to bring us a cold lunch and watched a couple of the locals playing darts. It was too early for the usual customers, and there was only one other man there and he was sitting not far from the fire at the one long table. That bar was in deep shade which didn't make it too warm.

"Mind if we sit here?" I asked the occupant.

He smiled. "Help yourselves. Come along here, nearer the fire."

"Wouldn't dream of disturbing you." I said. "Just here will be fine."

His pint tankard was almost empty and I asked if he'd have a refill. The landlord brought three tankards, we lifted them to a good health and then settled down to our meal—a good country meal of ham, tomatoes, cheese and really good bread.

"You gentlemen natives of these parts?" our friend suddenly asked.

"Oh, no," I said. "We're just passing through on our way back to town. We knew this pub was a good place for lunch, so we arranged to pull up here."

"It sure looks good," he said. "Landlord, can you let me have a meal like these gentlemen here?"

He was a biggish man, his age maybe in the early fifties. He was clean-shaven and his hair a badger grey. He had a pale, but distinguished-looking face and his dark clothes, dark overcoat and the black Homberg on the bench by him had made me guess he was some well-to-do local resident, but his American accent had rather disproved all that. His voice was cultured and his smile delightfully friendly.

"You live here yourself?" I said in my wariest way.

"No," he said, "I'm over here on a short business trip, but my wife made me promise to look up some of my ancestors, if you know what I mean. They originally came from Laybrook, a short ways back. My name's Ashman, by the way."

"Nice to meet you, Mr. Ashman. My name's Travers. My colleague here is Hallows."

The landlord brought his lunch and he settled down to it like a man who's in need of a good meal. That two-mile walk from Laybrook had given him, as he said, a pretty good appetite.

"What luck did you have with your ancestors?" Hallows asked him.

"Not a great deal," he said. "Found a couple of tombstones and that's about all. I'd left my camera behind at the hotel, so I couldn't even take any pictures. Reckon I'll have to come back."

"What's your part of America?" I asked him. "You are American, aren't you?"

"Sure. I move around a good deal but my home town's Butte, Montana."

"Good Lord!" I said. "Montana's one of the few States I know really well. As a matter of fact I was there only last year at Missoula."

"Well, what d'you know!"

"I know Butte pretty well too," I said. "Been through it several times and had a meal or two there. Used to be a pretty hot spot in the old days, they tell me."

He smiled. "It's not exactly rural now. Nothing like the old days of course. You going back there?"

"Not for a year or two at least. Got to save up some dollars. Not that I don't like Montana. Between you and me I sometimes feel a kind of homesickness for all that foothills-of-the-Rockies country."

"I know," he said. "I've only been away a week and I'm beginning to feel that way myself. I don't like being hemmed in. Give me God's free air and the open range. That's what a man was made for." He smiled a bit wryly. "I reckon you think I'm a bit of a sentimentalist."

"Not a bit of it," I told him. "I've lived in London more years than I care to think of and I still have a hankering after the country. I suppose that's really why I dropped in here today."

All that talk had been between bites, so to speak. We finished eating in almost a triple dead heat. I offered Ashman a cigarette.

He thanked me but said he didn't smoke. I passed the case to Hallows, then got my pipe going.

"Did I hear you gentlemen say you were driving straight back to town?"

"That's right," I said. "You'd like a lift?"

He smiled gratefully. "That's mighty kind of you. I had intended to take the bus and get back by stages but now I've got to go back I guess I'd rather get along to town."

"Any particular part?"

I said we'd be going into town by way of Northwood and Harrow. He asked if there was a Tube station at Harrow and told me that'd suit him fine.

I liked Ashman. He was genial without being too hearty and, until we were into the outer suburbs, he told me a lot I didn't know about the old North-West. It turned out he was in copper and in England on business for one of the Anaconda group. As we approached North Harrow Station I suggested we might have a meal together if he could spare the time. Hallows, from the back seat, gave him one of our cards. Ashman almost gaped when he looked at it I had to laugh.

"Oh, yes," I told him. "We have what you call private eyes over here. We're chiefly in the insurance business."

He smiled. "For a minute you had me worried. A man can't be too careful."

The car was drawing up. He thanked us warmly and said he might take us up on that meal and a chat. But he was going to be a mighty busy man and we weren't to think him rude if he couldn't make it.

It had been a good trip, but meeting Ashman had made it all that better. When we got back to Broad Street we got to work on the report for United Assurance and it took us till very late in the afternoon. Hallows, who's our specialist on that sort of thing, was delivering that report to the director concerned in case of additional enquiries, and as I was sealing the large envelope he made a peculiar remark.

"What did you think of that American, Ashman?"

"Ashman?" I said. "Well, I thought him quite an interesting person. I enjoyed his company."

Then I gave him a look. "Why? Something on your mind?"

"Don't know," he said, "but something keeps telling me I've seen him somewhere before."

"You must be wrong. This is the first visit to England for nearly ten years."

"I know," he said, and frowned. "It's just a hunch." Hallows, like most of us, has his lucky hunches and those not so lucky.

"Any idea what was behind the hunch?"

"No," he said. "It was just that extraordinarily peculiar feeling. But did you notice anything about his clothes?"

I thought for a moment, then smiled.

"If you mean his weren't the clothes for the country—well, would a business man bring over country clothes?"

"It wasn't that," he said. "I first caught it in the pub, but there was a faint smell of mothballs."

There was an answer to that. He'd left America during the fall when the weather was still good. He hadn't worn thick clothes since the previous spring.

"Well, then, his shoes."

I hadn't noticed his shoes.

"Remember what it was like this morning?" he asked me. "A very heavy dew. It looked almost like a white frost when I was getting up. Ashman was supposed to have gone round a country churchyard round about eleven in the morning, looking at tombstones when the dew was still pretty heavy, and yet his shoes were as smart as if he'd had 'em cleaned five minutes before we clapped eyes on him."

I could only grunt.

"And did you ever know an American make a special trip to anywhere and forget his camera? He'd be more likely to forget his pants. And there was his face. Quite pale. Not like a man who's been through an American summer."

"You may be right," I said. "And it was all that that made you think you'd seen him somewhere before?"

"Don't know," he said. "But you were talking. I was sitting in the back, listening. I had a lot more time to think."

"Well, if your hunch is right, you may remember some time where it was you saw him. What might help is whether or not he rings me about that meal I mentioned. It won't exactly prove anything; not even that he prefers not to see either of us again."

Hallows shrugged his shoulders. "As you say, it won't prove anything. All the same, I wouldn't mind betting we'll never clap eyes on him again."

"Not with me!" I told him. "Sounds too much like a good thing."

But Hallows was to be wrong. It was exactly a week later, and at about ten in the morning, when Bertha buzzed through to say a Mr. Ashman was on the line and would like to see me. I told her to put him through.

"Why, hallo there!" came an enthusiastic voice as soon as I spoke. "How are you, Mr. Travers?"

"Nice to hear you again." I said. "I hope it means we're going to have that meal together."

"Well, no," he said. "What I hoped was you'd be able to carry out a little commission for me. You do handle that kind of job?"

"What kind of job?"

"Finding somebody. It's for a friend back home. Why can't we meet somewhere and work it out over a cup of coffee?"

"Why not?" I said. "Where're you speaking from?"

"Not far away," he said. "I had to see a friend in Cannon Street, so I'm ringing from his office."

"Then why not come on here?" I told him. "We make the best cup of coffee in town."

He said he'd be with me in ten minutes. Bertha rushed out to get cream. She needn't have worried: it was a good twenty minutes before he arrived. Hallows had left that morning on an assignment out of town, otherwise I'd have got him to Broad Street for another look at the client. You can't take too many precautions in our kind of job.

It was a blustery, rainy morning and Ashman's clothes were very different from those he'd worn that morning in the country. Except for the good quality and obviously English waterproof, they had quite an American air, especially the shirt and the necktie. Something else was different, too.

"You're looking pretty good," I told him as I took the waterproof and the soft-brimmed hat. "If you don't mind my saying so, you weren't looking any too well the other day: a bit peaked, as we say."

"Ah, yes," he said. "I'd had a mild attack of your English influenza. That's one reason why I made myself take the day off."

Bertha brought in the coffee.

"Just a minute, young lady," he told her. "Mr. Travers here tells me you make the best coffee in town."

He helped himself to cream and sugar. It wasn't too hot for a good mouthful. He was positively beaming as he looked up at Bertha.

"What d'you know. It's good. Real good!"

I remembered in time not to offer him the cigarette box.

"Now then," I said. "What's this job you want us to do? Something, I gathered, about a missing person."

"Yes," he said, and his voice was far more business-like. "It's to oblige a neighbour at home: a widow, name of Wale—W-A-L-E. Her husband died recently and she's taking it pretty hard. They had a pretty substantial business which Joe—that's the husband—used to run, and now she isn't too happy about leaving things to a manager. I think she's stupid. I know Fred Morgan, and, believe me, he'll handle things far better than Joe ever did. You don't mind me going into all this?"

"Far from it," I told him. "The more background, the better."

"Well, you can't get women to see things our way. What she wants is to have an English nephew go over there and see her. When I told her he mightn't know as much about the timber trade as I do—and that's damn little—she started talking about her own flesh and blood." He smiled. "It was Joe's flesh and blood, but that's the way it was. Also, the last time she heard from this nephew was about five years ago. Not even a card at Christmas. I told her he might be dead, or gone away or something. She's never even seen him. Joe was over here a few years back but she's never seen him. She hadn't even a photograph. All she knows is what Joe told her and what was in the occasional letter."

"And just what details have you got?"

He produced a paper from his wallet. "I've gotten them all written on this."

Harry Wale, aged about 40. Height about six feet, weight when Joe saw him about 170 pounds. Dark hair, good-looking. Married but no children. Wife's name Carol. When last heard from five years ago was continental representative for a hard-goods firm. Was living then at 34 Highland Way, Ilmoor, London.

"And all this was five years ago?" I asked him.

"I guess so. One thing I ought to tell you. A day or two ago when I had an evening free, I went to this Ilmoor place. No Harry Wale. The people had been there three years and the people before them weren't named Wale." He shrugged his shoulders. "It didn't take me five minutes to know I'd have had a real job on my hands, if I'd the time for it, which I haven't. I'm due in Birmingham this afternoon and I'll be back in town on the Thursday. Then I fly straight to Belgium and home from there."

"Doesn't give us much time," I said.

"You do your best and let me have a report on Thursday morning at the hotel. The Philippe—"

"I know it. Just off Dover Street"

"That's the place." He smiled. "I guess it seems kind of stupid, looking for a man who might be dead or gone to God knows where, and it's likely to be expensive—not that I mind the expense. Millie— that's Mrs. Wale—is a good friend of my wife. Between ourselves, all this is just as much my wife's doing as Millie's."

"Well, I'll do my best," I told him. "It'll mean at least a couple of men working all out. It'll cost you a hundred pounds. Strictly all in, but no results guaranteed."

He took out his wallet again and carefully peeled off twenty five-pound notes. Five minutes later he was putting his copy of the contract in the wallet.

"Deadline what time on Thursday?" I wanted to know.

"Midnight, shall we say? I'll be on the first flight for Belgium the next morning." He gave me that little confidential smile again. "That report's the main thing. Just something tangible to show my wife and Millie."

I had a little talk with Norris. Hallows, as I said, wasn't available till Thursday, which would be far too late. French was the only operative standing by and he could be ready by midday. I wanted to be at that Ilmoor address when the occupants of Wale's old house, and their neighbours, would be likely to be home, and one o'clock meal-time seemed as good a time as any.

I went back to my room and, before I hardly knew it, I was thinking about Ashman, and particularly in the light of those curious things which Hallows had noticed that day in the pub. For the life of me I couldn't find anything in the Ashman of an hour ago, or his story or demeanour, that—in spite of any possible misgivings on the part of Hallows—would make him an undesirable client. I still liked Ashman.

The time he had spent with me that morning had shown me another facet or two.

That slight attack of influenza, from which he had barely recovered that morning at Davenant Parva, had made him also subdued compared with the Ashman I'd just seen. There'd been something almost mercurial or kaleidoscopic about him: at one moment the serious man of business and then, when he was talking about the folks back home, a humour that was intimately dry. I wondered what that wife of his was like. I tried to imagine her, and the dithering Millie, and I found myself smiling. At the unsubstantial them? Or was it just Ashman?

I looked up Highland Way in the large-scale map. Years of driving in town have as good as qualified me for a taxi licence. Side streets avoided the main flow of traffic to the north-east and it was still short of one o'clock when we drew into that quiet, residential Ilmoor Street. There was something forlorn about it that morning, with the rain still coming down and the gutters littered with the broad leaves of the plane trees.

Number thirty-four was the near half of a well-built, red-bricked Edwardian house. I put it in the £4,000 class. Like its neighbour it had a roomy garage with a concrete run-in, a largish lawn plus rose-bed garden at the front and a miniature shrubbery beyond the side door and the garage, concealing what was almost certainly a quite large garden at the back. I went to the front door.

A quite pretty woman in the early thirties opened it, and there was the expected slight recoil as her eyes ran quickly over me. I gave her my best smile.

"I'm not selling anything. I believe you had a caller recently enquiring about a former owner of your house, a Mr. Wale, and you were unable to give him any information. I'm a solicitor and it's most important we get into touch with Mr. Wale. It concerns an important legacy."

She slowly shook her head. "Until the other gentleman called, I'd never even heard of a Mr. Wale."

"So he told me. What I'm wondering, though, is this. You've been here how long?"

"Just about three years."

I tried the same smile. "Then I'm sure you must have made quite a lot of friends. Among them there must be someone who's lived here quite a long time. Someone who must have known the Wales."

She frowned in thought. "Well, you might try Mrs. Fraser. She lives at forty-six."

A smile, thanks, a lift of the hat and I went back to the car. Number 46 was semi-detached and the very spit of the one I'd just left. The Mrs. Fraser was a business-like woman of about sixty. She had a good look at me and the look of chilly appraisal didn't disappear till I'd ended my spiel. But she didn't ask me to step inside till she'd peered round to look at the car. Even then we got no further than the tiny hall.

"I didn't know *him*," she told me, "except by sight, but I knew his wife. I met her at the hospital. I had to go in for a serious operation and she was very, very kind. She was secretary to the registrar, I believe."

"What hospital was that?"

"The Matthew Cooper."

"She had full-time employment there?"

"Yes," she said. "Her husband used to travel abroad a lot. I think I remember her telling me he was a sales representative for some electrical firm: refrigerators, washing machines and all that."

"What was the husband like?"

"Well, I never really met him. He was tall and smart-looking. Always drove an expensive car. Probably paid for by the firm, my husband said. I only saw him close once when I went by as he was cleaning the car. I believe it was a Humber. I remember he had dark hair and one of those little gigolo moustaches."

"Just one other question, Mrs. Fraser. When the Wales left, did you know they were going? Did she tell you?"

"No," she said. "I heard it from my husband. He went by when a furniture van was being loaded and told me about it. I rang up later but there wasn't any reply."

"And you never saw either of them again, or heard anyone mention them?"

"Never. They just disappeared. About a week later someone else moved in."

"You think you can remember the firm of house agents who dealt with the property?"

She frowned. "Afraid I can't. It's so long ago and I didn't know them all that well." Then her face brightened. "My husband might know. Would you mind waiting? I'll try to get him."

She went through to the lounge and I could just hear her voice as she telephoned. She must have been going over every word of our conversation, for it was quite five minutes before she was back. But she had something for me.

"Sorry to have been so long. My husband says it was Holder and Holder. You'll find them in the High Street."

3

THE QUEST FOR WALE

THE offices of Holder and Holder were closed from one o'clock till two. We'd had no lunch so the wait didn't matter. At a snack bar a few doors away we had sandwiches and coffee before we went our separate ways. French was to get all the information he could about the sale of the Highland Way house, then make the rounds of the local furniture removers. I was making enquiries at the Matthew Cooper Hospital and we'd collate the information back at the Agency.

I collected the car from the local car park and drove on almost through Ilmoor itself. The hospital, quite an old one, was at the end of a cul de sac just off the main road. Eyebrows were raised when I told Enquiries that I was in search of information about a Mrs. Wale who was working some five years ago in the office of the Registrar. A Registrar, if you don't know it, is a kind of aspiring surgeon who doubles for a consultant surgeon who happens, in an emergency, not to be available. You could say he's on the way up to being a consultant surgeon himself.

The Registrar, a Dr. Yeoman, was definitely in, but it took quite a lot of persuasion before I was taken up to his room.

He was much younger than I'd expected and, once I'd explained the call on him, most co-operative.

He spoke most highly of Carol Wale. He hadn't been Registrar at the time but he'd heard a lot about her from his predecessor. A charming, cultured and most reliable secretary, and he seemed to remember there'd been only husband trouble as the reason for her leaving.

"I know," he suddenly said. "Nurse Payne might be able to help you. I'll see if she can spare you a moment."

He courteously left the room at our disposal. Nurse Payne was in the thirties: a petite brunette with a delightful smile.

"I was her closest friend," she told me. "The only thing that hurts me is that she never sent me a single word after she left.

I can only think it was shame and wanting to cut herself clean off, if you know what I mean. She hated anything ugly or dirty."

"What exactly was it that happened?"

"Well," she said, "I don't know the details, but her husband tried to sell the house behind her back and when she discovered it, he just walked out and left her. He did it while she was here and she found the note when she got home."

That was all she knew. The disheartening thing was that she'd never heard a word of Carol Wale since she'd left. No one at the hospital had heard a thing or she herself would have been told.

"How long had she been married?"

"Only about two years," she said. "She didn't say much about it but you could tell she wasn't happy after the first few months. He was some sort of representative for an electrical firm and used to be away for weeks on the Continent. It wasn't the sort of married life I'd put up with myself. I'd like to have a husband I could keep an eye on."

The telephone went. She picked up the receiver and looked a bit surprised when the call turned out to be for me. It was French, calling from the house agent's office.

"Something you ought to know, sir, and Mr. Jack Holder is good enough to say he'll see you personally. Three o'clock if you can make it!"

I said I'd be there. I had twenty minutes to make it, which was plenty of time.

"Sorry about all that," I told Nurse Payne. "But we were talking about the husband. You knew him, too."

"I only saw him once or twice," she said. "A very attractive sort of man. Much younger than she was, or so I thought. I put him at not more than thirty-five, but Carol was over forty. She didn't look it, but she was."

I didn't ask her any more questions: after all, when I'd heard whatever it was that the house agent thought I ought personally to know, I could always come back. But on the way to Ilmoor High Street again, I couldn't help thinking about that marriage.

Shakespeare, I remembered, had some apt advice to offer about marriage and, if anyone should have known, it was he.

> . . . *Let still the woman take*
> *An elder than herself. So wears she to him:*
> *So sways she level in her husband's heart.*

My guess was that Carol Wale had been asking for trouble. What exactly the discrepancy was in ages I didn't exactly know, but if he was in the middle thirties and she in the early forties, there was discrepancy enough. The odds were surely against children, for one thing, and that meant no binding agent as still more years went by. Then there was his long absences which would make for suspicions and jealousy. Not that what I had learned from Nurse Payne had been any particular help. Maybe I'd have better luck with Holder and Holder.

Mr. Jack Holder, the senior partner, was a man of sixty: soft-spoken but most convincing. I hadn't been in his office two minutes before I appreciated why he'd thought it necessary to talk directly with me.

"I've been here all my life, Mr. Travers, and that Wale business was the most extraordinary I've ever come up against. It's very simple, really, and it boils down to this. As you'll see, I had to think a lot about it at the time and I've done a lot of thinking since.

"There's no doubt in my own mind that Wale had found some other woman and was thinking of leaving his wife, but he didn't want to leave empty-handed. But I should tell you about the wife first. A most charming and cultured woman, Mr. Travers. She really gave up her chances of marriage in order to look after her mother, who was a widow. The mother died some ten years ago and left her the house and contents and an annuity of about a hundred and fifty a year.

"You see the point? Mrs. Wale had her own banking account, so he couldn't touch her money without her knowing. What he decided to do was to sell the house."

"But how could he? It was hers."

He smiled. "I know. I know. But you have to take into account several things, above all his plausibility. You just took his integrity for granted, so when he approached me about the house, I never had the faintest reason for suspicion. You know what their family life was?"

"Probably not nearly as well as you."

"Well, he was away for weeks at a time on business. She was working at the hospital and so what you might call fully occupied. He also had periods of sometimes as much as a month when he was in England and then he used to take things easily. He'd have a lot of time on his hands—generally during the late summer. To compensate, he told her, for those periods abroad. That was why he was able to take us over the house: that was why he could later take prospective buyers over the house without her knowing a thing.

"I needn't go into all the details but naturally he had to resort to forgery. He had to forge her letter to the bank, asking them to give him the deeds of the house, and he tricked her into putting her name to a power of attorney. The whole thing might have gone through but for a clerk of mine who was handling some business for the hospital and came into contact with Mrs. Wale. She was in a dreadful state when she came to see me.

"The thing was that the house, as far as we were concerned, was sold. He had a solicitor and the only thing was the signatures on the documents and the payment of the balance. The tragedy might have been that the purchasers had sold their home and made all arrangements for the move, and that's where Mrs. Wale was so generous. She let them have the house. It was a wrench to leave her home but she did it. We had to be most discreet about the whole thing, mind you. and make excuses for the various delays, but that's what happened. Once everything was settled, Mrs. Wale left and we haven't heard a word from her since. Not, I suppose, that there was any need."

"A nasty bit of business," I said. "Her husband walked out on her. I expect you know that."

"Yes. I knew. But I mentioned his charm and plausibility." He smiled. "Think of a small boy, Mr. Travers, whose mother spoils him. He steals the tarts and he doesn't worry too much about getting caught in the act. He knows he can smile himself out of it."

"I see. But this was something Wale couldn't charm himself out of?"

"Exactly. She was a woman of great integrity. If you ever happen to meet her, I'm sure you'll agree."

That was virtually all I learned. As I told Holder, I was most grateful for his confidence. What, of course, I didn't tell him was that it hadn't helped at all in finding the absconding husband: in fact I'd have given all the time I'd spent that day, interesting though it was, for the present address of Harry Wale—and added a couple of ten-pound notes for good luck.

I did have a cup of tea with Holder before I left. He told me he had a grandson at Cambridge: not at my old college but it made a sort of bond. He occasionally had business which he'd be happy to pass on to us, so the afternoon wasn't altogether wasted. It was just after four o'clock when I left him, and when I got back to the office, French hadn't arrived. A few minutes later he did come in and he had news that compensated for everything.

At the second furniture removers where he'd made enquiries he'd struck oil. Mrs. Wale had had her furniture stored with them for about six weeks, and then had it removed to her new address. It was 38 Horburn Avenue, Kingsdale.

That was almost five years ago and things might have happened since then. I looked in the telephone directory but there was no Mrs. Wale at Kingsdale. But there were still ways and means. I got hold of Enquiries. In a few minutes I was told that the telephone number was 7723 Kingsdale. I rang at once but there was no reply.

I looked up the directory again and the name of the occupant was a Miss C. Nevett. The C. looked promising, so I took a chance and rang Holder. He ultimately told me what I'd hoped might be true: that Carol Wale's maiden name was Carol Nevett.

After that, French and I began working things out. An annuity of a hundred and fifty pounds wasn't a living. Carol Wale must be working somewhere and, in that case, she mightn't be home till well after five. Say six to be more certain. That meant we had best part of an hour to wait.

It was five-past six when I rang. Within a couple of seconds of my hearing the first ring, the telephone was picked up. "Kingsdale 7723."

"Miss Nevett?"

"Yes," she said. "Who's speaking?"

It was a beautiful voice: a warm contralto.

"My name's Travers, Miss Nevett—Ludovic Travers. I'm head of the Bond Street Detective Agency, and I'd like to speak to you most urgently about your former husband, Harry Wale."

For a good few seconds there wasn't a sound. When she did speak, her voice had quite a tremor. "What about him, Mr. Travers?"

"It's too long a story and too confidential for the telephone. I'd like to come and see you."

"When?"

"It's very urgent. Can we say tonight?"

"I'm afraid not. I do volunteer work at the local hospital and I have to be there in a few minutes."

"Tomorrow, then?"

She thought for a moment. "It would have to be at a quarter to one. I usually lunch at the works' canteen but I could come home."

"I'd be most grateful," I said. "I shall look forward to meeting you."

I was about to ring off but she was speaking again. "Tell me frankly. Is my husband dead?"

"Frankly, Miss Nevett, I don't know."

In the same moment I heard the click as she rang off.

I didn't know if French would be required but I took him with me in any case. Horburn Avenue was yet another road of semi-detached Edwardian houses, and once we'd found the house we wanted, we moved back and waited in the car. We were about ten minutes early but prompt to time we saw the lady arrive. We gave her three minutes and moved the car on.

Carol Wale was one of the most attractive women I've ever met. Ten years ago she must have been remarkably beautiful: now the years showed an age which she wasn't bothering too much to conceal. She was tallish and on the slender side. She had a lovely complexion, dark hair with still no trace of grey, and dark expressive eyes. Her voice, as I said, was perfectly delightful.

The interview took place in her lounge. I'd wanted her to make herself some lunch but she said she'd anticipated our call and taken sandwiches with her, which she'd eaten on the bus. She was now secretary, it emerged, to a director of Associated City Electric, whose head office was about a mile away on that depressing main road.

I began by telling her exactly why we were there. I've never seen anyone look more surprised.

"But that's absurd!" she told us. "My husband didn't have any relations. I'm positive if he'd had any relative in America to whom he'd been writing, he'd have let me know."

"Will you let me talk to you frankly?"

"Of course," she said. "It's what I want you to do."

So I told her about our enquiries of the previous day and all we'd unearthed. I hope I softened it by mentioning the opinions everyone had of her personally. Her cheeks flushed at the warmth of that praise.

"What I'm really getting at is this," I said. "Your husband was prepared to deceive you quite heartlessly, even criminally, in the matter of your house. Would he have had any scruples about deceiving you in minor things, such as relatives? How well did you really know him?"

She moistened her lips, but she couldn't speak.

"I'd hate to distress you," I went on, "and I'm most grateful to you for allowing us to come here, but might we start at the beginning? It might help. How, for instance, did you first meet Harry Wale?"

"It was just by chance," she said. "It was my day off from the hospital and I went to town to do some shopping and, just as I'd gone through the barrier at Liverpool Street, I twisted my ankle somehow. Harry helped me up. He'd been seeing off a friend. Then he insisted on taking me home in his car. The next day he called with some flowers and then—well, within a month we were married."

"What did he tell you about himself?"

"Very little really. There didn't seem much to tell. He hadn't any living relatives. His father was an army officer who was killed in the war and his mother died soon afterwards. He was at school in India because his father was stationed there. Then there was the firm he worked for in town. I forget the name but their works were near Rochester. That's where he was living when we met."

"He was generous?"

She smiled slightly.

"Now I come to think of it, he was. He always insisted on paying his share of the household expenses whether he was home or not. And he always brought little presents back after one of his trips abroad. Personal things mostly."

"And what went wrong with the marriage? I take it, it did begin to go wrong?"

"Yes," she said. "It was those continual trips of his. It all seemed so unnatural. And he was always so secretive about things. I got the feeling he was keeping all sorts of things back. That's why we began quarrelling."

She hesitated.

"I don't think you're going to believe this, but he finally owned up that he'd been deceiving me all along. About his work, I mean. What he really was, was a government agent. All the same, I was still to let my friends think his job was a foreign representative for the Rochester firm."

I almost allowed myself to smile. "You believed him?"

"I think I did. After all, it was more credible. He was also a good linguist. He was always bringing foreign newspapers to the house when he was home." She smiled. "I'm afraid I'm no linguist myself. What little French I had is practically forgotten. Oh, and later on there was the visitor. That was about a fortnight before he finally went. There was an unexpected change of duties at the hospital one morning when I got there and I was asked to make it my day off. That's why I came back unexpectedly, and there was Harry with this visitor. They both seemed very surprised. He was a Monsieur Armand: a man of about forty-five or so, and looking very foreign. I don't know what made me remember the name, but I did. His English was quite good and he looked quite a charming person. Naturally I made an excuse to go out again, and when I came back they'd both gone. Harry told me afterwards he was a colleague."

"It's still all very queer." I said. "I know there have to be intelligence agents and your husband might well have been one, but how does that explain his trickery over selling the house?"

"I don't know," she said. "He did try to explain it in the note I found the day he left. I think now he was trying to justify himself and throwing the blame on me."

"How?"

"Well, there were obscure hints about his soon having to live abroad and how he knew I'd never part with the house and so he had to force my hand, if you know what I mean. If I was told about it when it was all over, then I couldn't help myself."

"You didn't believe it?"

She was silent for a moment.

"I don't believe it now. But it wasn't a question of believing it then. That wasn't the problem. Mr. Travers. You see, whatever he'd done, I was still in love with him. The problem was a sort of compromise. To keep him, and to keep the things I believed in. and he solved it for me by just disappearing out of my life. I neither believe it now nor disbelieve it. because I've also managed now to shut him clean out of my life. That's why it was such a shock to me when you rang me last night."

"Yes," I said, "and I'm sorry. But it seemed at the time something that just had to be done. And you've not the faintest idea where he might happen to be?"

She was most emphatic. "None whatever."

"And you knew of no other friends of his besides that Monsieur Armand?"

She smiled wryly. "None at all. That was one of the troubles with our home. Everything always seemed wrapped in some big secrecy."

"You have a photograph of him by any chance?"

"I haven't. There's nothing whatever in the house that could ever remind me of him."

I got to my feet. "And now, thanks to me you have to start forgetting all over again."

"It won't be too hard." she told me. "But may I ask something? If you ever do find him, will you let me know?"

"I will. I promise faithfully I will. And if by any chance you should hear from him or of him, will you let me know?"

We left almost at once. A couple of hundred yards away in the shopping centre a confectioner's shop was open. I bought a large box of chocolates and they promised to deliver it at once. Though I'd learned nothing that would help me to find Wale in time, it was a trifling thing to do compared with the deep impression Carol Wale had made on me. Even French, as we discussed the case on the drive back, seemed to have been impressed by her, too.

I asked him what his views were about Wale's connection with M.I.5. All he could say was what I'd told Carol Wale: that there were intelligence agents and Wale might have been one of them. The snag, of course, was that nasty business of the attempt to sell the Ilmoor house.

"Couldn't you find out from M.I.5 yourself?" French asked me.

"Never a hope," I told him. "They'd never divulge the name of an agent: not even to far more important people than me."

I spent the rest of the afternoon drawing up the report for Ashman. It was a very much edited version of what had happened during the last twenty-four hours, but even the essentials made quite an impressive show. I left the delivery till after dinner, when I thought I'd be sure to find Ashman at the hotel. They had him paged but there was no sign of him, so I left the report at the desk, together with my private telephone number.

Bernice, my wife, went to bed, but I sat on in case Ashman should ring. It was nearer twelve than eleven when he did so. He was full of apologies. All I wanted to know was if he was satisfied with the report.

"Sure I was satisfied," he told me. "All I needed was something to show back home. Guess they'll get a thrill out of that secret agent stuff."

"Well, so long as you're satisfied, that's everything," I said. Bed was calling and I didn't want a chat.

"Everything was fine," he told me. "Sorry we had to miss that meal. Better luck next time I'm over."

"Happy dreams, then, and a fine trip home."

"And happy dreams to you," he said. "It's been great meeting you."

So that was the last of Ashman and an assignment well and truly paid for. We'd done the best we could though some people, after reading that report, might have thought it not good enough. But Ashman hadn't been worrying about results. What he'd wanted was something to satisfy the folks back home. I was wishing we had a few more clients like him.

The next morning Hallows came in from the Midlands after finishing a fairly routine job. I happened to see him when he came out of Norris's office, and called him in.

"If I hadn't been a coward I might have won a nice little bet from you," I told him. "We've been working for Ashman ever since you left. Like to see our copy of the report?"

He read it carefully through. I added the reason why Ashman had wanted Wale.

"A queer business," he said. "This Wale's very much a mystery man, so that makes two."

I had to think quickly to get his allusion. "You mean Ashman himself?"

"That's it," he said. He smiled a bit deprecatingly. "If this hadn't cropped up I'd never have mentioned it, but I thought I'd come back this morning much the way we came the other day. It wasn't all that far off the regular route. I just wanted to check something for my private satisfaction."

"Such as what?"

"Those two tombstones of the Ashman family that he said he'd unearthed in Laybrook churchyard. That churchyard, so the woman told me who gave me the keys of the church, had been cleaned up this summer and all the tombstones cleaned too. I went over the whole lot methodically and there wasn't a single Ashman. Then I tried inside the church and there wasn't a single monument or engraved stone with that name. The same woman who gave me the keys, and she was well over seventy, said she'd never heard of any Ashmans in the parish."

"So he was lying," I said. "He must have had other business at Laybrook."

Hallows gave me the same deprecatory smile.

"I don't know. As it was on my way I pulled up at that Davenant Parva pub. The landlord told me Ashman had got off the Petcham bus, and that was the first one of the day. That bus takes the same route we did, so all Ashman knew about Laybrook was the name which he saw as he went through."

"But why lie and bolster the lie up with circumstantial evidence?"

He shrugged his shoulders. "Don't know. Also I can't remember where it was I saw him before."

"Well, thank heaven it isn't an assignment," I said. "Ashman should now be in Belgium and he's flying home direct from there. It's ten to one we'll never see him again."

"Give me twenties and I'll risk half-a-crown with you."

"Right," I said. "It's a bet. Better have a time limit, though. Within the next two years?"

Within the next two years it was. That half-crown was as good as in my pocket, even if I did proceed to forget all about it.

4
THE INFORMER

THE very next day a nephew of mine was visiting us from New Zealand. He's my wife's only living relative and, as it was his first trip to England, the event looked like being a notable one.

But before we get down to the events that arose out of that visit, I'd like to get a few things clear. However irrelevant they may seem, they're not padding. With some of them you may be already acquainted, but with most you're definitely not. All, at the moment, seem to me essential both as background to, and immediate part of this case, the one that I'm calling *The Case of the Three-Ring Puzzle*. The very title seems to imply involutions, or, should I say, a series of baffling attempts to reconcile and rationalise apparently unrelated problems. It was little of the sort. What appeared baffling, as it may possibly appear to you, was actually nothing of the kind, if—and it's quite a big if—we'd only recognised the puzzle for what it was.

You, for instance, are probably familiar with the puzzle of the three metal rings, apparently tightly and intricately bound together. The problem is to separate them. Just as difficult is to put them together again, ready for somebody else. What we had to do in the long run was not to separate the rings but to put them together. And what's so hard about that? Well, in our case, just this. We weren't presented with the three rings at the same time. It was not till we had all three rings that we realised they must be part of the same puzzle, and only then could we really get to work on a reassembling.

But about those things I ought to make clear and the people with whom you should get more closely acquainted. The first is Bernice, my wife. Bernice Haire was a classical dancer, a profession that nowadays in England seems as dead as the dodo, even if we still rapturously receive the troupes from such countries as Spain. She still loves dancing, even if it's only such things as tangos at occasional private dances or on the floors of certain special restaurants.

Bernice Haire and her younger sister, Joy, toured practically all the cultural world. The sister was a singer and impersonator in the Beatrice Lillie class. Both sisters were extremely well-connected, as we say: both were products of Roedean and a Swiss finishing school. How on earth then, you will say, did anyone like Bernice Haire come to marry anyone as questionable—I was almost going to say as sordid—as a private detective?

Part of the answer to that is that in those far too far-off days I wasn't anything of the sort. I'd had the good fortune to be left very well-off: among my other inheritances being the property later developed into a block of flats, in one of which I've lived most of my adult life. My hobby was criminology and I even was occasionally called in as an unofficial expert by the Yard. I met the Haire sisters at a private party. Bernice and I had quite a long chat that evening and the next day she rang to ask if she might consult me professionally.

I was later to write about that case, using disguised personalities and names. Let me admit that it isn't relevant to this story: all the same, I think you'd like to hear it. It was one of the most amazing of all my experiences.

The sisters had been on a tour of India and had given during the course of it a private performance for a certain wealthy maharajah. They returned to England on the same liner in which this maharajah was also and unexpectedly travelling. One evening he asked Bernice to inspect a collection of jewels in his cabin, and there he offered her a perfectly fabulous diamond ring—on conditions you may easily guess. She indignantly refused. Two mornings later, Joy appeared at breakfast wearing the same ring! It had been, she said, a present from the maharajah.

What conclusions could Bernice help but draw? It was the estrangement that at once arose that was worrying her into almost a nervous breakdown and it was about that that she wanted to see me. It was ultimately proved, of course, that Joy's ring had definitely been merely a present, and a nicely calculated revenge on the part of a man with a cunning and sadistic mind. Bernice was grateful and a few weeks later we were married. She never danced professionally again.

Joy married a New Zealander named Millery and died when their son, Tom, was still a boy. It was he who was visiting us. His father had a relative or two in England and Tom was spending some time with them. As his stay was one of only a month, we were lucky to get a very long week-end of his time. We had a photograph of him which showed a nice-looking boy—or should I say man?—of twenty-two. He favoured his mother rather than Bernice, though he had Bernice's dark hair. Joy had never been the absolute beauty that her sister had been, and Tom had his mother's high cheekbones and mobile mouth. But his passion was dancing and, when he got back home—so he wrote—he was thinking of forming his own band.

All that, as Chaucer once said, has been a long preamble of a tale, and where it has led us is to the Mayland Restaurant in Vickery Street, Soho. Bernice and I did a lot of talking about that visit, and finally it was decided that we'd dine out every evening and, during the day, Bernice would show Tom the sights of London. He'd also expressed the wish to see everything historic and my contribution would be to lunch him one day at my club, with Jewle, and later get Jewle to show him round the Yard. The three of us—Bernice, Tom and I—would also have lunch one day at Cambridge and visit my old college.

The problem was to choose the evening restaurants. The essentials were those with a good clientele, a good band and a good dance floor. Not that it mattered to me. Between ourselves, I loathe dancing, and, if there's a worse dancer—of modern dances, that is—I'd be glad to pin the medal on him and shake him by the hand. Bernice loves it, as I said, and, though we stay at home more than we used, we still dine out about once a fortnight. That adds up to quite a knowledge of London restaurants. I thought that Genetti's in Jermyn Street was as good as any. Bernice said the floor was much too small.

"What about the Mayland?" I said. "It's quite close for one thing and the food's good."

She frowned for a moment, then agreed. During the last year the Mayland was the place to which we'd many times returned.

"I think that's a splendid idea," she said. "It must be a month or two since we were there."

I'd known the Mayland a good many years, especially in the days when Charlie Mayland ran it himself. The clientele had been colourful, if questionable, and Charlie had had one or two encounters with the police. Four or five years ago he'd dropped dead of a heart attack in his own restaurant, but a few months later the lease had been acquired by Louis Marquette. His father had been French and his mother English, and for years they'd owned a hotel in Toulouse. Louis literally turned the Mayland inside out. He must have spent quite a decent fortune on it, but a year after he'd taken over, it had a name as good as any in town. That it should be on the Soho fringes didn't matter. If the Mayland had been on the fringes of Bethnal Green it'd still have been full every night.

How did I know all this? Well, Louis was one of the old type restaurateurs who know the value of personal contacts. From time to time every night he would move slowly through the two dining-rooms, staying for a moment at every table. He also had the essential memory for names. I think it was only the second time I was there that he addressed me by name and since then he'd treated us—we didn't flatter ourselves that we were the only ones—as honoured guests.

He was a man who looked about fifty: rather an imposing figure with a Louis Napoleon face and beard, and a very slight middle spread. His manners were charming, never gushing but always the right shade of deference or intimacy. I imagine his French was perfect but his English had occasionally a false intonation which was rather attractive. Bernice liked him: maybe—I didn't dare say so—because he was always complimenting her on her dancing. He even once jocularly offered her a professional engagement!

About a year previous to the night I'm going to talk about, we actually did a job for him. He had suspicions about his then head-waiter who was keeping a table or two up his sleeve and taking big tips from guests who hadn't booked. It was an old enough racket, worked in collusion with the desk cashier. Hallows had a couple of evenings there and managed to get the proofs needed. That, of course, made for a still closer association between Louis and myself. And so to the evening when Tom and Bernice and I were shown to the table that had been reserved for us at the Mayland. It was a Friday, the second evening of Tom's stay.

One of the things that Louis Marquette had done was to throw the two dining-rooms of the original place into one large room. Since his charges were pretty stiff, he could afford to have fewer tables. That made for a larger dance floor which attracted more patrons. Any after-theatre custom was absorbed by serving no meals after ten-thirty and having instead cold snacks in the bar. That meant that by eleven the dining-room tables could be cleared back, giving room for the augmented band. Up till then a trio used to play near the cloak-room angle.

We had quite a good table that evening, and we'd just handed our things over at the cloak-room when Louis spotted us and came across from the passage that led to his office. I guessed afterwards that he'd actually been on the look-out for us, so apt was his appearance. I was having at that moment a slight argu-ment with the remarkably pretty girl in charge of the cloak-room, who'd put, as I'd thought, the wrong hats with the wrong coats. It was quite a friendly argument. During our visits I'd come to know her pretty well. Everyone knew her as Doris. A nice girl. Plenty of tact with the charm. The other girl, who shared the duties with her, was Lorette. I'd seen her far less often than Doris.

Louis was ushering Bernice and Tom to our table. He was holding the chair for Bernice when I caught up.

"Ah, Mr. Travers," he said. "It is a pleasure to see you again, and to make the acquaintance of your nephew."

"Mr. Millery plays a pretty good note on the trumpet," I said. "You'd better keep an eye on him later or you may find him in the band."

Tom blushed. Bernice was reprimanding me with a shake of the head. Louis only laughed.

"Perhaps it can be arranged. You would like the Tavel Rosé as usual?"

I said that'd be fine. He told us he'd see to it personally.

We had a very good meal. Bernice and Tom danced between courses to the music of the trio and later, just as we were finishing our coffee, Louis came to the table again.

"You permit, madame, that I take your husband for a few minutes? A little private matter about which I'd like his advice."

"Why not?" Bernice told him. "Provided you don't keep him the whole evening."

"Only a few minutes," he assured her. "Meanwhile anything you wish, just ask."

I followed him past the desk to the office. He asked me to wait for a moment outside, but he left the door wide open.

Frank Gledmill was just finishing his meal at a side table. I ought to tell you about Frank.

Frank was public school and Oxford, the son of a country vicar of very moderate means. He had burst like a meteor, as they say, on the boxing world of twenty years ago, and he's still rated the best light-heavy who ever stepped into the amateur ring. The crowd loves a killer and Frank was certainly that. Soon after he came down from Oxford he turned pro. and in a year or two was right up among the title contenders. A year later he won the European championship from a Frenchman named Stalmann. I saw that fight. Gledmill kayoed him with a terrific left uppercut in the third round. The next year I saw him fight a tough, coloured American boy in the final eliminator to the world championship. He took the biggest hammering he'd ever had and, though he got the verdict, he was in no shape to box again. An eye had been permanently injured, and it was said that he now wore contact lenses.

He must have made quite a bit of money and when next I heard of him he was with Charlie Mayland at the old Mayland. It was said he'd bought a partnership. I could well believe it. Charlie was a horse-player with the big killing always just a head away. Frank, of course, brought in custom—and there was no need to waste money on a bouncer. I never liked him, and not because of the unpleasant rumours that sometimes went the rounds. I thought him a man who couldn't live with success and whose favourite dish was adulation. That's why I was pretty surprised to hear that when Louis reopened the Mayland, he'd taken Frank over as well.

Frank got to his feet when Louis went in. He was a fine figure of a man: about a hundred and seventy pounds, deep-chested, slim waisted, just over six feet in height. His blond hair looked almost white where the light caught it.

"All right, Frank," Louis told him. "Just going out again."

He went across to the safe, unlocked it, took something out, slipped it into his breast pocket and locked the safe again.

"We'll go upstairs to the flat," he told me as he closed the office door behind him. "More comfortable there."

There were only two floors to the Mayland: the first floor housed the kitchen and quite a good-sized flat. I'd never been up there before, though I'd guessed something of the layout. The bedroom where we were to do our talking was at the back, which kept the noise of the Vickery Street traffic to little more than a hum.

"What will you drink?"

"Nothing for the moment," I told him. Bernice drinks very little and Tom not at all, so I'd already disposed of virtually a bottle.

He poured himself a drink at the little corner bar, looked at it, drank it down and came slowly back to his chair.

"I'm going to tell you something which I never thought I'd tell to a living soul," he said. "I want your advice but on one condition: that under no circumstances whatever will you ever reveal anything I say in this room."

"I see. But may I put it another way? You wish that what you're going to tell me should be strictly confidential. It's never to be divulged to a third party."

"To me, that's the same thing. I also wish you not to make what they call a—a snap decision. Put yourself in my place, Mr. Travers, and don't judge me by what you'd have done yourself."

"Very well," I said. "You have my word. Absolute secrecy and no snap judgments."

I give you his story in my own words. He told it dispassionately but quickly, as if it were something he wanted to eradicate from his whole self. It related to the French Resistance. In 1944, not long before the Allied landings, he was a member of a group, and a valuable one, since the Germans used that Toulouse hotel and he was always careful to be sympathetic. Then one day he was suddenly whisked off to Gestapo headquarters. It appeared he'd been suspected for some time. What he was faced with was a dreadful alternative. Either he told all he knew or his parents and his wife would be shot with the hostages that had been selected after a Resistance raid in the outskirts of the city. He knew about those hostages and there wasn't any doubt that his interrogators would live up to their word. After a couple of days of intensive questioning, he gave in.

Exhausted though he was, he still had enough strength of mind to include in his information an element of warning.

Even then something went wrong. His group was surprised and what prisoners were taken were shot out of hand. A couple of days later he was released, only to find that his parents and his wife were not at the hotel. In fact, he was cynically told that they were being held and would only be released if he virtually acted as a spy. Occasionally he was brought in again for further questioning, and on one such visit he managed to escape. But he was caught and, until he was released at the German retreat two months later, he was kept in close confinement. He then learned that both his parents and his wife had long since been shot.

In spite of that he felt among his old associates an undercurrent of hostility, and after a few months he managed to sell out and move to Paris where he acquired another hotel. He did well there and sold out only when he'd made up his mind to come to England.

It was on the eve of the reopening of the Mayland that he had a telephone call.

"You are Louis Marquette?"

"Yes," he said. "Speaking."

"Then listen, M. Marquette. In the post is a photograph as a specimen of various others in our possession. When you've had time to look at it, I'll call you again."

He took the photograph from his breast pocket and handed it to me. It seemed to have been cut down to a size that would fit an ordinary small business envelope and it showed two men in the act of parting in a street. Behind them was the door of some building. Each man was turning away and one was giving a kind of valedictory wave of the hand. Each was dressed in civilian clothes. The big man on the right, spade-bearded and wearing gloves, was Karl Freudig, a Gestapo agent, the one who usually escorted Louis from the hotel to Gestapo headquarters. The one on the left, giving that wave of the hand, was Louis himself, though I'd never have recognised him.

A day after he'd received that photograph, the telephone went again. The price of those photographs was five thousand pounds, after which he'd never be troubled again. The alternative was that they'd be sent to the French authorities.

"You see what it meant for me?" he said. "He told me things about betraying that group and how he'd been looking for me—he and his friends—for years. Also I'd been a fool, Mr. Travers. I'd never applied for naturalisation, so there'd be no difficulty about—what do you call it—?"

"Extraditing you?"

"Yes, extraditing me."

"So what did you do?"

"I paid," he said. "Arrangements were made and I paid. It was just after I had all these expenses here, and I hadn't the money. That's why I took Frank in as a partner."

"You told him about your trouble?"

"No, no," he told me quickly. "Also I burnt all those photographs except this one which didn't reveal anything to anyone who didn't know."

"They were damning photographs?"

He shrugged his shoulders.

"There was a secret observation post opposite Gestapo headquarters and every one who came was photographed. Some, like this one, were what you called damning. Very damning."

I thought for a moment. Something was puzzling me. "But now it's all over, so where do I come in?"

"I'll tell you," he said. "Two days ago I was rung up again. They held back the negatives of the photographs and they want another payment. This time ten thousand pounds. And it's money that I don't have. Also at any time it may start all over again with more copies. So you see: I can't go to the police because that would mean telling the truth. After all, I did betray that group."

"I don't think you've much to reproach yourself with there," I told him. "It was a cruel decision you had to make and I'd probably have done what you did. But where do I come in in all this?"

"You must get the negatives and any photographs."

I stared. "But how? In God's name, how? What is there to go on?"

"Only this," he said. "I have another week in which to find the money. Also I was told that I'd be under constant watch in case I tried any tricks, as they said. That means that whoever it is must frequent my restaurant"

"Yes," I said slowly. "Did he tell you anything else about himself? How he knew what he knew?"

"Yes," he said. "He said he was a British intelligence agent serving at that time with the Resistance. Also I was foolish. I should have changed my name. Once he knew I'd left France, all he had to do was look in the telephone directories."

I had to do some more thinking.

"All right," I said. "Let's suppose we do spot a man and track him down. What then? If he denies everything, we can prove nothing. We can't cosh him and search wherever he lives. Even if we took such a fantastic risk, it's a hundred to one we'd find nothing."

He slowly shook his head. There was nothing he could really say. The whole thing bothered me. I hate the insolvable problem. I hated even more to see a blackmailer get away with honest money.

"Very well, Louis," I said at last. "I don't promise you a single thing. Remember that. Still, you know Mr. Hallows. I'll arrange for him to have all his meals here for the next few days. If he should be lucky enough to spot a likely man—well, we'll take it from there, if you know what I mean. You realise that he'll have to be told the whole story?"

He shrugged his shoulders. "Mr. Hallows is an honest man. I trust him like I trust you."

I went back to the dance floor to have the mortification of not having been missed. Tom said later that he'd had the evening of his life. His aunt was a marvellous dancer and he'd also stood in—I think that's what they call it—as trumpet in a number he knew.

"You really should make an effort and take some dancing lessons, darling," Bernice told me. "Fancy being at a place like the Mayland and spending half the evening talking nonsense with Louis Marquette."

Which goes to show. I don't know quite what, but it shows it.

5
MORE OF WALE

I DO quite a lot of thinking during the interval between getting into bed and reaching the borderland of sleep. I find it helps sleep to come, provided always that what is thought about is not the persistence of something that has been worrying me seriously during the day. What I like to think about are trifling things like a television show I've just seen, or a missing crossword clue, or a film, or something I've been reading.

That night I was thinking about those revelations of Louis Marquette and the French Resistance, and I'd got as far as my own job in the war when I fell asleep. When I woke there was the sub-conscious, busy as a bee all night, ready with something unexpected. One moment it wasn't there, and before I'd hardly had time to yawn, there it was. The blackmailer had said he'd been a British agent in France. Wale had told his wife he was an intelligence agent. Was Wale the blackmailer?

There then was the problem, hitting me as abruptly as I've written it, and making me suddenly wide awake. Then, almost as quickly, I was shaking my head. It wasn't that I was afraid of coincidences but that Harry Wale seemed hardly to fit. And yet I didn't know. In 1944 he was just in the twenties and he might have been working in Intelligence. According to his wife he was very much of a linguist. Another moment and I was shrugging the whole thing off. Things, I told myself, just didn't happen that way. In any case I'd never seen Wale, and, for all I knew he might turn up a dozen times at the Mayland without any risk of identification.

We weren't meeting Jewle till lunch time, so I went to the Agency to arrange about Hallows and then back to Soho for another word with Louis Marquette. The Mayland didn't open till noon but there's a kind of unloading passage leading off Vickery Street, and a service door with a lift up to the kitchen. A chefs assistant heard me and let me in. Louis was out—probably marketing for the weekend—but Frank Gledmill was in the office. He told me Louis was due back at any moment, so why not wait.

"Too early for a drink?" he asked me.

"If you mean coffee, no," I told him. "But don't let me disturb you."

He'd been working at accounts and a lay-off, he said, would do him good. When coffee came down he swivelled round in his chair.

"If I'm not being curious, you and Louis were having a long palaver last night?" He treated me to his little twisted, ironic smile. "Or were you cooking up something behind my back?"

"Now, wait a minute," I told him. Frank was always a man of pretty uncertain temper. "If you and Louis don't happen to be hitting it off together, don't try to pick any quarrel with me."

"All right, all right," he told me impatiently. "Who said we weren't hitting it off together? And who the hell are you, in any case?"

"Now you're being offensive."

"All right," he said. "So I'm being offensive. What am I supposed to do? Apologise?"

"That's up to you," I told him. "What I'd rather say is that if there's anything *you'd* like to have a palaver about, well, I'm here."

"Forget it," he said. "I'm a bit on edge. To tell the truth, Louis has been acting a bit queer lately. He's got something on his mind. Every time I tax him with it, he puts me off."

"It isn't the business?"

"You know damn well it isn't," he told me. "But tell me. Just what were you two talking about last night?"

Louis came in before I could think up an answer. I wasn't going to sit down again before I got something off my chest. Louis had looked very surprised to see me, and I thought I could get him off balance.

"Frank here has been telling me he's sure you've got something on your mind," I said. "If you have, don't you think you ought to tell him about it?"

He looked at me as if I'd betrayed him.

"He's your partner," I said. "Either you trust him or you don't. If you don't, then I'll be on my way. I'm not getting Frank round my neck."

"You mean. . . ."

"That's right. I think he's a right to know. What I came here for was to ask you a question or two, but if it's going to go on making bad blood between you and Frank, not to mention me, then, as I said, I'll be on my way."

He dropped pretty heavily into his chair. He still didn't like things. Maybe they'd been too sudden.

"Well," he told us at last, "maybe I was wrong."

"That's fine," I told him. "But tell him as soon as I've gone. Sorry to be in such a hurry but I happen to have an important

engagement. So suppose you tell me again just what that telephone caller told you."

He went over it again: a bit reluctantly and spasmodically,
and always with glances across at Frank, but there didn't seem
to be much that I'd missed. The ex-Resistance, in collaboration
with the authorities, had a list of war-time collaborators, a great
number of whom had already been brought to trial. The search
for the others was still going on. Louis' name was on that list.

"What sort of voice did the caller have?"

"An English voice," he told me. "What you call upper class."

"An old voice?"

He shrugged his broad shoulders. "How can you tell? Of my
age, perhaps. If you mean a grown man: well, he was a grown man."

"You'd recognise the voice?"

He shrugged his shoulders again. "These things are hard to
remember. A voice on the telephone: a voice that talks with you.
Two different things."

"Well, try," I said. "Make your rounds of the tables and listen
hard. Take care never to miss a single guest. Get them to talk to
you. Hallows will be here from Monday's lunch on, but I think
you can do more than he can. And just one other thing. When you
paid over that first money, just how did you pay it?"

"Money?" Flank said.

"You keep out of this." I told him. "When I'm gone you'll hear
the whole thing. How did you hand over the money, Louis?"

"In a parcel." he said. "All old notes. I was to go into St. Anne's
Church and leave it and go out."

"Thanks." I said. "Obviously he took good care not to be seen."
I held out my hand.

"Goodbye. Louis. And thanks. Don't be too optimistic, but
we'll do our best to straighten all this out. Goodbye, Frank. Be
seeing you some time."

"Sure," he said. "And thanks. Sorry we had those few words."

I couldn't help smiling as I went back to where I'd parked the
car. An apology and thanks from Frank Gledmill in one breath
was definitely an event. I'd heard he'd been getting a bit morose

of late and I'd had a lot of luck in handling him. Mind you, I was still dead sure I was right in advising Louis to make a clean breast. Whatever else Frank wasn't, he was a loyal enough partner. And Frank, for all I knew, might help. Frank might always have been his own enemy, but no one could deny that he had plenty of brains.

I went home and collected Tom. Jewle met us at the club, and as always when I'd spent an hour in his company, I couldn't help thinking again what a great fellow he was. There's something shiningly genuine about him. Like most big men, he's quiet. There's nothing about him that he ever tries to parade and yet he's always surprising me by the things he knows. A friend, it seems to me, is someone with whom you know you could never conceivably quarrel. Jewle was just that kind of friend.

We had that conducted tour of the Yard. When we came out, Tom remarked in his apologetic way that as we were so close, couldn't we look round the Abbey.

"You run along," I said. "There're always guides doing tours. We'll expect you at the flat when we see you."

"A nice boy," Jewle said. "I expect Bernice is very fond of him."

"We both are," I said. "But now he's gone I've remembered something. Could we go back to your room? I'd like to ask a favour."

On the way up I was trying to fabricate a water-tight story. Then I decided to say virtually nothing at all. He sent down for a pot of tea and I didn't broach the subject till he'd handed me my cup. What I told him was that I had a client who had fraternised with the enemy during the war and had been recognised recently by an ex-intelligence agent who was attempting to blackmail him. Like all people in his predicament, he was resolutely refusing to go to the police. It so happened that I had a likely suspect, a man named Harry Wale. All I needed was to verify if Wale had been an agent of British Intelligence in 1944.

"He might have been in M.I.5 or in general Intelligence," I said, "and, if so, he was working with the French Resistance at that time. As you know, I don't stand a chance of getting anyone to hand over information to me, but you people here are different."

"Harry Wale," he said. "How do you spell it?"

He reached across for a note-pad and wrote the name down. "Age?"

"In 1944 he was about twenty-one or two."

"That's quite a time ago," he said. "Any known description?"

"Tall, well-spoken, dark-haired, good-looking. A very plausible manner. Afraid that's all."

He wrote it all down. He gave me his slow smile. "Well, I'll see what I can do. Might be a day or two. These fellows always take their time."

The Sunday was a quiet day. I stayed home with cross-words and a book while Bernice and Tom went to the Zoo. Monday saw a change of plans. We'd always been of the opinion that no visitor should ever be allowed to leave England without seeing Canterbury Cathedral, so off Bernice and Tom went to Canterbury. In the evening we were dining out for a final fling.

In any case I'd have had to be at the office that Monday morning in order to brief Hallows. He was waiting for me when I arrived and straight away we got down to business.

He, too, had known the Mayland in Charlie's days but hadn't patronised it since Louis had taken over, except for the assignment I mentioned, so it took quite a time to get the whole set-up clearly in his mind. Even then, as I had to agree, it was about the queerest assignment he'd ever been given—to be on the look-out for someone who might never appear and to have nothing by which to recognise him if he did.

I hadn't had time to open the few letters on my desk, but as I ran an eye over them, I noticed that one was an air-mail letter from New York. I opened it first and my eyes almost shot from their sockets when I saw who'd written it. I didn't wait to push the buzzer but nipped out of my chair in pursuit of Hallows. I needn't have worried. He was talking to Bertha.

He grinned when I told him what had happened.

"This ought to be good," he told me. "Wonder what he's up to now?"

I read the letter to him: very slowly, since I wanted to digest it thoroughly myself. It was quite a long letter.

Dear Mr. Travers,

You'll be surprised to hear from me so soon, but when I reached Butte it was to a sorrowful homecoming. Millie Wale had died from a stroke the day before I arrived.

Joe was always a secretive man and no one knew his exact circumstances when he died and Millie never let it be assumed that she was left other than comfortably off. In her Will I was named executor and it was a great surprise to me to find the estate will amount to somewhere in the region of a quarter of a million dollars. The important thing is that fifty thousand dollars was left to her nephew, Harry.

What I urgently want you therefore to do is to continue the search for him and I am empowered to spend immediately up to five hundred dollars—a draft for which is enclosed—to cover such a search. What with my own responsibilities and those arising out of the executorship, I shall be busy in the coming weeks: far too busy to come to England, so I shall assume you are undertaking the search. I shall not expect miracles, so spend the dollars enclosed and no more. Should you however feel that further expense will bring definite results, then continue after notifying me in the way I shall suggest. In that context I am happy to tell you that during a thorough examination of papers, documents, etc., left by the deceased, I came across what may be a valuable clue. It was a letter written some eighteen years ago by Joe's brother Alfred, Harry's father. Alfred was then owner or tenant of the Bull Inn, Upcliffe, Sussex, England.

If you should track Harry down, please put him in touch with me at once. The quickest way will be a notice in the New York Times which you can fix in London. Almost wherever I happen to be over here, I can get the Times. Suggested wording is "—ASHMAN—H.W. will be in touch with you"—or "ASHMAN—regret to report further progress impossible." I am sure this will be a far quicker means of communication than by letters or cables which may have to follow me from one State to another.

Unless such a notice appears, I shall take it you are undertaking a new search. I am temporarily in New York, as you see.

Sincerely,

CHARLES ASHMAN.

I looked at Hallows.

"Well?"

He grinned.

"Well, whatever ideas we may have about Ashman himself, he's sent five hundred good reasons why you should take the job."

"Yes," I said slowly. "But the worrying thing is this. Those lies he told us about his activities at Laybrook may have been for a very good reason. There may be a perfectly simple explanation. After all, this is a straightforward, lucid business letter. On the face of it there's no swindle like the Spanish Prisoner racket. He's paying *us*."

"True enough," he said. "But may I make a suggestion?"

"Why not?"

"Then why not send a letter or a cable to your New York agents. Get them to make certain enquiries. You can carry on looking for Wale meanwhile, till you know there's no hope or till the dollars are gone. A reply should be back long before then."

We drafted a letter. By air-mail it would reach McGuffie Investigations in three days. Instructions were:

1.—What is known in Butte, Montana, of a Charles Ashman, said to be executor of the estate of a Millie Wale, lately deceased.

2.—What is known of a Timber Company in Butte, said to be owned by the late Millie Wale.

3.—What is known of Charles Ashman at the Cavendish Hotel, 178 W. 198th Street, New York, where he was ostensibly staying on about the 11th instant.

We got that letter off at once. Hallows asked me if I'd be going down to Upcliffe myself. I said I'd probably be going the next morning. I had to see my nephew off and then I'd be free.

"Look," he said, "There's plenty of time for me to get dolled up for the Mayland, so why shouldn't I slip along to Somerset House and take a look at Harry Wale's birth certificate?"

Maybe I was losing my grip. It was something we ought to have done long since. However, I handled the rest of my mail, then I had a look at the motoring handbook. Upcliffe had a population of 4,000 approximately, and it had two hotels. One, the Royal Oak, had two stars: the other, with a modest one star, was the Bull. The Royal Oak had twenty-four bedrooms and its charges were appreciably higher than those of the Bull. It had only twelve bedrooms. Bertha got the number.

"Bull Hotel," a woman's voice said.

"My name's Travers." I spelt it for her. "Have you two single rooms available for tomorrow night and the next?"

She told me almost at once that she had. I said we'd be arriving for lunch.

"Something I ought to mention," I said. "I'm a solicitor, enquiring about the heirs of the late Alfred Wale—"

"But he died years ago!"

"I know," I said. "We're trying to get information about his son, Harry, so if you can pick up anything between now and the time we arrive. I'll be most grateful. Naturally I'll be prepared to pay for any really helpful information. What is your name, by the way?"

"Greeve," she said. "My husband's the manager."

I thanked her, confirmed the time of arrival and rang off. I took Ashman's letter and cheque to Norris and talked things over and by then it was coffee time. Hallows was with Bertha when she brought it in.

Hallows had found what he'd been looking for. Harry Wale was the son of Alfred and Ethel Wale, and he'd been born at Upcliffe on April the 22nd, 1920.

*

If Ashman's draft went through, and I anticipated no difficulty about that, I had about a hundred and seventy-five pounds with which to work. It might mean a pretty tight budget if anything was unearthed at Upcliffe: if there weren't, then, in fairness to the Millie Wale estate, there might have to be a refund. Not that that was worrying me at the moment.

French and I went down in my car and got to Upcliffe just before noon. It ought to have been called Undercliffe, since it was tucked in nicely under the Downs, but there's no accounting for those old names. I'd been through it years before and remembered it only vaguely: a quiet, rather straggling little town: a community oasis surrounded by arable land and hop gardens. We passed the Royal Oak soon after we entered the High Street. The Bull, a much smaller place, was on the tiny market square. Its stuccoed front almost certainly concealed Tudor timbering and, as soon as we went inside, the ancient beams of the little reception room were there to prove it.

Mrs. Greeve was at the desk. She gave us both a good look before the welcoming smile. After we'd signed the book she told me her husband would like to see me when it was convenient and I gathered what she meant. At the moment he was in the bar. French parked the car and brought up our bags. Each bedroom was heavily beamed, and the ceiling of mine was so low that my six feet and more instinctively ducked whenever I changed position. They were comfortable rooms: everything spotlessly clean.

We went down for a drink. There were quite a few people in the bar: locals apparently and of various social strata. Bert Greeve was a man of about sixty: of medium height and rather stout. He gave me a quick look and no more when I asked for two pints of bitter. I asked him what time the bar closed and he told me the usual two-thirty. He must have gathered what I was driving at, for after lunch, at about twenty to three, there was a knock at my room door and there he was. I did the formal introductions. There was only the one chair in the room and I made him take it. There was room for French and me on the bed.

"So you're a solicitor, sir?"

It was a wary kind of opening.

"And was I right in thinking you were after information about a Harry Wale?"

"That's right," I said. "He's come in for quite a lot of money and that's why we're prepared to pay for any helpful information as to his whereabouts. And for any trouble you yourself may have taken."

"That's all right, sir," he said. "No need to worry about that yet." He brought out his wallet and selected a small sheet of paper. "I have here a couple of names for you. Bob Goodson, he used to be handyman here, and what he doesn't know about the Wales, nobody knows. He's eighty-five. Then there's Dick Ramus of North Farm. He was in the bar when you were there, though of course you wouldn't know who he was. He was at school with Harry Wale."

He handed me the paper.

"What school would that be?"

"In those days it was the Old Grammar School, sir. Now they've built a whole lot of new rooms and they just call it The Grammar School."

"I'm most grateful to you," I said. "But about yourself, Mr. Greeve. What do you know personally about the Wales?"

"Not very much, sir, but I'll tell you. This used to be a free house and it was part owned by some Lewes people. Alfred Wale ran it, and so did his father before him, till he died. That was in nineteen-forty-four. Alfred, so I'm told, never talked a lot about his private business, because, when he died, it had to be put up for auction and it was bought by British Hotels Limited. Maybe you know them, sir."

"I do," I said. "I even happen to hold some of their shares."

"Well, that's all right then, sir. I came here in forty-six after they'd spent no end of money on it and I've been here ever since. In Alfred Wale's time it wasn't much more than a pub and a sort of eating house. Used to cater for the market business chiefly. According to what I've been told, young Wale was thinking of making changes here himself till the war put a stop to it. And, to tell the truth, sir, that's about all I know."

"And a good start too," I told him. "But these two people: what'll be the best time to see them?"

"Bob doesn't get about much nowadays," he said. "You could see him at any time. The same with Dick Ramus, except he may be working on the farm somewhere. Anyone would know where he was."

I handed him two five-pound notes.

"No, no, sir," he said. "There's no need to do that."

I made him take them. If he mentioned the fact it might be good publicity. Someone else might come forward with something worth while. At any rate, we went downstairs and he showed us how to find Goodson and Ramus. Bob Goodson's cottage was only a couple of hundred yards away: Ramus's farm was a good mile. French and I talked it over, and he took the car. I walked on through the town to Warble Cottages.

6
END OF TRAIL

OF THE three small cottages, Goodson's was the nearest to the town. When he opened the door at my knock, I could hardly believe my eyes. It had turned out a dull afternoon with imminent rain, and, in the dark of his tiny parlour, I took him at first for a son. But it was Bob Goodson right enough. Almost eighty years ago he'd got a job as ostler at the Bull, and now he had the look of a wizened jockey. A knee, long ago kicked by a horse, was crippled with rheumatism, but he was cheerful enough. And shrewd enough, or am I giving him too much credit? At any rate, he spotted me at once as the gentleman from London who wanted to know about Harry Wale.

He offered me his own grandfather chair but I insisted he keep it and took another instead. It was cheerful enough in that tiny room, with quite a fire going in the old-fashioned grate. I'd kept my overcoat on, but it wasn't long before I was glad to take it off. There'd been a smell of tobacco in the room, so I offered him my pouch. He knocked out the dottle from his pipe.

"Don't often get tobacco like this, sir."

He packed the pipe so full that it was hard work to get it going. Then he gave it up.

"Think I'll save this for later on," he told me. "And you want to know about young Harry, sir. Is it right he've come into a fortune?"

"Quite a big sum of money," I said. "All we have to do now is find him. You've no idea yourself where he is?"

His wizened old face wrinkled still more as he thought. "Must be best part o' twenty years since I seed him. In forty-four, it was. He was in the army and he got leave to come and see to things. In November it was, just sort of a day like this when he come into the pub."

"Wearing uniform?"

"No, sir. Just ordinary clothes. He was a captain, so he told me. Quite altered he was from when he joined up at the beginning of the war. The second war, sir, if you understand. He only stayed just long enough to square things up and, far as I know, no one's ever clapped eyes on him since."

"Of course you remember him being born."

He chuckled. He even remembered Harry's father being born. After all, he'd had no schooling after his eighth year and had gone straight to the Bull. That was one of the great ages—the apotheosis, one might almost say—of the horse. For Bob, the last nail in the coffin was when the old stables were turned into the present garage. That was Harry's doing, he said. He was always wanting his father to get what he called up-to-date. Wanted to make the Bull as good as the Royal Oak.

"What sort of a boy was he?"

"A crafty one," he said. "Used to twist his mother round his little finger. Regular young liar too. Could lie himself out of anything. Then when his mother died, Alfred made a regular fool of him too."

"He did well at school?"

"Yes," he said. "I will say that for him. Reckon he was one o' the smartest they ever had. Alfred wanted him to be a doctor, or lawyer, or something, but Harry knew he'd be coming in for the pub one day and that was good enough for him. You're a lawyer, aren't you, sir?"

"In a way, yes."

"Briars we always call 'em. Like them old briars in a hedge what cling to you. No offence meant, sir."

"That's all right, Bob," I said. "I know what you mean. And you'd say that at the time war broke out, Harry was as good as in charge?"

"Well," he said, "I suppose you could. Always making what he'd call improvements."

"Then why did he join up?"

He gave me quite a crafty look. "You never knew about Mabel Clark?"

"Never heard of her in my life."

"Well," he said, "everyone knew about it and I don't suppose it'll do no harm talking about it now. She was chamber-maid at the Bull and Harry got her in the family way. It didn't come out till he'd gone. Alfred saw she was looked after all right, but Harry never showed his face here till that time when his father died."

"Harry was one for the girls?"

He chuckled. "A regular ram, sir. I could have told some rare tales if I'd been so minded. Rare smart-looking he always was. A regular gentleman."

I let him ramble on about the old days, hoping he might let something else fall, but he didn't. About Harry Wale there was precious little else to tell. Maybe it had been an hour wasted. I didn't know. One never does know. Something he had told me might chance to be of use. Everything he *had* told me certainly fitted the Harry Wale who had married Carol Nevett. He looked quite startled at the tip I gave him—only a couple of pound notes—and for a moment I thought he was going to spit on them for luck.

*

French didn't get back till after five. I ordered tea for us and over it we talked. Dick Ramus, as we'd been told, had been a contemporary of Harry Wale at the Old Grammar School, and remembered him well.

"He told me no end of tales about him," French said, "but they all added up to just a few things. He wasn't much good at games, but they had a Cadet Corps at the school and he was a sergeant. That's about the top rank, I believe. And that's why he got a commission almost as soon as war broke out. He sent Ramus a postcard of himself in uniform and that's all he ever heard of him."

"Any other characteristics?"

"Yes. He'd be at the back of escapades and generally managed to shift the blame on to someone else. Also he must have had a very good brain. Ramus reckoned he might have been almost anything if he'd only set his heart on it."

He had a look at his notes.

"One thing that may be important. He left here hurriedly after getting a girl in the family way."

"Old Goodson told me that. A girl named Mabel Clark. You might try to follow that up in the morning. There's just the faint chance Wale might have made contact with her after the war. Anything else?"

"Yes. He gave me a name that might be useful. The Reverend James Balfry who used to be headmaster of the school when Wale was there. After he retired he took the living at Croft Green. He's still there. Address is The Rectory."

"That's fine," I said. "I'll see him in the morning. Tonight we'll spend most of our time in the bar. Everyone'll know by now what we're here for."

For the expenditure of little more than a pound that night on standing treat, I heard quite a lot about Harry Wale, but little that was new. Not a soul mentioned Mabel Clark. In the morning I looked up the Reverend James Balfry in the telephone directory and gave him a ring. He said he'd be delighted to see me. There would be coffee at around ten-thirty if I could make it by then.

It was a cross-country drive of about twenty miles. The village was little more than a hamlet but the church looked large enough to seat most of Upcliffe itself. The rectory too was enormous: a relic of those days when mostly the moneyed entered the Church. Balfry had closed down most of it and was using only three or four of the rooms. He was a widower and it was his elderly housekeeper who showed me into his study.

He was tall, rather thin, but a most imposing man. Except for the side whiskers, he reminded me of Charles Kingsley. But he had quite a sense of humour and we got along fine, even if he was an Oxford man.

"So Harry Wale's come into money," he said. "I always thought he'd either end up in jail or as a millionaire."

"He had a good brain?"

"A brilliant boy. One of those lucky people who can do in his sleep what most people have to work hard at."

The housekeeper brought in the coffee. It wasn't too good but at least it was hot and sweet.

"That mention of jail in connection with Harry Wale," I said. "Would you mind telling me what prompted it?"

"Just an unlimited astuteness," he told me smilingly. "To tell the truth, he was completely unprincipled and the astounding thing was I could never—well, as the modern idiom is, pin anything on him. He could look one in the face and tell the most plausible story. You knew it was a lie and yet you could never prove it. He left school at sixteen, by the way. I'm sure he could have walked away with one of our two major scholarships, either of which would have taken him to Oxford, but he was crazy to leave. To tell the truth, I wasn't so sorry to see him go."

"Someone or other at Upcliffe was telling me he did good work in your Cadet Corps."

"Perfectly true," he said. "Anything he really liked to do, he did exceptionally well. Languages, for instance. In those days we had an exceptionally good language master: a man named Henrikson, a naturalised Swiss: a great believer in spoken German and French as opposed to the old-fashioned teaching of my young days. Henrikson always said he never had a pupil like Wale." He shook his head. "Henrikson was an interpreter during the war. Poor fellow: he was killed in the final advance. I think it was in Holland."

Before we finished with the coffee, he had quite an idea. Was I in a hurry? I said I wasn't.

"Well," he said, "I have some copies of *The Upcliffian*." He leaned back for a moment with eyes closed. "Oh, yes. Wale was under me from 1932 till 1936. Those will be the relevant years. Perhaps you'd like to look through them yourself."

I said I'd be most grateful. Once again I was thinking those copies of his school's magazine might contain a clue that might subsequently lead me to Harry Wale. Each issue consisted only of some sixteen pages, so it didn't take me all that long, and the only things of interest that I learned were these, and they were only confirmations. There were Wale's various gazettings in what might be called the school's Part I Orders, through lance-corporal and corporal, to sergeant in his penultimate year. At the Prizegiving at the end of his second year he received the junior prize for German. The next year he won the senior prizes for both German and French, and won them again in his final year. Henrikson, during those last two years, took about twenty senior boys, with a younger master, on Easter visits to Salzburg and Paris respectively. On that last trip Wale was mentioned as being the life and soul of the party.

It was about midday when I left Croft Green and I was making for Lewes to interview, I hoped, the firm who had handled the 1944 sale of the Bull at Upcliffe. They, I also hoped, might put me in touch with Alfred Wale's solicitors. If the auctioneers didn't close till one, I had half an hour before lunch. As it turned out, they no longer had any records of that sale, except a diary entry, but they did give me the name of the solicitors—Fletcher and Poole, three doors down in the High Street. I left them till after lunch.

It was the managing clerk whom I ultimately saw. Luckily for me, he'd been with the firm for over forty years and had a first-class memory. A few minutes' search and he came up with a file. The upshot was that I learned that as a result of his father's death, Harry Wale had come in for a sum of approximately eleven thousand pounds. This, at his request—he was abroad at the time of the final settlement—was transferred to an account at Barclays Bank, Piccadilly.

I had plenty to think about on my way back to Upcliffe that late afternoon. Wordsworth said the child was father of the man: a paradox that was more of a truism in the case of Harry Wale. Everything we had learned and surmised about the man had been true of the boy. One thing he hadn't lied about was his gift for languages, and those foreign newspapers that Carol Wale was always seeing in the house hadn't been brought there to give an impression of a knowledge which he didn't possess. The problem was, had they been designed to bolster up a lie—that he was an agent for British Intelligence?

In connection with that there was something else. Five years ago Wale was still claiming to be doing the same work. That was in late 1955. But in 1945, only ten years before, he had received the sum of eleven thousand pounds. Reasonably invested, that should have given him at least the hard core of a living. Where had that money gone and, if it hadn't gone, why was he still working? And why was money so essential that, when he'd planned to leave his wife, it had to be with the proceeds from a surreptitious sale of her house?

As soon as I got back to the Bull I rang Norris. I brought him up to date with the case and suggested a personal call on the Barclays Bank branch. Naturally he wouldn't hope to find that Wale still had an account there. What he might hope to find was that, if the money had been withdrawn or transferred, just how those transactions had been effected. I said I'd be in at about noon the following day and maybe he could have the information by then.

French had unearthed only one thing—why people were a bit hesitant about recalling the Mabel Clark episode. It appeared she'd married, after the birth of a son, an assistant boot and shoe repairer, and he now had a shop of his own next door to the chemist's in the market square. Their family now amounted to five.

Just as we'd finished a belated tea, I had a telephone call. I thought it might be Norris, but it was Balfry.

"Ah, Mr. Travers," came his brisk voice. "About the gentleman we were discussing this morning. I remembered something after you left. I've been looking for it, but can't find it. A photograph of himself in uniform that he sent to me in, I believe, March 1940. On the back was a very flippant message. As far as I remember it was 'How's this for the black sheep of Upcliffe?' Words to that effect. Just a bit of adolescent boasting."

"Trying to get a rather cheap revenge?"

"That's right," he said. "Telling me that he knew I knew, if you know what I mean."

"Exactly. But do you remember the regimental badges or anything that would connect him with any particular regiment or corps?"

"I don't," he said. "All I remember is that he was facing slightly sideways and had that imperturbable, enigmatical sort of look I'd seen so often. I do remember he was a second-lieutenant and had a very shiny Sam Browne."

That was virtually the end of the Upcliffe enquiries. We again spent best part of the evening in the bar. We didn't mention Harry Wale's name and nobody else mentioned it. As far as Upcliffe Bull was concerned, the brief wonder was at an end. The next morning we left for town soon after ten.

I calculated that even with expenses and overheads I'd spent less than a hundred and fifty dollars, and I had the uneasy feeling that what we were going to run out of was not money but ideas.

When we got back, Norris had the information from the bank. The Harry Wale account, opened in 1945, had been closed in 1950.

"Closed," I said. "Not transferred."

"And a far less healthy account too," he told me. "The original eleven thousand plus had shrunk to just over two thousand."

There are times when figures can be both graphic and loquacious; these weren't. An average spending of under two thousand pounds a year couldn't be called an orgy of extravagance. A new quality car and an exchange to a later model after four years would account for a good slice of it. Maybe a car was useful to an intelligence agent, but, if so, why wasn't it provided by the government? And if Wale had been in employment during those five years, why did he need to spend at the rate of an extra thousand a year?

The bank, Norris said, had had no communication from Wale since the closing of the account. His own idea was that Wale had decided on a change of occupation, and probably a shady one. He could have left just a few pounds with the bank and so kept the account alive for any future emergency. Surely the usual practice, too, was to let a bank transfer one's account.

"Let's face it," I said. "Wale withdrew every penny and, as far as we're concerned, disappeared. Then he popped up as a married man at Ilmoor five years ago, and disappeared from there. Nothing we unearthed at Upcliffe gave a clue to where he went after the first disappearance and nothing at Ilmoor gave the smallest clue to where he went after the second. Very well then. Let's do what we could have done in the first place if we'd only had the time—advertise for him."

We chose eight papers in whose personal columns we'd insert an appeal. We've had to do that kind of thing before and it's done by arrangement with our solicitors. The wording was:

> If Harry Wale, only son of Alfred and Ethel Wale, both deceased, and late of the Bull Hotel, Upcliffe, Sussex, will communicate with Price, Price and Morland, 349, Chancery Lane, London, W.C.2, he will hear of something to his advantage.

At an average cost of fifteen shillings a line, even for three consecutive insertions, it wasn't all that expensive, and it was Ashman's money we were spending. Norris said he'd see to it at once.

Hallows had ascertained when I'd be back from Upcliffe and he rang me soon after I'd left Norris. It was only to say that nothing so far had happened at the Mayland. Something was to happen before his orgy of free meals had gone, but it's better to leave it, and what arose out of it, till the end of the Wale enquiry. Keeping the two enquiries separate avoids overlapping. And your own confusion.

What happened first was a call from Jewle the afternoon of my return from Upcliffe.

"The man you asked me to enquire about. No one of his name appears in the records of the Intelligence Corps or has ever been employed by M.I.5."

All I could do, of course, was to thank him, and that ended that. The trouble was that I couldn't very well call on him again. Two other things had occurred to me, provided I still had any faith in Wale's claim to have been doing work for Intelligence. One was to try to find out if what had been the old Free French headquarters still had any kind of existence, and records, and if it could find out if a Harry Wale had been seconded to them from a British regiment for work in 1944 with the French Resistance. Or I could try to obtain from the War Office the full military record of Harry Wale. In both cases it seemed to me I should need some influence. Information of either sort wouldn't be likely to be divulged to a detective agency.

What I decided to do was wait till a possible reply was received from those advertisements. Two days after the last of them had appeared, no one had come forward. There was still time, of course, but then something else happened. As far as I was concerned, it was like a smack on the skull from a sledgehammer. It sent the whole thing to Limbo as effectively as if the devil himself had kicked it endways.

It was a cable from McGuffie Investigations.

Charles Ashman not known in Butte Montana stop no Millie Wale lately deceased stop no Millie Wale known stop no timber company as described in your letter stop no Charles Ashman at hotel at dates mentioned stop McGuffie.

You see what a facer that was. It reached me just after one o'clock and I'd been finishing a job in the office or I would have been away to lunch. I rang the Mayland. It was Frank Gledmill who answered, and he actually seemed quite pleased to hear my voice.

"What can I do for you, Travers?"

"Is Hallows with you?"

"Came in about ten minutes ago. I saw him myself."

"Then there's plenty of time," I said. "Ask him, will you, to see me here when he leaves. And, by the way, Frank, what did you think of what Louis had to tell you?"

He gave a grunt. "He certainly got himself in one hell of a mess. The only thing is to get him out of it, and me."

"How d'you mean?"

"What I say. Parting with that kind of money's going to hit me as well as him. I'd like to talk to you about it some time."

"Drop in when you like," I told him. "Just ring beforehand to make sure I'm here."

Hallows must have cut short his lunch for he was with me just before two. He just couldn't believe that cable. He had to read it a second time.

"It's fantastic," he said. "Everything he told us was sheer fabrication."

"But why?"

He was frowning while he lighted his cigarette.

"Don't know. Only one thing is absolutely clear. He wants to find Wale. First he planked down a hundred pounds. Then he sent five hundred dollars. To me that says he wants him really bad."

"And equally important is that Ashman doesn't want his own real identity known. It's a hundred to one Ashman isn't his name."

We took our coats off, so to speak, and had a look at the whole case from the beginning and, very slowly, a kind of pattern began to emerge. When we'd had time to examine it, we knew that pattern was true.

Ashman wanted Wale. He'd gone to the Davenant Parva area that morning because he had hopes of finding him, or information about him, there. He hadn't been successful but he'd gone on with his private enquiries. They'd led him to Ilmoor—a clue he might have picked up in the Davenant Parva area—only to find that Wale had long since gone. He either hadn't the time or the ability to follow up things from there, so he had come to us. We'd been no more successful, but in the time between receiving our negative report and the letter he'd ostensibly sent from New York, he'd had sense enough to go to Somerset House and discovered that Wale had connections with Upcliffe.

"It was probably a friend of his in New York who sent that letter to us," Hallows said. "Ashman sent him a cheque and he sent the draft to you, and a copy of the letter, and the friend typed it on the hotel notepaper."

"Maybe," I said. "But that draft was on a New York bank. I wouldn't be surprised if Ashman flew there. He must have money and he's prepared to spend it to find Wale. If it's a matter of life and death to him, what's a few hundred dollars for a flight to New York?"

"Yes," he said, then suddenly looked up. "Are you prepared to spend any more money?"

"On what?"

"Well, you could get Bob McGuffie to make enquiries about that cheque. You could find out if Ashman really did fly to New York."

I smiled. A bit ruefully, but I smiled.

"And do that for whom? As far as we're now concerned, Ashman doesn't exist. No," I said, "I know it won't work but we'll try to flush him once more into the open."

"How?"

I picked up a pencil and reached for the note-pad.

"Here's how. I put a notice in the London edition of the *New York Times*. Just as he suggested. It's a hundred to one he's still over here. We've had that *New York Times* trick played on us before; just a convenient way of establishing an alibi."

The final draft of the notice was this:

ASHMAN—regret case abandoned. Collect balance two hundred dollars.—L.T.

I might as well tell you now that that notice in the *New York Times* had no sequel. The pseudo-Ashman neither rang us nor wrote us. That notice might never have appeared. Also the Harry

Wale, who could have heard something to his advantage, was as dumb as the grave. Both men, as far as we were concerned, might never have existed. All that remained of the case was a special account in our bank: two hundred dollars being held in the name of Charles Ashman.

7
BACK TO THE MAYLAND

FRANK Gledmill did drop in to see me. When Bertha buzzed through to say that he was there, I'll own I didn't feel too happy. I wondered, in fact, why I hadn't kept my mouth shut. I hate scenes, and with Frank Gledmill one never quite knew what was going to happen. But I needn't have worried. When he left the office that morning, I almost liked him.

He'd actually walked from the Mayland, and that was a tidy step, and he was proposing to walk back. He said he liked keeping himself in shape and every morning, rain or shine, he took an hour's brisk walk. Sometimes he took another in the late afternoon: it all depended on how he felt. That, and the weather.

He certainly looked remarkably fit and I couldn't help thinking what he might have done if it hadn't been for that trouble with his eyes.

"Almost my time for coffee, Frank. You'd like a cup?"

"Guess I would," he said as I took his coat and hat. He didn't smoke, so I didn't offer him a cigarette.

"You've come to talk about Louis," I suggested.

"It's necessary," he said bluntly. "By the way, I'm grateful to you for making Louis put me wise. It was mighty decent of you."

"It merely seemed at the moment the right thing to do," I said. "You're either his partner or you're not. It's as simple as that. In any case you know the way we're trying to handle things."

"Yes," he said, "and I can't say I like it. Not that I'm trying to teach you your business."

"Well, what's wrong with it?"

Bertha brought coffee in. When she'd gone he told me what was wrong.

"You're backing a thousand to one chance when you're trying to find whoever it is that's keeping tabs on Louis. I don't think there's a particle of truth in it. That yarn about having him watched was just to scare Louis. He's there, isn't he? Why should he bolt? What would it prove?"

"Very well, Frank. Let's make the criticism constructive. Just what would you do yourself?"

"What Louis ought to have done in the first place," he said. "Instead of calmly handing over five thousand pounds' worth of notes in that church, he should have contacted someone like me. As soon as that packet was picked up. I'd have had the one who did it."

"And suppose it wasn't the actual blackmailer but only an agent?"

He smiled. His fingers came together in a clench as he thought of it.

"Would it have mattered? By the time I'd have finished with him he'd have told me who was employing him. And that's when the real fun would have started."

I winced. Suddenly I was seeing again that last fight of his and the bloody faces of the two men beneath the lights of the ring.

"Guess it would," I said. "But not for him. And that's what you're proposing should be done this time? Even when you realise that this Operation Gledmill, or whatever you call it, takes place at the very last moment?" I shrugged my shoulders. "Still, there's plenty of time before then. Play it my way, Frank. If that fails, then there's your way left."

He seemed to agree, so I switched to Louis and how he was taking things.

"That's what I nearly forgot to mention," he said. "I think he's keeping something back. He knows a lot more than what he's admitted."

That was a nasty surprise. I must have looked quite startled.

"Knows a lot more about what?"

"About the bastard who's blackmailing him. Louis is far more on the surface than you'd think. Didn't I tell you I knew he had something on his mind? Well, he's still got something on his mind, and it's more than parting with that money."

"That begins to alter things," I said. "If he knows the black-mailer—"

I had a sudden idea. "Wait a minute. Let's work this out logic-ally. Louis didn't know the man, or the man didn't know him, all the time he was in Paris, or else he'd either have been apprehended or blackmailed. He didn't meet the man till he'd got the Mayland as he wanted it, years and years after what happened in 1944, and then he seems to have paid up without anything more than an argument. That makes me think like you. He knew whom he was dealing with, and the man he was dealing with was someone he knew in 1944. That seems to give us three choices: a British agent serving with the Resistance, a German who was mixed up in it all at the time, and an ex-member of the Resistance."

"Sounds good sense to me," he said. "But there's another side to it. All this business has been done over the telephone. That means he doesn't know Louis has recognised him. Also he's prob-ably got something of his own to hide."

"True enough," I said. "The real problem is to think out what we're going to do about it."

"No use talking to Louis," he said. "I asked him bluntly if he knew who it was and he swore to God he didn't. All the same"—he gave me one of those ironic looks—"I don't know that I shan't do a little detecting myself. It isn't all that hard, you know."

"Oh?" I said blandly. "What's so easy about it?"

"Come off it." he told me. "You fellows make a mystery of it because it pays you. But take what that man of yours, Hallows, is doing. I'm in a position to do it far better than he is. And all the rest of it. Asking a question or two. Putting two and two together. What's so hard about that?"

"Nothing at all," I said. "In fact, why not just call it a racket. But about this detection work you're going to do. It's going to be strictly on your own? Nothing said about what you might discover? To me? or Louis?"

"You're jumping ahead," he told me irritably. "Let's leave it there, shall we?"

"Suits me." I said. "What about another cup of coffee?" He got to his feet. "Thanks, no. Time I was getting back. Oh, and one other thing. Don't forget I'm in this with Louis. What affects him affects me. Just a reminder in case you might think all this is something just between him and you."

I didn't like the way he said it. I couldn't miss the implied threat.

"I'll remember it," I told him. "You and Louis and me."

"Now you've got the right idea." He smiled as he held out his hand. "It's been a nice chat. Maybe I'll drop in again some time."

"Always glad to see an old friend," I told him. "Especially when he suddenly becomes a colleague."

If there was an irony, he preferred to ignore it. He was still smiling as he went through the door.

I wasn't sorry to see him go. It pays to be wary of people as touchy as Frank Gledmill: at one moment all smiles and affability and then, before you hardly know it, bridling at some imaginary offence. And when the one concerned has the physique and the quick temper of Frank, it pays to be doubly careful. Maybe he had his grievances, but haven't most of us too? The world didn't owe Frank a living. It hadn't treated him so badly after all.

But what he had told me was far more important. He knew Louis intimately: far better than I, and, if he said that Louis hadn't told us the whole truth, then there had to be something in it. What was it then, that Louis was keeping back? All I could think was that he had been guilty of a lot of self-glorification. Perhaps he'd really been a collaborator and finally he and the Germans had double-crossed each other. Whatever the truth, I didn't like the way things had suddenly begun to shape. After all, there are three people to whom you have to tell nothing but the truth: your Father confessor, your doctor, and your private detective if you have the misfortune to have to employ one. Some people would add a fourth: your lawyer. About that I've certain reservations of my own.

There was another thing about which I wasn't too happy: that intention of Frank to start doing detective work of his own. Handling a blackmailer is a remarkably ticklish business, and the more cocksure he was the bigger fool he was likely to make of himself, and us. Then I thought that perhaps he hadn't been too serious. Maybe the whole thing had been some sort of private and sadistic baiting arising out of some resentment he still felt about Louis having confided in me rather than in him. You never knew, as I've said, with Frank.

What took my mind off the whole thing was a call I had from Hallows just before I was going out to lunch.

"Glad I caught you," he said. "There's something I think it would be worth while for you to do."

"Yes?"

"It concerns an old friend, Brian Jedmont."

"Good Lord! Brian Jedmont. What about him?"

"Listen carefully," he said. "I haven't got all that much time. He's lunching here, and it's the second time since I've been here. He still has that office in Wingram House, Lauder Street. He may have seen me, so I can't do the job myself, but I'd like you to be in the neighbourhood of Wingram House within the next twenty minutes so as to run into him casually. He always was a talker, so he may tell you things."

"Right," I said. "Any particular things?"

"Just things. Sorry I've got to ring off now."

A taxi mightn't get me there in time, so I took the Underground to Leicester Square. I went along to Shaftesbury Avenue and cut left and I was five minutes' early when I took up my stand across the road from the office block and looking down Acton Street. If Jedmont were coming from the Mayland straight back to his office, then down Acton Street was easily the nearest way. If he *was* coming straight back. I didn't see how Hallows could possibly have told. Even if he'd followed him once himself, that didn't make it a certainty.

As far as I was concerned, the whole thing was a mystery, not that you mustn't give me credit for having thought that, as a photographer. Jedmont was necessarily connected with photographs. But how he could possibly be connected with photographs taken in Toulouse by the French Resistance in 1944, was altogether beyond me. Not that the dates couldn't be fitted in. Jedmont was in the middle thirties. In 1944, at nineteen or twenty, he could have been in a branch of the service. He could have been in Intelligence, and in Toulouse, and yet I very much doubted it. He'd never given me any cause to think he was any expert in languages. Also he was a boaster. If he'd done anything whatever of note during the war, he'd certainly have contrived to let it slip. And then when I thought of him as a whole, it seemed more than ludicrous that Intelligence should have employed him. He just wasn't anything resembling the type.

It was a good ten minutes later than Hallows' deadline when I caught sight of him, coming towards me from Acton Street. I hastily crossed the road and deliberately bumped into him practically on the steps of Wingram House.

"Sorry, sir."

Then I let myself recognise him. "Good lord! It isn't Jedmont?"

I held out my hand. He took it, and he wasn't looking displeased to see me.

"What're you doing in this part of the world?"

"I have an office here. Come in and I'll show you."

He'd changed quite a lot. Beards are the fashion now among a certain set, and his was a beauty, coming down straight from the ears to a point at the chin and linking up with the silky moustache on his upper lip. His hat was widish of brim and his clothes smart but not gaudy. In every way he looked more mature.

We took the lift to the second floor. Across the lobby he unlocked the door on the frosted glass of which, in stylish lettering was:

MONTY JEDLAND
ART STUDIES

"This is you?" I asked him artlessly.

"Yes," he said. "In this game you have to keep up with the times. Brian Jedmont didn't mean a thing. You have to think of something more snappy."

We'd stepped straight into what was probably his office: quite a large room with the usual desk and telephone, but the walls practically covered with photographs, most of them in colour. On the desk was an expensive-looking cine-camera, and in the right corner was a tripod on which was another. There was a book-shelf that occupied the whole of one wall, and it was chock-a-block with books and magazines. Other magazines littered the desk. There was also a filing cabinet and a couple of modern, Swedish looking chairs.

"You're not what an old fogey like me would call an ordinary photographer," I told him. "Just what sort of work do you do?"

"That kind of thing." He was taking off his coat and paused to wave a hand at the wall. "High-class stuff for the picture magazines. Competition stuff. Anything that appeals to me. Stuff that pays."

"Mind if I have a look?"

He showed me around. This had been taken for such-and-such a magazine and this had won such-and-such a prize at a certain competition. I'm no photographer, but even to me they were high-class jobs. I couldn't conceive of any better, and I told him so.

"Only a beginning," he told me. "Between you and me, I've done remarkably well. Now I'm going to branch out. You acquainted with how things are in the television racket?"

"Can't say I am. All I suspect is there ought to be quite a demand for film stuff."

He smiled. He leaned sideways, slipped a thumb into a corner of his jacket pocket so as to open the pocket wide.

"See this? I'm standing at the bottom of a chute and down it is coming money. It's pouring down. Your pocket's full before you get another one open." He smiled again. "That's television. All you have to do is give them the stuff, and collect."

"And that's what you're going in for?"

"That's right," he told me more soberly. "I'm negotiating now for an old studio out Denham way and I'm going to start off with shorts and cartoons. You fancy my chances?"

"Turn yourself into a public company and offer me some shares," I said.

He laughed. "A bit early for that. Still, you never know."

I let my eyes go once more round that office. "This can't be your only room?"

"Oh, no." He waved a hand at the far door. "There's a dark room and what I call the workshop. And my secretary's room."

That door suddenly opened. The smart-looking brunette looked as startled at the sight of me as I was at her.

"Oh!" she said, and was drawing back.

"It's all right, Gay. Come in. This is Mr. Travers, an old friend. Gay Lavalle, Mr. Travers. My secretary. And my favourite model."

We smiled at each other as we shook hands. She was a most attractive girl—or should I say woman—in the early twenties: full-lipped and with hair worn in that rather taking mop that one sees everywhere these latter days.

"I think I've seen you before," I told her smilingly.

"You have?" she said. "Where?"

I waved a hand at the wall, with here and there its artistic nude.

"Ah, those," she said, and laughed. "Just part of the day's work. Be seeing you later, Monty." She held out her hand. "Goodbye, Mr. Travers. Nice to have met you."

She disappeared through the door. I told Jedmont I'd have to be going and we moved towards the outer door. I stopped.

"Mind if I ask you a question?"

His look was suddenly wary. "Depends what it is."

"Well, all this must have cost you a considerable sum of money and I was wondering if that aunt of yours—what was her name, now?—Mrs. Coome, had financed you. You remember that little job we did for you?"

He looked quite relieved. "That was a long time ago. Five years, wasn't it?"

"About that."

He nodded gravely. "Well, she died about two years ago. I didn't get all her money, but I got quite a lot. Enough to get all this going."

"Fine," I said. "I'm glad it turned out so well."

I held out my hand. "Nice to have met you again. And I'll be glad to hear how that pocket of yours gets on at the bottom of the chute."

He laughed, and on that happy note we might have parted, if I hadn't thought of something else.

"That reminds me. A friend of mine was asking me the other day to look out for any original and interesting pictures to do with the war. He's writing a book and I know he'd pay pretty well. Did you take any yourself in the war?"

"Me?" he said. "How old do you think I actually am?"

"Well, that beard makes you look older. I'd say getting on for forty."

"I shan't be thirty-eight till January."

I smiled ruefully. "Damn silly of me. I ought to have worked it out closer than that. But what about your military service? Did you see anything exciting there?"

"I didn't do any," he said. "I had a mother to look after so I was excused. And my lungs weren't all that good."

There was something else he wanted to say. I waited.

"I suppose you're the only one I've ever told this to since I began to get on, but you remember me from the old days, and even you didn't know much about me. My elder brother was killed early in the war and I had to look after my mother, who was an invalid. In Stepney, that was. I had to leave school and I got a job as office boy. At Mandel's, the photographers."

I said I remembered the name.

"They were doing very well. Had virtually all the Jewish business but that didn't do me much good except to make me have ideas about getting on in the world. And being a photographer. You hear a lot nowadays about the pocket money children get. You know what I had? Twopence a week. It took all the rest to keep us going. I was seventeen before I had my first camera. When my mother died I saved every penny so as to get started on my own. You were one of the first people who gave me a job."

His lip drooped ironically.

"That aunt of mine was ashamed of us. She'd married pretty well and we didn't even know where she was. When I began to get on, I got into touch with her. I saw the notice of her husband's death when I was with the *Record*."

"Sorry," I said. "I didn't know all that."

"Well, that's how it was," he said. "People come up here, Mr. Travers, and tell me how lucky I am to have a place like this. You know what I'd like to say to them? 'Don't make me laugh.'"

"Yes," I said. "That's one of life's little ironies."

There was an awkward silence: then I said I'd have to be getting along. I did add that I wasn't being patronising when I said he deserved everything he had. And I wished him luck again in the new venture.

I walked back to Leicester Square and the Underground. When I walked into the Agency, Hallows was waiting for me. We went through to my room.

"Well, young fellow," I said. "What's all this hullabaloo about Jedmont?"

He smiled a bit sheepishly. "I suppose you could call it a hunch."

"Because he had lunch twice at the Mayland?"

"Look, sir, you'd better let me explain."

When Bob Hallows is deferential, it means he's got a lot on his mind.

"It's a whole series of things," he told me. "Things—and ideas. For one thing, I've never trusted him. He's tricky. You know that."

"He's also touchy," I said. "But I'll explain that."

"All right, then. He's tricky and he's touchy. I still think he was double-crossing us in that job we did with his aunt."

"How?"

"Well, he could have given that Hubert Courtney a private tip, which was why he'd left when we got down there. He made twenty-five pounds over it, if you remember."

"Maybe you're right. But that was five years ago."

"I know," he said. "But it makes a kind of background. Once you have a certain opinion of someone, you don't change it till it's proved otherwise. That's why I took an interest in him when I saw him in the Mayland the first time. And still more when I saw him the second time."

He leaned forward.

"You see, he did himself extraordinarily well. A half-bottle of wine and a liqueur with his coffee. I reckon each lunch cost him about three pounds. And his waiter seemed very gratified with the tip. I just wondered where the money was coming from."

"A pretty sound question. Anything else?"

He smiled wryly. "Well, that's where the hunch comes in. I know he's only five minutes' walk from the Mayland but I was—well, I was almost startled to see him there. Then—you know how your thoughts run on—I began thinking of him as a photographer. To cut a long story short, I wondered if he had anything to do with those blackmailing photographs."

"He couldn't have." I said. "He was only fourteen when war broke out, and only nineteen in 1944. And he was exempt later on from National Service. But let me tell you just what happened this afternoon."

I told him everything I'd seen and every word, as far as I could remember it, that had passed between Jedmont and myself. I even mentioned Gay Lavalle.

"So you see." I said. "He's made money and there's no need to wonder where it comes from. We know he has a tricky streak. That's nothing uncommon when a man's had home circumstances like Jedmont's, and meant from the word go to get on. You're still unconvinced?"

"About his upbringing and so on—no." he said. "It agrees with what I knew about him when I first recommended him years ago. Also I agree he couldn't have handled those incriminating photographs in 1944. But there *is* another way to look at it."

He waited a moment, thinking something out.

"I'll put all my cards on the table," he told me. "There *was* one thing I'd have preferred to work out, but you might as well hear the lot. First there's the hunch. You know even better than I do that you can't afford to ignore hunches. What I'm getting at is this. After what you've just told me, that hunch is stronger than ever. If Jedmont's not mixed up somehow in all this, my name's not Hallows."

8
MONTY JEDLAND

"JUST give it some thought yourself," he said, "then ask if everything isn't remarkably opportune. After he got the sack from the *Record* he went down and down. Then he began to get back a little as a free-lance and that was when he employed us on that job. If he managed to ingratiate himself with his aunt after what we found out, well and good. She found the money to set him up in Wingram House. But that doesn't fit. You had a talk with her before you left the Farina and she wouldn't hear of Courtney being a crook. If I remember rightly, she was absolutely indignant, so, if she wouldn't believe you, why should she suddenly believe Jedmont? She wasn't all that fond of him."

"What you're getting at is that he got the money for that place of his at Wingram House from somewhere else than from his aunt. The dates fit. I admit that."

"At exactly the same time. When Louis Marquette was handing someone five thousand pounds, Jedmont was still hard-up. Shortly afterwards he wasn't."

"Get back to the photographs," I said. "How do you explain them?"

"By contact. I admit it's all very vague, but Jedmont happened to meet the one who had them. Call him X. X was hard up too. And maybe the original photographs were just small snaps, so when X wanted to cash in on them, he went to Jedmont to have them blown up. What happened then is anybody's guess."

He raised a quick hand.

"Just a minute. You're going to say that's all pretty flimsy. So it is, but there's something else. Louis parted with five thousand pounds and Jedmont went to Wingram House. Now Louis is being asked for another ten thousand and Jedmont's talking about branching out again. Even negotiating for an old studio. If that isn't opportune, what is?"

He was right. It could be a coincidence, but at that moment, like Hallows, I didn't think so. I said I'd do some striking while the iron was hot, so I asked Bertha to get me Tom Holberg. Tom's a very old friend and he has what's probably the best theatrical agency in town.

I was lucky. Tom himself came on the line. We had a private word or two before I came to the point.

"Tom, I've got a client who's talking of buying an old studio for the purpose of going into the television film business. On a fairly modest scale. Just shorts and cartoons. What are his chances of buying?"

"Two years ago? For a song." I could see him spreading his free palm. "Now? Well, as Jimmy Durante used to say, everyone wants to get into the act. You might get a short lease for a few thousand. I don't know. It isn't in my line. You want I should give you the name of an agent?"

"Don't want to give you any trouble, Tom. Just what'd be the price for the lease of a smallish studio?"

"I'll ring you back," he said. "But how long is it that you're in the property business? Things are bad?"

"Couldn't be worse. Expecting the brokers in at any moment."

He told me I should worry. He was still chuckling at the joke as he rang off.

I gave Hallows the gist of the talk. "Anything else was there that helped along that hunch?"

"There may be nothing in it," he told me diffidently, "but Jedmont didn't pay either of his lunch bills. When his waiter brought the bill he merely signed it. I don't know why it should have struck me as peculiar, but it did, so I said to my own waiter when I was paying my own bill, that since I was having my meals there regularly for a time, wouldn't it be more convenient to sign the check and pay up the total when I stopped coming? He was very emphatic. The Mayland never did that. I wouldn't do such a thing, of course, but anyone could disappear before the bill was due."

I thought for a moment, then rang through to Bertha. She was to get me the Mayland.

"Something else we can clear up as we go along," I told Hallows, and then, almost at once, the Mayland was on the line. It was Frank Gledmill who spoke.

"Nothing serious, Frank, but I've been thinking about our man Hallows. He pays his own bills so as not to call attention to himself, but wouldn't it be more sensible if he just signed the check? He may be staying on for longer than we originally arranged."

"Can't make you out," he said. "That'd be the very way to call attention to himself. We don't go in for that kind of thing here."

"Pardon me, but you're wrong." I said. "Hallows saw one of your regulars signing his check."

There was a silence. I gave Hallows a significant look, and then Gledmill was speaking again.

"One swallow doesn't make a summer. We do have a very small number of customers who've been vetted and who prefer to pay monthly. But that isn't going to apply to Hallows. Get that well into your head."

"As you wish," I said. "Merely a suggestion. Be seeing you, Frank."

So that was cleared up. Frank, as I told Hallows, should know. He was the one who handled the accounts. Then, before we could get down to Jedmont again, Ruth, Tom's secretary, was on the line. Small studios were very rarely on the market. A short lease—say ten years—might cost anything up to ten thousand, plus annual rental. Everything depended on size, site, facilities and a dozen other things.

"There's something we didn't understand about your client," she went on. "If he's merely doing shorts and cartoons, why an old studio? Any largish building would do and he could adapt it to suit himself."

"Thanks, Ruth," I said. "I'll pass all that on to my client."

"Jedmont definitely mentioned a studio," I told Hallows. "Of course, he may have been trying to impress me. We could find out, of course, by enquiring of every likely agent in town, but we haven't the time, or anybody else's money."

"So what do we do?" he said. "Forget about Jedmont?"

I thought for a moment.

"Not altogether. There's just one thing that might be checked: how much money his aunt left him. There may have been enough to set him up in Wingram House and enough left over to get him started on this new venture. I'll get busy on it in the morning."

Hallows left then. He wanted to get home before returning to the Mayland for dinner, and he wouldn't even stay on for a cup of tea. Bertha brought a cup in for me, but even relaxing after it with a pipe, I wasn't feeling happy. Hallows had given me an awful lot to think about and, if Somerset House had still been open, I think I'd have gone there straight away.

As soon as Somerset House opened its doors in the morning, I was ready to inspect the Last Will and Testament of a Mrs. Harriet Coome, for which probate had probably been granted in 1959. I had a twenty-minute wait, only to be told that no Will existed. I had another look at the application form in case I should have made a slip, but it was in order.

I was on my way back to the Agency, walking for the sake of exercise, and I'd got as far as Norfolk Street when it suddenly struck me that I could approach things another way. Perhaps Harriet Coome had died intestate. I'm no lawyer and I never before handled a case involving the intestacy of anyone, but it did seem to me that intestacy might have made difficulties about the depositing of a Will. After all, if there's no Will, how could Somerset House have a record? A record, perhaps, about the subsequent distribution of the estate among the relatives, even if in this particular case there'd only been one—Brian Jedmont.

What I'd do, I thought, was establish first the exact date of Harriet's death, and the place, and then proceed from there, so back I went and filled in another application form. This time I had a much shorter time to wait. What I was told was an absolute facer. There was no record of any such death!

I set off again for Broad Street, thinking things out as I walked. Behind the thoughts was a certain excitement: the kind you always get when you begin to see daylight after groping about in the dark. What I had ahead of me was a long spell of telephoning, and I got down to it as soon as I was back. The first call was to the Farina Hotel, Sandford.

It was to be just as long-winded as I'd thought. The reception clerk said that there was no guest of that name. I said the matter was extremely urgent and had the hotel any forwarding address? After all, Mrs. Coome, up to at least five years ago, had been a regular resident. He said he'd call me back. It was a quarter of an hour before he did so. The last forwarding address the Farina had was the Whitelock Hotel, Beachhaven. Mrs. Coome had left the Farina for Beachhaven on the 7th of July. 1956.

I did some more thinking before I asked Bertha to get me the new number. My impressions, made at the time of the visit to the Farina in 1956, had been that Harriet Coome had stayed in the south for the winter and then moved north for the summer, and I'd been definitely of the opinion that she hadn't been intending to stay at the Farina longer than a very few weeks after my visit. And yet she had stayed on for almost four months, well into what we had of a summer.

The answer to why she had stayed on seemed fairly obvious. In that March, as I'd ruefully discovered, Harriet Coome had had all the confidence of a besotted woman in the charming, assiduously helpful Hubert Courtney. He'd gone but he'd be back. After all, his going had been as much in her interests as in his own, and so she stayed on in the Farina. The hope became a little fragile. It turned to worry and at last she left. But when Hubert returned, as he certainly would return, he'd get into touch with her through the forwarding address.

Bertha got me the Whitelock Hotel. Mrs. Coome wasn't actually there but they were expecting her at the end of November. She'd paid, I elicited, regular visits for a number of years.

"It's most urgent that I get into immediate touch with her," I said. "Can you give me the address from which she last wrote to you?"

A couple of minutes and I had what I wanted. The letter had been written from the Quinton Hotel, Cove Bay, which was where she presumably still was. *Was* was what they call the operative word. No wonder I hadn't found a Will or a death certificate. Harriet Coome was very much alive. Jedmont had lied right and left. The money hadn't come from his aunt. Where it *had* come from one couldn't be dead sure, but the chance existed that it had come from either a certain five thousand pounds, or a share of it.

Then something stopped me dead. Wasn't I very much jumping to conclusions? Suppose, for instance, that what had been done at the Farina in March 1956 had ultimately led to a reconciliation between Jedmont and his aunt. He would have claimed to have unmasked Courtney, and she hadn't believed him. She'd known that Courtney was coming back. Then, slowly, she'd realised she'd made a fool of herself. She'd even begun to feel a certain gratitude and at last there'd been the reconciliation. Jedmont had saved her quite a lot of money, and it wouldn't have been too hard for him to have induced her to finance him in the move to Wingram House.

I looked at my watch: it was still only a quarter-past eleven, and Cove Bay was only forty miles away. Just over an hour's drive separated me from knowing once and for all if Jedmont had got that money from his aunt. If there'd been any hesitation about what I was going to do, let me say that I hate loose ends. The unfinished and the unsolved always nag at me, and that morning I just had to know. I didn't wait: just told Bertha where I was going and went back to St. Martin's to get my car.

It was a quarter to one when I reached the smallish seaside resort of Cove Bay. The Quinton Hotel was just off the front and when I'd parked my car in the yard behind it, I looked it up in the motoring guide. It wasn't large but its charges showed it as definitely select.

At the desk the pleasant middle-aged receptionist confirmed that Mrs. Coome was staying there. I asked where I'd be likely to find her. She glanced at the clock. Mrs. Coome rarely came down to lunch before one o'clock so she was probably still in her room. She glanced at me as she reached for the telephone.

"What name shall I say?"

"A friend of Mr. Hubert Courtney."

Somebody answered and the message was delivered. There was quite a pause before I was being told to go up. The room was number 7, on the first floor.

I took the stairs instead of the lift and I'd scarcely rapped on the door before Harriet Coome opened it. The five years had aged her. The face had wrinkles that no beauty treatment could iron out or conceal. The eyes were more sunken and the unashamed hair was a greyish white.

The look of anticipation went. A quick bewilderment took its place.

"Haven't I seen you somewhere before?"

"May I come in?" I said. "Sorry to trouble you, Mrs. Coome, but I shan't keep you more than a moment or two."

I didn't sit down till she was seated, and by then she'd remembered me.

"You're the man who was at the Farina Hotel. A long while ago."

"That's right," I said. "My name's Travers and I ventured to warn you about a certain Hubert Courtney. It can be a cruel thing, Mrs. Coome, to remind anyone of a past mistake, but I do think you know now that I was right. I take it that you've never heard a word since that date about Hubert Courtney?"

"No," she said. "No, I haven't."

She wasn't looking at me. I thought I'd better do some embellishing.

"A man's only allowed to write so many letters when he's in jail and then they're very carefully scrutinised."

She took it well. The years had brought a grievance: not against herself—she'd never be that kind of woman—but against the man who'd tricked her.

"You said you were an enquiry agent. I mean, when I last saw you. You were paid for what you did?"

"Surely you knew that," I told her. "I was acting on behalf of your nephew. Didn't he tell you that?"

"Would you tell *me* how much he paid you? I've thought about it a lot and I'd like to know."

"If I tell you, will it be in strict confidence? It isn't ethical to give such information about a client."

"Of course," she said, with just a touch of the old impatience. "I just want to know."

"Well, he had to find a hundred pounds. Later I gave him a rebate because the work hadn't taken so long as we'd thought."

"So that was it," she said. "It was my hundred pounds, Mr. Travers. He borrowed it from me just before. He said he had to have a special sort of camera."

I nodded gravely. "I see. But may I tell you very quickly what I thought happened after I left? I thought your nephew claimed for himself all the credit for—well, saving you from losing a lot of money. That was his original idea. You were going to be grateful and, since he was your only living relative, you'd make him your heir."

"You are right," she said. "I see now that that was what he was doing. Only then I didn't believe him about—about Hubert Courtney. Also I had every reason to disbelieve Brian. He'd already forged my name to three or four cheques and, if it hadn't been for the publicity, I'd have taken legal action. He was utterly unscrupulous."

"And when did you see him last?"

"The following weekend after what happened at the Farina. I told him that if he didn't pay back that hundred pounds, I should prosecute him. And I said I'd consulted my lawyers about those cheques. And I haven't seen him or heard from him from that day since."

I hoisted myself up from the depths of the easy chair. "Thank you," Mrs. Coome. "That's all I wanted to know. I really came here, as you've guessed, to get information about your nephew. There're certain matters about which I'd like to talk to him myself. Unluckily you can't help me. Not that I'm not grateful to you for sparing me your time."

"If I should hear from him, and I hope I never do, how could I let you know?"

I gave her an Agency card. I found another hotel at which to have lunch, and in my mind was not so much a satisfaction at having learned all that I'd thought I might find, but every now and again a queer sort of depression at the thought of Harriet Coome. Old age was not too far away and life for her would go on being little more than a series of caravanserais. No real friends, but only a series of acquaintances, and against each brief, superficial pleasure or content, the dark cloud of memory and the months once spent at a Sandford hotel to which she'd never had the moral courage to return. I wondered how well she slept. Not too well, by the looks of her. The sedative stage was probably already there. And all that was why I was also feeling a sudden hatred of Brian Jedmont. That was what I was to tell Hallows when I saw him that evening at the flat.

I'd rung him at his home and asked him to drop in on his way to the Mayland. The Mayland isn't all that distance away. You cut through to Tottenham Court Road and then left again, and at once you're in the heart of Soho.

It was about half-past six when he arrived. Bernice likes Hallows, but after a word about his wife and small daughter, she left us to ourselves. He wouldn't have a drink in view of the dinner ahead, so I didn't open the can of beer for myself. What did surprise me was the placid way in which he listened to my news.

"He took me in too," he said, "otherwise I'd never have recommended him." He was referring, of course, to Brian Jedmont. "Then various things happened and—well, you know what I think of him now. He's a smooth twister. And something's telling me he's either at the back of, or up to the neck in, this whole damn business. I'd say he ought to be concentrated on."

"But how?" I said. "Let's keep a sense of perspective about all this. The fact that Jedmont lied about where he got the money doesn't make it anything remotely resembling a certainty that he got it by blackmailing Louis Marquette. All it definitely means is that he doesn't want it known where he did get the money from. And one other most important thing remains. He could not conceivably have had anything to do with taking those Resistance photographs."

He was about to say something.

"Let me finish what I was getting at," I said. "I agree that he might have acquired the photographs from somebody else: in fact, that's the only way he could have got them. But from whom? How're we going to find that out? If we don't, how can we establish any connection between him and the photographs?"

He smiled. Hallows has a placidity that often reminds me of Jewle.

"I know," he said. "But if you ask me my opinion, I'd say we oughtn't to get hot and bothered. Many a time we've just had to do nothing more than keeping someone under observation and hoping for the best, and then something turned up merely out of doing just that And it isn't as if we're on a tight schedule. There're still quite a few days left."

"Maybe you're right," I said. "He'll be under observation from now on. It may lead us to the one from whom he obtained the photographs or with whom he's actually working." I gave a sort of half-grunt, half-chuckle. "Always remembering we're working only on suspicions. I've the nasty feeling Jedmont mayn't be connected with that blackmailing business after all."

"It's a chance you've got to take," he said. "It'll cost money but that's Louis' headache."

"Which reminds me," I said. "Everything's been verbal so far. About time I got his signature on a contract."

He got up to go and I was helping him on with his overcoat when he too remembered something.

"Something I wanted particularly to mention to you and then it slipped my mind."

He gave me his dubious sort of smile.

"According to Louis, the voice told him on the telephone that he was going to be always under observation, which is why I'm now off to the Mayland. Then at lunch today I had an idea. Like that Father Brown story of Chesterton's and the postman who wasn't seen because everybody took it for granted he was a kind of natural part of things. See what I'm getting at?"

"You mean someone like a waiter?"

"More or less," he said. "But waiters come and go. I'm thinking of someone who's been there ever since the place opened. Two people. Those two girls who have the hat-check concession—Doris and Lorette. Especially Doris."

I don't quite know why, but I had to smile.

"You mean she's the one who's keeping an eye on Louis?"

"Could be," he said. "Just an idea. She might just be worth keeping our own eyes on. If the funds rise to it."

I didn't give myself the chance to forget once more. As soon as he'd gone, I rang the Mayland. It was Gledmill who answered.

"Frank," I said, "I'd like to see both you and Louis in the morning. Will you suggest a time?"

"Why?" he said. "You've got something?"

"Possibly a whole lot of things. They have to be sorted out: also they're none of them stone-cold certainties. I'd like to talk things over before I go any further."

"Half-past ten suit you? The front entrance'll be open."

"Fine," I said. "By the way, how're those personal enquiries of yours getting along?"

"That's my damn business," he told me, and rang off.

9
MORE JEDMONT

FRENCH was available for the Jedmont job but there had also to be a relief. The only man Norris could think of was Drew, a youngish operative who'd been with us only a couple of years and whose hobby was photography: at least he was always something of a joke with Bertha whom he imagined to be as enthusiastic as himself. Things go on at the Agency of which I'm utterly unaware till something brings them to my notice. I didn't know Drew was an amateur photographer but Norris did. So did Bertha. She was always having to look at prints and colour stills.

Nothing could be done till I'd seen Louis and Frank. I had to be pretty brusque about it when I saw them that morning. A waiter must have been on the look-out for me. He opened the front door and said the boss was waiting for me in the office. Louis greeted me as if I'd come to bail him out. Frank, working as usual at the desk, merely looked round and gave a nod.

I said I wouldn't keep them very long. Louis' face fell.

"You're not making any progress?"

"Don't know yet," I said, "but I'm spending quite a lot of money and time. Oughtn't we to have a proper agreement?"

Frank swivelled the desk chair round so as to face me.

"He's right, Louis."

He left it there. With a pose of aloofness he began manicuring his nails with his pocket-knife.

"Very well," Louis said. "What's fair to you is fair to me."

"Why not be a little adventurous for once," Frank said, still busy on his nails. "You save us ten thousand pounds. What about a percentage? Five per cent or nothing. Five hundred pounds is a pretty big sum."

"Sorry," I said. "I don't do business that way. What I'll do is meet you. The lowest possible rates plus a bonus."

"I still prefer a percentage."

I picked up my hat and stood up. "Nothing to do, then, but wish you good-day. I'll let you have the account for what we've done so far."

"You can't do that." Louis was getting to his feet "What's the matter with you, Frank? You didn't say anything of this to me."

He gestured helplessly. Frank hadn't stirred.

"Only trying to protect both of us, Louis. They tell me Travers always gives a fair deal but that's no reason for throwing good money after bad. Doing it my way gives everybody a chance."

"I don't run a gambling outfit," I told him. "We give the best we can for a fair return. So make up your minds."

Louis shot a look at Frank. There was no reason to ask who'd become the dominating partner. "I'll pay it. Out of my own pocket."

"Very well," I said. "A hundred pounds retainer and twenty pounds a day. Try elsewhere if you like but you won't get rates anything like as low anywhere in town. And I've typed in a clause to the effect that either party can call the whole thing off at a day's notice."

I took out the agreements. Louis shot another look at Frank.

"Might as well sign, Louis," Frank said calmly. "You heard what the man said."

A couple of minutes and I was putting my copy back in my breast pocket.

"There's just one other thing, Louis, and don't take offence at it. Will you give me your solemn word that you've no idea whatever who the blackmailer is?"

"I don't. I swear it. I tell you it's driving me crazy."

"What about you?" Frank said. "You've nothing to show for what you've done so far?"

"Nothing. At least nothing tangible. I've got ideas but they want sorting out. I'll let you know one way or the other in two or three days' time: then, if you wish to call me off, you can. It's all in the contract. There *are* two alternatives. You could tell the blackmailer to go plumb to hell—"

"But the publicity! And what would happen—"

Frank cut him off. "Shut up. Louis! Let the man finish."

"The second alternative is to wait till the actual moment of handing over the money. How that's going to silence the black-mailer I don't know. If you don't pay, then he talks. On the other hand, deprive him of the original negatives, and he's got nothing left but wild, unsubstantiated accusations. His word against Louis'."

"It's the best way, Frank. I told you it was the best way."

Frank shrugged his shoulders. "Very well. Let the man carry on. There's always the escape clause."

He swivelled the chair round again with a show of indifference. Louis gestured with a kind of helplessness. But he did give me his personal cheque for a hundred pounds. We said goodbye. Frank waved a curt hand from the desk.

It was a long time since I'd been so unhappy as when I walked back that morning towards Leicester Square. The air of that office had had an unpleasant veering of currents and I had the feeling that what hadn't been said was more important than what had. All the same, it was hard to pin anything down.

I did have an idea or two by the time I got back. Frank, I now thought, had suggested that results or nothing business because he was reasonably sure I could never uncover the blackmailer. But since, in his own interests, that blackmailer *had* to be uncovered, the real reason behind his suggestion must be that he was now fairly hopeful of doing the job himself. Or it might be that he was relying on trapping the blackmailer at the moment of his picking up the money.

There was something else: something I liked even less—that Frank deliberately wanted to throw Louis to the French wolves. I hadn't even a vague idea of the partnership terms, but there might be a clause in the agreement to the effect that the survivor took all. Or, if one partner withdrew, then the other had the option of purchase. But, as I said, I didn't know, and I had no means of finding out. What I did know was that Frank Gledmill, even in his short career as a professional, had made a great deal of money, and that since his retirement he'd been a slow spender. Now, living as he did at the Mayland. he was spending virtually nothing at all.

What I should have done when I reached the Agency was to have had the courage of my various depressions and have rung Louis to say that I'd changed my mind and was exercising my right to call the whole thing off. I think it was only that insatiable curiosity of mine that stopped me. I was involved, and what I just had to know were the whys and wherefores, and how the whole affair would ultimately resolve itself. And there were people in whom I'd become deeply interested: people like Monty Jedland.

I briefed French and Drew. They'd be working in shifts, with Drew taking the first. If Jedmont came out of Wingram House with a friend, the friend was to be followed when the two parted. Just before five o'clock both operatives would be on duty. If Gay Lavalle and Jedmont left separately, each was to be followed till their addresses were known.

I had my usual cup of coffee and set about putting into operation something of my own. Among the things I've picked up in the course of my life is an early eighteenth-century miniature of a man. I'd had an expert opinion on it. The artist couldn't be definitely named but I was advised to insure it for a minimum of fifty pounds. It was in the original frame and had all the things one looks for: brilliancy, grace of line, deft touch and fine, transparent colour. At the sales I've seen inferior miniatures make much more.

I rang Jedmont. I mentioned the miniature and asked if it'd be beneath his dignity to make me a colour reproduction.

"Sounds interesting," he said. "Why not let me see it?"

"When?"

"Well, why not now? I don't say I'll do the job now but I'd like to look at it."

Twenty minutes later I was pushing the bell at the side of the Jedmont door. It was Gay who let me in.

"You're looking very pleased with yourself?" I told her. "Someone left you a legacy?"

She laughed. "No such luck. But why shouldn't I be pleased?"

I gave what I hoped was a humorous grimace and a shrug of the shoulders. I was beginning to like her. Cheerfulness is rarely a jar. I'd seen her previously for only a minute or two but now I was having a kind of personal look at her, and I was thinking she was far too good for Jedmont.

"Monty's expecting you," she said. "I'll tell him you're here. About a miniature, isn't it?"

"Yes," I said. "I'd like you to see it too. I think it's pretty good."

She went through the far door. A couple of minutes and Jedmont came in, Gay with him. He was in what I'd call studio clothes and was wiping his hands on a small towel.

"Ah, Mr. Travers. You've brought the miniature?"

I took it out of my overcoat breast pocket, unwrapped it carefully and handed it to him. Gay was peering over his shoulder.

"Nice," he said, and gave her a look. The look stayed for a moment and became a smile.

"What do you want me to do?" he asked me.

"What I said. Make me a couple of exact copies. Any idea of what it'll cost?"

He pursed his lips. "Tricky work. It'll cost you ten pounds."

"More than I'd hoped," I said, "but it's a bargain."

He smiled.

"Wait a minute. It needn't cost you a cent. I could use something like this. Give me permission and you can have your two copies for free."

I thought it over. It wouldn't do me any harm if that miniature had a certain amount of publicity. If I ever decided to sell it, it might do me good. Gay had taken the miniature and was looking at it. Jedmont was smiling at her and that was when something struck me. Good lord, I thought. A miracle's happened. Jedmont's in love!

"You could do lots of things with this, Monty," Gay told him.

"Perhaps," he said. "What about it, Mr. Travers?"

"Suits me," I said. "When can I have it back?"

"Tomorrow. I'll give you a ring."

That was virtually all. He gave me a special receipt and then I left. Gay had gone through to her room and it was he who showed me through the door, and I was thinking he was a pretty shrewd man of business. It had never occurred to me that he might want to use that miniature himself, and now I had the idea that, compared with that ten pounds of mine, what he'd make would be infinitely more. Somehow I hadn't seen that miniature myself till I'd just seen it through his covert enthusiasm, and Gay's far more unconcealed delight.

But let me end that business of the miniature here and now. It'd be merely confusing to let it trail on. I did get my copies, and there were three of them, not two. Each had been taken in a different light. The frame had not been tampered with, and how he'd got over the difficulty of reflections from the glass I didn't know. And he'd done a magnificent job. Each of those reproductions was worth a frame of its own.

Let me add something else. I thought up that business of the miniature only in order to make contact with Jedmont again and get more background. What I did get from that short call on him was to prove to be about the only thing that could possibly have solved the whole case.

Something else happened that day. I'd got back to the flat just before six and it was just short of seven, when we were waiting for the service to send dinner up, when French rang me. Nothing had happened during the day.

"Then something turned up tonight, sir, which I thought you might want to know about at once. The two left together and walked to Piccadilly Tube Station and took tickets for Knightsbridge. They went into a block of flats near Knightsbridge Station, a place called Hepworth House. They have Flat Twenty-one in the name of Mr. and Mrs. Jedland. A furnished flat and they've been in occupation only about six weeks."

"An expensive place?"

"I'd say so. I couldn't risk making myself too conspicuous."

"Where're you ringing from?"

"A call-box at Knightsbridge Station. I didn't know if you wanted us to keep the place under observation."

"No need," I said. "You've done extraordinarily well. Pack it up and go home. I'll see you in the morning."

I don't know why that news should have made me so angry, but it did. It wasn't a question of morals and there's no law against cohabitation. I think it was the thought of that particular man and that particular woman: the man with whom she'd become so closely involved and the wonder whether she had even a suspicion of the exact kind of man he was. That started me wondering what would happen to her if it was proved he'd blackmailed Marquette.

I forgot all about it till the morning and then it woke up with me. Curiously enough, and thinking back to the previous day's visit to Jedmont's studio, I began to see things in a different light. But I forgot it again when I began reconsidering the whole affair, prior to seeing French and Drew. Somehow I couldn't avoid a feeling of utter futility. Sum the whole thing up and all I had was suspicions. There was no point in it at all. To try to find the one from whom Jedmont had obtained those photographs seemed sheer lunacy.

I wasn't even sure that Jedmont was the blackmailer. If I saw him and bluntly accused him, he'd indignantly deny the whole thing. He'd probably dare me to make the charges before a witness and risk a libel action. Or suppose that I was dead sure he was the blackmailer, how could I obtain the negatives? As I'd told Louis, breaking and entering, or personal violence, weren't in my line. In other words, everything I was doing seemed pointless, and professional integrity demanded that I should withdraw from the case.

What I did was to give it one more day. What French and Drew were expected to find out I didn't know, but I put them on double shift till Jedmont and his secretary left that night. Their instructions were to follow Jedmont wherever he went and to make as full a note as possible of any contacts. After that I caught up with arrears in the office and it was well after eleven o'clock when I began thinking again of that Knightsbridge apartment. A few minutes later I made up my mind. I paid yet another visit to Somerset House. I didn't think the officials there were encouraged to be talkative, but the one who gave me the copy of the marriage certificate did make a remark. I'd expected at least a twenty minute wait. As it was, my man was back in no time.

"Pretty quick work?" I said.

"As a matter of fact," he told me, "we had the same enquiry only about an hour ago."

"You did? A man or a woman?"

Maybe he realised he shouldn't have spoken at all. His tone was almost frigid.

"Sorry, sir. We're not allowed to give out information."

Once again there was plenty to think about as I walked back to Broad Street. Those loving looks I'd seen in Jedmont's office had been the genuine thing. Brian Jedmont (37) and Gay Lawson (26) had been married at the Register Office, Kensington, on the 10th of October last. To check on the two witnesses would almost certainly be a waste of time: they'd been found in all probability by the Office itself. What I did wonder was why Jedmont wasn't letting it be generally known that she was other than a secretary-model. Maybe his business had to be surrounded with an aura of glamour, with a pretty secretary far more effective than a wife. And with a name like Lavalle instead of the prosaic Lawson.

But that was his affair, and hers. Much more mine was the question of who was that other enquirer into Jedmont's private affairs, and, rack my brains as I might, I couldn't even begin to find a satisfying answer. Had Jedmont acquired those French photographs and negatives from, say, X and had he double-crossed X in the process, and was it X who was now prying into Jedmont's private life in an effort to recover them? Was it Jedmont himself who had been at Somerset House that morning? If, as usually happens, his wife held the marriage lines, did he, surreptitiously or otherwise, need a copy for himself? And if so, why? Might he need a copy for some matter of insurance?

I didn't see why. I didn't see anything at all. All I had was the same uneasiness. I told myself that Jedmont's marriage was quite outside the case and therefore no business of mine. After that, a lunch at my usual pub did put the whole thing out of my mind. Till French rang me, and that was just after two o'clock. He was reporting on Jedmont's movements that morning and asking for further instructions. Hallows dropped in while I was listening and I motioned him to wait.

The two operatives had arrived outside Wingram House just in time to see Jedmont leave. He was carrying a camera and had another in a case round his shoulder. He took the Underground at Piccadilly Circus and ultimately emerged at Aldgate. After that he spent the whole morning, and it was the finest we'd had for days, just walking around and taking pictures with both cameras. Some, to French, at least, were of the oddest things: belated flowers on a bomb-site and a puddle of water under some trees. He also snapped a paper-seller outside the Bear, and, later on, a crowd of young children coming out of a school. He'd taken one of the children, a girl, and posed her for a special picture. At about twelve-thirty he'd worked his way back to Aldgate Station and had dropped into a near-by restaurant for lunch. He'd taken one more picture, of a bus unloading passengers, and then he'd returned to his office.

I told French to call it a day and report back in the morning. As I told Hallows, all Jedmont had been doing that morning was using the tools of his trade. What to French had been unusual, was to Jedmont the essential.

"By the way, has he been at the Mayland recently?"

"No," he said. "Must be three or four days now since he was there."

I told him the time had come for a complete reappraisal and went carefully over everything that had happened since we'd last talked. We agreed that what we'd been doing had brought us into a dead end. The only thing was to turn around and go back—or home. I had no new approach to suggest, neither had he.

"I know it doesn't seem very relevant, considering how things stand," he said, "but there's one question's been bothering me. Mind if I go back?"

I waved a hand.

"I'm Jedmont," he said. "I acquire those photographs and see how to use them. That was four-and-a-half years ago when Louis was just reopening the Mayland. I get five thousand for copies, which is pretty good money. I hang on to the negatives. Why?"

"Hoping for another squeeze later on."

"But why wait four-and-a-half years? You'll say because I now want to expand. I say I'm not that kind. That talk about getting into television was sheer blether. Two or three years ago, after Independent Television started, was the time to get busy. Nowadays there must be the devil of a lot of competition. I'm impatient. I'm always being driven by the urge to get on. By the time I've been a couple of years at Wingram House, it's too small to hold me. And yet I wait for another two-and-a-half years. If you really know me, that doesn't make sense."

"Put it like that, and it doesn't," I said.

But it did give me an idea. "There's one way of finding out a few things about Jedmont that we've neglected. You knew why Jedmont had left the *Record*. Does that mean you have friends there?"

I always knew he had plenty of friends in Fleet Street, but from end to end, that street's a pretty long place.

"I did have," he said. "You know what things are like in the newspaper world. They come and go. You want me to get anything I can on Jedmont?"

"It's something to be doing. He couldn't have been very popular there. You can ring Louis and say you're skipping dinner at the Mayland. Or just not turn up. I'll have to see him and Gledmill in the morning in any case."

While he was ringing the Mayland I thought of something else. "Did you ever find out anything more about Doris?"

"A few things," he said, and took out his notebook. "Her name is Doris Finkel: calls herself Francis. She took on the concession at the Mayland when it opened and she's been there ever since. Works just for tips, and there's that little cigarette and cigar stand which brings in a good bit too. Lorette, who acts as relief, has only been there about a year. Her name's Seaman. The two girls share a small apartment above a junk shop in Wardour Street. Almost on the Mayland doorstep."

"Isn't it a long while for Doris to have held that concession?"

"I wouldn't say so," he told me. "She's getting a bit long in the tooth but she's still attractive. And she definitely knows her job. And Louis hasn't got any headaches. He's getting everything for free. I'd say he thinks himself damn lucky to have anyone like Doris."

"Right," I said. "You spend the evening in Fleet Street. Drop in here in the morning and we'll talk things over before I call on Louis."

Then I had to say one last thing.

My mother died when I was twelve but I remember her well and I have a portrait of her hanging above my desk at the flat. Every time I look at it I remember something. She was always reprimanding me for being too sure, and I don't necessarily mean cocksure. When I announced that I was going to do something or go somewhere at a future date, she'd always check me with the reminder that there was such a thing as Divine Providence. What I had to say was, *"All being well I'm going to Such-and-Such a place."* It's a habit with me still, and Bernice often laughs when I say that, all being well, we'll do this or that. I think it's an asset, if only because it makes one stop for a moment and think. It checks me in the act of jumping to conclusions. That's why I added a postscript as Hallows was leaving.

"Mind you, we've always got to keep one thing in mind. All this time we may have been barking up the wrong tree. Everything we've unearthed about Jedmont so far may have been just coincidence."

He didn't laugh. He just gave me a wry sort of smile as he went out of the door.

10
LOUIS REFUSES

I'M ENOUGH of a low-brow not to like things I don't understand: abstract painting, for instance or modern music. Ballet is something I can like in patches but an evening of it is something I wouldn't care to face. Bernice, of course, adores it. She was spending that evening at Covent Garden with a friend, and, though I'm pretty sure she sees clean through my various excuses, she has long since ceased to argue the point.

So I had a bachelor evening. I felt almost resentful when the telephone went just after nine o'clock. It was Hallows.

"I've found out a few things," he said, "and I wondered if you'd like to hear them. I might be a bit late in the morning." He said he was calling from a Soho call-box. Why he was so far from Fleet Street I didn't know, but I told him to come along. It turned out he'd had nothing to eat, so I sent down for sandwiches and had ready two tins of ice-cold beer. As soon as he came in I knew he'd prefer hot coffee. In November you have to pay a stiff price for a sunny day, and the fog was getting pretty thick outside. I suggested he use our spare bedroom, but he'd already rung to say he'd be home late.

This is the story of his evening, told with no recorded interruptions of mine.

Who should I run into at the 'Record' but Fred Elston: you remember him, one of their crime reporters. He and Jedmont used to have to work a lot together in the old days so I stood him a drink and we got to talking. The first thing he said when I told him about that posh office of Jedmont's was that the bastard must have had his hands in someone else's pockets. Then, believe it or not, he wondered where Doris was.

"Doris?" I said.

"You didn't know her?" he said. "A very smart piece. Cashier at that coffee house next door to the Drovers. She and Jedmont kept house together. Last I heard they were still together. Must have been four or five years ago."

As you're guessing, that was all I wanted from him but I couldn't drop him straight away, so I told him about Jedmont's marriage. He'd never heard of a Gay Lawson or Lavalle. He did say he hoped to God she'd slip arsenic into his coffee. At any rate we yarned for ten more minutes or so and then I had to be going. First thing I did was to ring the Mayland.

I wanted to speak to Doris: I was using a different voice, of course, but it was one of her nights off. She's on the telephone so I called her and she was in. She didn't remember my name but she knew me when I described myself. When I said I wanted to see her on a private matter she told me to come along.

A cosy little place she and Lorette have got there. Doris was all dolled up in a red blouse and black jeans and she'd had the television on. I didn't want her to have any ideas so I kept my overcoat on. Said I wouldn't keep her more than a few minutes.

"I'm an inspector for a big insurance company," I said. "My job is to check up on new clients. I've only just been appointed to this district which is why you haven't seen me before last week at the Mayland. You understand that this is all in strict confidence?"

She swore blind nothing would ever pass her lips, so I told her I had to investigate a new client, an old friend of hers, so I'd been told. I waited a second till she was all keyed up, then I told her he was Brian Jedmont. Was she surprised!

We sparred a bit about how did I know and all that, then I asked her if she knew he'd recently married.

"I should worry," she told me. "He dropped me like a hot potato about three years ago. Who's he got his hooks into this time?"

I told her. She'd never heard of a Gay Lawson alias Lavalle. She didn't even know Jedmont had an office at Wingram House. That looks as if he dropped her just before he rented the place. That'd be more like four years ago. Three years, four years she said: What did it matter?

I asked her if he'd been a regular patron of the Mayland all the time she'd been there. She said he used to drop in at intervals the first few months she was there and then she didn't see him till about a week or so ago.

"What was he like?" I said. "I mean after that dirty trick he'd played on you. Did he make up to you at all?"

"What him?" she said. "Handed in his hat and coat and took the check just as if I wasn't there. Every time he left, he tipped half-a-crown. Just trying to impress. Do you know what I'd like to have done with it?"

I told her I could guess. Then I asked her how she came to get the Mayland concession.

"I admit that was him," she said. "I don't know how he knew it, but he told me it was going and I was to go along and see, and, sure enough, Mr. Marquette was willing to try me out. But you know what that bastard Jedmont did? Reckoned he'd been my agent and used to take about a third of what I picked up. Not that I didn't rig things sometimes. That was before I got another girl to help me. If I had all the money he had out of me from time to time, I could damn near buy the Mayland, Mr. Hallows."

That was about the lot. I got her to swear she wouldn't mention the marriage or even move a muscle when she saw him at the Mayland again. I said that what she'd told me had been a great help and, since my company was paying, I thought she'd earned a couple of quid. She said since that was how it was, she'd take it. I warned her not a word to Lorette, and then I left.

"That seems to clinch things," I said. "Jedmont must have had sufficient hold over Louis to have got her that concession. Yet I don't know. It could have been all above board."

"I can't believe it," he said. "It isn't as if we've had one coincidence. We've had three or four. The way I see it is that Jedmont or our old friend X—the original owner of the photographs—simply added another clause to the blackmail terms. Doris had to be employed to keep an eye on Louis. And Louis daren't get rid of her, even if he'd wanted to, from then on. I admit that Jedmont took good care to profit financially from the arrangement."

"But why did Jedmont drop Doris?"

"Because he was on the up and up. He was getting delusions of grandeur. As soon as he'd decided what to do with the five thousand pounds, she no longer fitted in. Also he wouldn't want her asking awkward questions as to where all the money was coming from."

"And he didn't go to the Mayland because it might have been awkward meeting her?"

"I'm glad you asked that," he said. "I think it fits in with something I mentioned this morning. There's no doubt in my mind about his keeping a casual eye on the place, but he didn't go there because he didn't need to. Remember? Nothing was going to happen for another four years."

"And the time's now up," I said. "He waited, and what he waited for has happened. Something that has put him in a position to blackmail Louis again. And this time he's giving the screws a double twist."

What that something was we couldn't even begin to guess, so we had a word or two about my attitude when I went to the Mayland in the morning. We agreed it would be foolish to mention Jedmont's name. Either Louis or Frank—Frank especially—might be tempted to do something dangerously drastic. The best thing was to leave everything till the black-mailer announced the method of handing over the new demand, then we'd be in a strong position. Every move that Jedmont made could be watched.

That's where we left things. I went down with Hallows and the fog was thick, and the odd pedestrian on the other side of the street was little more than a blur. Hallows wasn't worrying. He was taking the Underground and his house was only a short way from where he'd get off. He'd report to me in the morning at about midday, just in case he was still lunching at the Mayland.

Bernice didn't get home till after eleven. I wasn't asleep, and she told me the fog was the worst we'd had for months.

Lullaby thoughts that night were about that fog, and the sunny days we'd had, and a sunny day in the country where we'd had lunch in a country pub. I wondered what Ashman's real name was, and where he was. I wondered if he'd employed some other detective agency to find Harry Wale, and what series of lies he'd had to fabricate. Not that I bore Ashman any grudge. He hadn't been the first to fool me and he certainly wouldn't be the last. Besides, he'd paid not too badly for the privilege.

A queer thought—something almost in the nature of a coincidence—was with me while I was getting dressed in the morning.

Two people were eager to find someone: Ashman to find Wale and Louis to discover who was the blackmailer. Which reminded me of something I ought to do before I saw Louis. It was to do with that gap of some four years between the blackmail jobs. I agreed with Hallows that the long wait must have a significance: also there was a factor which Hallows hadn't particularly stressed, but which now seemed to me to have its own importance—why the blackmailer now, after those four-and-a-half years, knew himself to be in a position to double the first demand.

That was why I rang our solicitors as soon as I got to Broad Street. I put a hypothetical case. The French Government, possibly backed by a post-war Resistance Organisation, had a list of collaborators; spies, traitors, etc., whom it was still anxious to apprehend. Five years ago it was looking for them. During those five years, and particularly at this very moment, had the search become more intense? Had, for instance, some new law been passed, or was one in the act of being passed? Or had other factors arisen to make the apprehension of such traitors more important than it had been five years ago?

I was told the partners would have to consult and they'd ring me back. They rang about ten o'clock when I was just about to set off for the Mayland. I'd already rung Louis. What I was told was that they'd put the case to the French Embassy and were hoping to give me an opinion later that day. I told myself a bit ruefully that, had I had the sense to think of it, I could have done that job myself.

The fog had as good as gone when I left the Agency and it looked as if we were in for another sunny day. That the fog would as certainly come down again that late afternoon wasn't troubling me at the moment: there was always the chance that it wouldn't. And I had other things to think about: what reception I'd get at the Mayland when I announced the change of attitude. I needn't have worried.

Louis was putting on a fair pretence of calm, even when he told me that he'd had the expected call only a few minutes before I'd arrived: not the final call but an essential preliminary. He'd been told two or three things: not to be so silly as to go to the police; not to ask questions, and, above all, to get busy at once on having the money ready. It was to be in used notes of five pounds upwards. Final instructions for handing it over would be given in two days' time.

"You heard the message, Frank?"

"Yes," he said. "I listened in."

"You didn't find the voice in any way familiar?"

"Should we? You're not giving him credit for very much sense. What about yourself? What've you been doing except banking Louis' cheque?"

In our job one has to be pretty thick-skinned. And, as far as possible, the customer has to be always right.

"I've got one good lead," I said. "But tell me something, Louis. What was the exact method of handing over that original five thousand pounds?"

It had been simple and quick. The money was to be in a suit-case, about eighteen inches long and dark in colour. He was to step inside the church at exactly ten o'clock in the morning—there wouldn't be many people there then—take a step to the right, put the case against the wall behind him and stoop down to tie up a shoelace. He was then to make as if he'd forgotten the case and walk slowly towards the choir, taking about two minutes. He was not to look back. When he did get back, a somewhat similar case was there, the photographs inside it.

"It didn't strike you at the time that the photographs were useless if he was still retaining the negatives?"

"Don't ask damn silly questions," Frank told me. "It ought to be obvious, even to you, that he didn't. What the hell's the good of blethering about what happened? Quit stalling and get down to what's happening now."

"Very well," I said. "I've got my own reasons for not telling you how, but I think I can get my hands on the man, whatever method he thinks up for collecting the money. It won't be money, of course: just bundles of paper, but we can work that out later."

I swivelled round a bit to face Frank.

"Now you tell me something. I get the man red-handed. What good's it going to do Louis? You can't hand him over to the police. All he'll do is consider himself double-crossed and get his revenge by telling the authorities all he knows. Unless—and it's an unless we haven't got time for—we've learned enough about him to incriminate him too, so that he daren't open his mouth. You answer me that one."

He smiled.

"Doesn't need answering. You put the finger on the man and your job ends there. We'll see to the rest. As a matter of fact, we prefer it that way. Isn't that so, Louis?"

"That's what you suggested, Frank."

"God-dammit!" I think if he'd been within range, he'd have struck him. "What the hell's got into you? Is that the way things have got to be done, or isn't it?"

"It is, Frank. It is. That's the way it ought to be done." Frank leaned back again in the swivel chair. The room was very still till he spoke again. This time it was quietly.

"Right," he told me. "Now we understand each other. You put the finger on the man. The rest is up to us. Understood?"

"Understood," I said. "As a matter of fact, it suits me fine."

"Right," he said, and got up. "Soon as we know how the money is to be handed over, we'll let you know."

I was a worried man as I walked to Leicester Square. I found a restaurant, ordered some coffee and did some more thinking, and there wasn't much prefacing of *all being well*. All I'd told Louis and Frank Gledmill had been true. The contract had been carefully worded. All I'd been called on to do in return for such and such a sum of money was to find a missing man. Once I'd proved beyond doubt that Jedmont was the man, then my responsibility was over. I just dropped everything, like dropping a red-hot poker.

But could I? If I knew Frank Gledmill, his idea of a taking over from then on would certainly include what I preferred to call an absolute finality. Mayhem? Murder? I didn't know, but if murder, things might so turn out that I had to tell the police what I knew.

Louis was the weak member and, if he talked, he'd hardly be able to keep my name out of things, and keeping back vital evidence in a murder case might endanger the whole future of the Agency.

The whole thing was so immediately alarming that I took the coward's way out by trying to divert my thoughts to something else. What the solicitors would have to tell me, for instance, about that curious gap of four-and-a-half years. And that was when I thought of something else in practically the same connection. I didn't wait. It doesn't pay to when you've found an answer to all the problems, so I gulped down the rest of my coffee and went out in search of a taxi. I was going to the French Embassy.

I had to fill in quite a large form. Full particulars, for instance, about myself and the precise business on which I was there. I didn't know how to word that vital question, so I took a chance and wrote, "Actions taken against French collaborators in the last war". The man at the desk read the form, pursed his lips, gave me a look and asked me to wait. When he came back I was told to wait again.

Half a dozen people were in the waiting-room. There was no notice about smoking, so I lit my pipe and began looking at the magazines, most of them French. If I was given an interview—something that, after a quarter of an hour, I was beginning to doubt—I wondered how my French would stand up if that was the language in which I'd have to make myself clear. I needn't have worried.

The youngish, alert-looking man who saw me might have been of any nationality and his English was as good as my own. He got me seated, offered me a cigarette, said he too preferred a pipe, and then gave me quite a charming smile. My application, he said, had been rather puzzling. Perhaps I'd like to elaborate. So I elaborated. As head of a private detective agency in good standing I had all sorts of clients and had to listen to all sorts of confidences. Could he assure me that what I was going to tell him would also be in the strictest confidence?

I think his must have been some kind of legal department, for the simple question led at once to all sorts of legal difficulties: the gravity of offences involved and the uses to which I would put any possible information obtained. I had to compromise. He'd hear what I had to say and then judge accordingly. I didn't know what that precisely meant but I took a chance.

I mentioned no names and I presented the whole thing as one of a man struggling with his conscience. The story itself was almost word for word as Louis had told it to me, even if I also took care not to mention Toulouse.

"My own opinion's this," I said, "and I know the man well. He's been an acquaintance of mine for some years. I think he should give himself up to your authorities. The main thing that's worrying him is the publicity, and what might happen to his business while his case is being heard. If he can prove his innocence to the satisfaction of the authorities, his troubles ought to be at an end."

"But he did supply information?"

"Under terrific pressure," I said. "And all for nothing. It didn't stop the killing of his parents and his wife. I may be wrong. I'm not familiar with French law but it seems to me that there are overwhelmingly exonerating circumstances. Maybe I oughtn't to ask you this, but oughtn't any punishment to be correspondingly lenient? Or none at all? He's very small fry compared with some of your traitors."

"I'm inclined to agree," he told me. "That's off the record. But about this other man: the one who's blackmailing him?"

"I'm glad you mentioned that," I told him. "You serve the ends of justice two ways. If my client gives himself up, then the blackmailer can be handed over to the police. His claws will be cut and that'll be the end of him."

He leaned back in his chair. He smiled.

"You're a very persuasive man, Mr. Travers. Perhaps you wouldn't mind waiting here while I consult a colleague. Do smoke if you wish to."

The wait was as long as before. When he came back he apologised.

"The position is this," he told me. "Your client should most certainly surrender himself. That, as you pointed out, will settle the matter finally. If everything he told you is true, then he should have very little fear of an enquiry. After all these years there should be a certain leniency. There is one thing, however, on which we must insist. It seems more than probable that the blackmailer himself may be an ex-collaborator. You will have to give us his name at the very earliest possible moment so that we may make our own enquiries." I said I definitely would. As soon as my client decided to give himself up we'd have means of unearthing the blackmailer. It was rather ironic in a way, unless Jedmont could be made to tell the source of the photographs. In any case the interview was over. I thanked him warmly and left.

I hadn't far to walk to my club, so I had lunch there. Soon after I got back to Broad Street, the solicitors rang me. The de Gaulle administration, they said, had in no way changed things as regarded the prosecution of collaborators and no immediate changes were contemplated. So much for elucidating the mystery of that strange gap of four-and-a-half years. The information did give me one quick uneasiness. My interviewer that morning had been suave and shrewd. When he had conferred with a colleague, he had probably discovered that mine wasn't the only question put that same morning on the question of war-time collaboration, so maybe the Special Branch at the Yard would be asked questions about me. Not that that was an immediate worry. The real problem was Louis himself.

I rang him. I said I had to see him urgently. Him and Frank. He wanted to know why but I wouldn't say, and finally we fixed the interview for four o'clock. When I walked into the office, he was very much on edge. Frank laid aside the newspaper he'd been reading.

"Well, what now?" He raised his eyebrows when I said I'd thought of a way to end Louis' troubles.

"This isn't some trick to cover up? Because you've done nothing at all and want to kid us you have?"

"I'm getting pretty tired of you, Frank," I told him. "Why don't you listen before you start opening your mouth?"

"You open yours," he told me. "And make it good."

"I will," I said. "I'll make it the absolute truth. And straight from the horse's mouth. I didn't give a thing away to get the information. No names; no nothing. Just a decision from the highest authority."

I told him, but it was Louis I was watching, and Louis' face had fallen as soon as he began to get the first drift. But he didn't interrupt, neither did Frank. It was Frank who made the first comment.

"Sounds interesting. What d'you think about it, Louis? Just the formality of turning yourself in. You don't want to worry about here. I can run things till you get back."

"No," Louis said. "No. I can't do it."

Frank's look narrowed. "Why can't you do it? You heard what the man said? Just a formality. And the other bastard gets what's coming to him at the same time."

Louis was still shaking his head. "You couldn't stop the publicity. It would ruin me."

Frank sprang up from his chair.

"What the hell's come over you! Who says there'll be any publicity? Even if anything's reported in the French papers, it wouldn't get out over here. For God's sake tell him, Travers."

I couldn't tell Louis anything. His toes were dug in. I talked at him. Frank talked, cursed him and almost threatened but he wouldn't budge. Nothing, he said, would make him give himself up. Besides, that other way looked foolproof. That was the way he wanted it played.

I picked up my hat.

"It's up to you, Louis. If you change your mind, let me know. If not, we'll carry on from this morning. Wait till your friend makes the final contact, then get to work."

Frank followed me out. I'd never known him so reasonable. "What the hell's the matter with him?" he asked me. "He gets the easy way out and he just won't see it."

"Can I say something in strict confidence?"

He gave me a quick look. "Why not?"

"Suppose the version we heard of that French business was Louis' version, edited specially for us. Suppose he wasn't all that innocent after all?"

He scowled. "My God, you're right! It's the only damn thing that can explain it."

"Keep it to yourself," I said, "but that's what I'm pretty sure of myself. You're not going to let it affect things?"

"No," he said slowly. "It's no skin off my nose. He wants it played his way, so we play it his way. If he should change his mind I'll let you know."

Hallows was at the office. He'd missed me in the morning and I hadn't thought to leave a message. I brought him right up to date and there wasn't a thing with which he didn't agree. The only reason why Louis wouldn't take my advice, and Frank's, was because he had far more to hide than he'd ever divulged. The last thing he wanted was an official enquiry.

11
FIASCO

THOSE of us who've lived in London for most of our lives ought to have ceased of recent years to dread the fogs of early November. I've never got the facts from a meteorologist but it looks as if the sun has still enough strength to dissipate them. There's always a struggle between sun and fog. It starts at around nine and then it's a question of may the best man win. Sometimes the sun does practically breakthrough, then it retreats and the fog takes over. Then, usually around ten o'clock and just when you think that for once the fog is going to win, out comes the sun again. In as little as five minutes the fog has gone and the only trace of it is a faint and not unpleasant autumnal mist. That was how it was to be that particular morning.

It hadn't been easy getting to the office and, even there, I never had got used to the artificial light. My room has one large window that gives ample lighting, so when I have to switch on the light at nine in the morning the very unnaturalness always brings a depression. It's as if you're hemmed in: as if you've lost your mental freedom. Not that I had any particular problems to solve that early morning. All I was doing was pottering about with accounts. Then, at exactly a quarter to ten, Frank Gledmill rang. He sounded as if he were in one of his better moods.

"Can you get along here straight away? I've got some news."

"The fog's still pretty thick here," I told him. "I'd rather not make it till half-past ten."

"Fog? What fog? There's hardly any fog here. And when did you start worrying about fog?"

I said I'd make it as soon as I could, and then, as soon as I'd rung off, I saw the fog had definitely thinned. I switched off the light, and, sure enough, I could see across the fifty yards of laid-out open space between us and the block of office buildings. A couple of minutes and I was on my way to the Underground.

Frank was alone in the office when I reached the Mayland. He was looking strained and tired. You notice it in a man like him, who always prides himself on keeping fit. I'd never taken him for any kind of Puritan, so I thought that maybe I was seeing him after one of his occasional nights of gladness.

"Take a pew," he told me. "And what about some coffee?"

Coffee, I said, would be fine. He rang for it. He said to make it plenty.

"Louis out?" I said.

"No," he said. "He isn't here. I made him go away."

I must have stared.

"The best thing to do," he told me. "He was a damn nuisance. He was losing his nerve. I just couldn't stand it. Another day like yesterday and I'd have been driven clean up the pole."

"He didn't want to go?"

He gave a dry smile.

"Not till I pointed out something else to him. If things go wrong, he can bolt. Between ourselves, he's down at Brighton. He could even slip across to France. That's the last place they'd think of looking for him. Soon as things had blown over, he could come back. I can run everything here." How things could possibly blow over I didn't know. Once the French authorities knew all about him, his case wouldn't be dropped till it was finally cleared up. But I didn't tell Frank that. Something was telling me to be very, very careful.

"And that made him change his mind?"

"Fairly jumped at it," he told me. "How a man can lose his nerve like that, beats me. It isn't a pretty sight to see a man literally shaking with fear."

The coffee came in. Frank took his black. Mine was too hot for more than a sip. He took a good gulp and didn't seem to notice.

"The final instructions came this morning," he told me over his cup. "The curtain goes up at ten tomorrow. That's why you and I had to have a talk. The time's gone for stalling. We've got to get down to facts."

"Who's doing the stalling? And what facts?"

"You see?" he said, and waved his free hand. "You're still stalling."

"Look," I said. "Let's quit this beating about the bush. What's biting you? What's on your mind?"

The sneer had gone. Suddenly his tone was almost placatory.

"All right," he said. "I'll give it to you straight. You know who this blackmailer is, so who is he?"

"I'm not telling you. It isn't in the contract. I have a suspect and he'll be shadowed till the moment he picks up the money. You'll be there. What happens afterwards is no business of mine."

He looked as if he couldn't believe his ears.

"I'm sticking my neck out pretty far as it is," I told him. "It's the sort of job I never ought to have taken on, and the sooner I get shut of it the better. You can take it here and now that that's my last word."

I thought he was going to blow up again.

"That's a hell of a line to take. Why do you think what's good enough for Louis is good enough for me? You know me. You tell me who he is and then it's between you and me."

"You haven't got a leg to stand on, not logically," I told him. "As soon as we pick up the man you'll know who he is. If I'm wrong about him, it's still no matter. Someone'll pick up that money and he'll either be the man we want or he'll have to lead you to him. What happens after that is no concern of mine. It'll be your business to conclude some sort of deal."

For a moment or two it was touch and go, then, reluctantly enough, he had to agree.

"All right," he said. "Let's get down to details. Everything's set for tomorrow morning at ten o'clock. The same old suitcase trick. This time at St. Paul's. That narrow strip of gardens along the south side, just beyond the bus stop. The case is to be left on the path, close up to the end of the first seat. That looks to me as if the one who picks it up can make a quick getaway back to the front."

"We'll take care of it," I said. "There'll be no getaway. He'll have to be carrying the replacement case which makes it all the easier. You stipulated for photographs and negatives?"

"There were only three photographs. I stipulated for all the copies he might have taken, and the negatives."

"Only three photographs? I gathered from Louis there were quite a lot."

"Louis made things look worse, just for his own ends. I made him tell me just how many photographs there were and he owned up there were only three."

I thought it good enough as an explanation but it was then that something else occurred to me: something quite startling.

"You seem to have had quite a long chat with our friend. How come he didn't get suspicious when he found he was talking to a stranger, not to Louis?"

He grinned. "You people haven't all the brains. When he rang up asking to talk to Louis, I guessed who he was. I said Louis was still in bed, suffering from laryngitis. He said it was very urgent and Louis would know that, so could I put him through. I told him to hang on for a minute, then I carried on the conversation in a croaky voice that might have been anyone's. He swallowed every word of it."

I had to smile. Frank certainly had brains.

"All's well that ends well, but you certainly took the devil of a risk. Now what about getting down to details?"

It meant a quick visit to the actual scene.

"Might be quicker to go in my car," he said. "It's garaged only a few doors up. You might as well wait here. A thing or two I must see to before we go."

I'd no idea he had a car. It turned out to be a last year's three-litre, Mark 2 Jaguar, green with green upholstery. But for a certain spattering of mud, it looked as good as new.

"Didn't know you drove," I said as he moved the car off.

"Quite a lot in the summer," he told me. "Now only occasionally at weekends. As you know, we don't open on Sundays."

He seemed a good, careful driver. Visibility, of course, was good. Even the faint mist had gone and, but for a cold north-east wind, it might have been a late summer day.

"The eyes don't bother you?"

"Almost as good as new. I had a check-up about a month ago."

The traffic was heavy and no detours could dodge it. The Underground to St. Paul's would have taken a quarter of the time and it was half-past eleven when we found a parking spot a hundred yards on. We strolled slowly, as if talking business, past the actual seat. Whoever picked up that suitcase would have a choice of exits: a side one or on to the front. Each would be visible from across the road. It didn't take more than a minute or two to make a plan of action as we sat in the car. Then I walked on to Broad Street. When I looked back a hundred yards on, there was no sign of Frank's car.

That afternoon I briefed French, Drew and Hallows, and I first saw Hallows alone. It takes a good few years for an operative to be trusted with every detail of a case. Walpole said that every man was potentially venal, and you have to accept the fact that the same holds true today. In any case it would be folly to present a man with the chance of lucrative blackmail, however trustworthy you may have come to think him to be. Hallows was an exception. With him it was a matter of knowing, not thinking.

That afternoon he raised a point which Frank and I had already gone into. There was every sign that the fog would soon be down. If it persisted beyond ten in the morning, everything might go haywire.

"As a matter of fact, a little fog might be a great deal of help," I told him. "Gledmill may have kidded the blackmailer that he was talking to Louis, but Louis won't be there to put that suitcase down by the seat. It may sound cloak and dagger business but Gledmill's getting himself rigged up as near to Louis as he can: false beard and all that. The two are roughly the same build. If there's a little fog he'll get away with it. He might get away in any case but fog'll make it more sure."

We went over the details before calling the other two in. There were to be two cars: mine and Hallows'. The perfect spot for parking was alongside Pawsons and Leafs, across the road, but there might be difficulties. To obviate that, we had to be early on the job. Both the cars would be parked at half-past eight, when there was almost the certainty of space. I would be in my own car and Hallows and French in the other. As the clock struck ten, Gledmill would put the suitcase down and, after a minute's wait, go out by the side gate. He would go on towards the city but take advantage of traffic to cross the road and work back to either car. If both were empty, he'd know the blackmailer had already been caught, in which case he'd get back as quickly as he could to the seat, ready to identify the man. What we had to avoid was argument or a fracas.

French and Drew came in. Drew was to be outside Jedmont's apartment at eight o'clock. He'd already had a good view of him, and should be able to keep him in sight If Jedmont went to Wingram House, his time of leaving was to be noted, and if he was carrying a suitcase. Then he was to get back to Broad Street. French's instructions were simple. He had to meet Hallows at St. Paul's at half-past eight and Hallows would tell him what to do. Everybody was to make ample allowances for fog.

I had a rather uneasy night and woke of my own volition well before my usual time. I got up at once, had a good breakfast and took care to take both my newspapers with me to the car. The fog wasn't all that bad except in the dip before Ludgate Hill, and traffic was light. There was ample room to park the car and there'd be plenty for Hallows if he arrived almost at once. He did, and it was still ten minutes short of the half-hour. In my mirror I saw French emerge from the mist to the left and get into Hallows' car: then I settled down to the long wait.

Hallows too had brought along a newspaper: reading it till the time came to use it as cover. I wished I'd brought along a flask of hot coffee. Once the car heater had cooled off, it was pretty cold in spite of my heavy overcoat. Then at about a quarter past nine the sun made a real effort to get through. I could see for a few moments right along between the bombed site and the new office blocks a good hundred and fifty yards, and then, almost at once, the fog closed in again. There was still a visibility of about fifty yards, and I hoped it would stay that way till ten.

I began doing a crossword but found I couldn't concentrate, so I watched pedestrians and the traffic instead. Cars and vans turned in behind and in front, and came and went. Buses drew in at the stop or went by to the stop at the top of Ludgate Hill. People went by, most of them hurrying. The time went by too, and then it was a quarter to ten. That quarter of an hour was the longest, and just before Great Tom struck the first note of ten, the sun began getting really through.

I saw Gledmill first when he was almost at the seat. When he sat I could see only his head, not that it mattered. What did matter was when he moved. Then he went quite slowly to the side gate and was in full view as he stepped through it. On the pavement he was momentarily hidden by traffic and then, fifty yards on, I saw him making a jerky way across the road. After that I had to keep my eyes fixed on the seat which he'd left. As far as I could see, he'd been the only one in those gardens.

I saw him pass the car, then nip quickly back and slip through the off rear door.

"Nothing happened?"

"A bit early," I told him, eyes still fixed on that seat.

Five minutes went by and nobody entered that garden. Another five minutes and it was clear that something had gone wrong. To have left that suitcase at the mercy of any casual entrant would have been lunacy. It had to be picked up within a minute of Gledmill's departure or not at all: all the same, I gave it five minutes' more and then I walked back the few yards to Hallows' car. I told French to pretend to find that suitcase, to have a good look at it and then bring it to me.

Another five minutes' and Gledmill and I were on our way to the Mayland. Hallows and French were going back to Broad Street.

"I can't understand it," Gledmill kept saying. "Everything was done exactly as I was told."

I couldn't do much talking till we waited at the traffic lights at the foot of Ludgate Hill.

"When did Louis go away, Frank?"

"Last night," he said. "I think I told you."

"Maybe you did and maybe you didn't, but that may have caused the slip-up. By this morning practically all your people must have known he'd gone. If the blackmailer knew it, that laryngitis trick of yours just didn't work."

"But it did," he said. "He didn't say a thing to show he knew he wasn't talking to Louis."

I left it at that till we got back to the restaurant, then I rang the Agency and spoke to Drew.

"Just give me a quick idea of everything that happened this morning."

"Nothing happened," he said. "Nothing different from what you said he usually did. I picked him up at ten to nine and—"

"He was alone? His wife wasn't with him?"

"No," he said. "He was alone. I followed him in the Tube to Piccadilly Circus and then on to Wingram House. He got there at just before half-past nine and he didn't come out."

"Not at all?"

"Well, not before half-past ten. That's when I left."

"What about his wife? Did she arrive at all?"

"I can't say," he told me. "If she did it was after I left."

I was about to ring off when I had another idea. "Is there another exit there?"

He didn't know. I told him to get back there and find out. I gave him the Mayland number: he was to ring me as soon as he knew.

I'd never seen Frank Gledmill so subdued. He didn't rear up even when I brought up that laryngitis business again. The caller couldn't have suspected anything: that's what he just kept on insisting. Then he had an idea. He undid the suitcase. But there hadn't been any mysterious substitution. That case had its crumpled newspapers and two empty bottles. I knew it was a waste of time. If anyone had gone within yards of that case I'd have seen him.

He had coffee sent down and, while we were waiting, he began cursing Louis. Louis should have done what I suggested and given himself up. There he was, sitting on his fat behind at Brighton, while we were sweating our guts out.

"It's my own damn fault," he told me. "I should have let him stew in his own juice. I'm his partner, not his bloody nurse."

"No sense in getting hot and bothered," I told him. "I've wasted a morning too. So have three of my men."

Coffee came and he calmed down.

"All right," he said. "What do we do now? I don't know about you, but I'm not going on playing these monkey tricks for ever."

"Neither am I," I told him. "What should happen is that you should be rung again. If so, you'll be told where we slipped up. If not, then we'll just wait a day or two. If nothing happens then I withdraw from the case. If you want to carry on alone, that's your affair. If you do, I ought to tell you you can't go on with that laryngitis trick for ever."

"Louis'll have to come back," he said. "If necessary I'll go down there and lug him back. I'll have to ring him in any case and tell him what happened."

"I wouldn't," I said. "Let him do as you said—stew in his own juice for a while. For all we know, you may get a call at any time from our friend."

A few moments and there was a call, but it was from Drew. There was a second exit at Wingram House, an emergency one operating from all floors.

"But I don't think it makes any difference," he told me. "It comes out by stairs up from the basement, but, if you use it, you still have to come round to the front and I'd have seen him."

"What about the fog this morning?" I asked him.

"Pretty thick at his flat but much thinner when he got to his office. I couldn't see the front from across the road so I crossed to where I could see. By ten the fog had practically gone."

I'd kept my end of the conversation well guarded.

"That was one of my men," I told Gledmill, "the one who had our suspect under observation ever since he left his house this morning. Unless he's a miracle worker he couldn't have been anywhere near St. Paul's this morning. Either that, or he already had his suspicions and never intended to go. Or, of course, I may have been all wrong. He wasn't the right suspect after all. Not that it changes things all that much."

"But you were pretty sure he was?"

"I oughtn't to be, but I still am."

"Very well," he said. "What about a confederate? Mightn't he have had his suspicions of you? If he had he'd be too clever to pick up that bag himself."

"Maybe. But the bag still wasn't picked up, confederate or no confederate."

I got to my feet. "We could go on arguing like this for hours. Let's do what I said—wait till you get another call." He shrugged his shoulders. "Perhaps you're right. If he does call. I'll get you at once."

I had to get back to the Agency. What to do about the three operatives I didn't exactly know, though it looked as if they'd be cooling their heels for quite a time. Then, while I was waiting at some traffic lights, I had an idea.

Gay Jedmont hadn't left the apartment that morning with her husband. Was she the confederate? I couldn't think of anyone else in whom Jedmont could possibly confide. If she were, then she wouldn't have left the apartment before Drew got there. If she had, then the only place she could have gone to was Wingram House, and Drew would have seen her leave later on with a suitcase. What she could have done was leave the apartment much later: just in time to reach St. Paul's before ten o'clock.

I moved the car on and it wasn't till the next set of lights held me up that I began to see the flaws. Even if Gay Jedmont was the confederate, why hadn't she gone through with things? And then I had a sudden thought that almost made my blood run cold. I hadn't been on the lookout for a woman, and my eyes had almost always been left towards the garden and not to the right. If she'd been told to reconnoitre, then she could have passed right by me on the pavement and, if so, I was the one she'd recognised. I was the one who'd scared her off.

I parked my car near the Agency and walked back, and I was still reasonably sure I was right. And yet there was something against which the whole idea seemed to be pushing and I'd turned into Broad Street before I knew what that mental obstacle was—Gay Jedmont herself. Somehow I couldn't see her as a confederate in a blackmail game. Or had she been? Mightn't Jedmont have pitched her some plausible yarn to account for things?

I didn't know. A few minutes later things happened again and took her momentarily out of my mind.

12
CURTAIN DOWN

I'D JUST stepped into Norris's room to tell him about the morning's fiasco when his buzzer went. Bertha said the call was for me, but she didn't know from whom. I said I'd take it in my own room.

The caller was Frank Gledmill.

"Can you get back here? I just had that call."

I thought for a moment. "You come here. I'm getting dizzy going backwards and forwards to you."

"God-dammit, how can I? You know how things are here. Lunches coming on and God knows what. You'll be paid."

"Right," I said. "Expect me when you see me."

As soon as I'd rung off I knew I'd been a bit childish, so I left word for the three operatives to stand by and made for the Underground. It took me only five and twenty minutes to get to the Mayland. Frank wasn't going the round of the tables. He was waiting for me in the office.

"All right," I said to him. "So you've had another call. What was it this time?"

"You'll never believe me," he said, "but the bastard told me the whole thing this morning was just a try-out. He just wanted to see if I'd do what I'd been told."

"A damn silly thing to do?" I said. "For all he knew, there was money in that case. We left it there a quarter of an hour."

"I know," he said. "He saw your man pick it up and he must have been a long way away because he took him for me. Wanted to know why I was so long. I said I'd slipped up when I was crossing the road and almost been run over and that'd held me up."

I let out a breath. "I don't know. The whole of this business is about the most amateur, bungled affair I ever knew. I'm not referring to you."

"Well, there it is," he said. "But of course he's an amateur. And he's probably scared. Realises he's bitten off more than he can chew."

"Anything else?"

"Good God, yes," he said. "The arrangement's for tomorrow morning. This time everything the same except it's in Trafalgar Square. Those seats under the wall across from the National Gallery. The nearest seat to those steps in the middle that lead down. You know exactly where I mean?"

"I ought to," I said. "I've been living hardly a stone's throw away for years. You said the same arrangements. Same time?"

"Everything the same."

"It can't be," I said. "For one thing, we can't park the cars. But wait a minute. Ten o'clock's when the National Gallery opens. Far as I remember there're generally people up there by the entrance watching what's going on in the Square. That might be a good observation point."

"It's up to you," he said. "What about this? If I don't hear from you to the contrary, I'll carry out instructions at ten o'clock tomorrow, deposit the case, sit there for a minute then have a look at one of the fountains and come back for the other case."

That was how we left it. I went to Broad Street and did the necessary briefing. It was latish by the time Hallows and I went to lunch. The office hadn't been the place to air his views, but as we walked towards the pub, he was finding the whole business incredible. As he said, it was all so damn silly. As far as Jedmont knew, there were ten thousand pounds in that suitcase and he'd let it be there for a quarter of an hour. Also there'd been quite protracted talks on the telephone between him and Gledmill and yet he'd gone on taking it for granted it was the laryngitical Louis who was talking.

We found a table for lunch. It'd have been more difficult if we hadn't been so late.

"You find the whole thing silly," I said. "I called it amateurish, but it's the same thing. Gledmill said there wasn't any getting away from the fact that we'd been dealing with an amateur. I wondered why he'd said that. That first pay-off, according to Louis, was a pretty slick business. It's in keeping with the Jedmont you and I know."

"May as well get it off my chest," he said, "but I have the feeling Gledmill's arranging things to suit his own ends. Perhaps he's trying to manoeuvre Louis out of the partnership. I don't know. I just have the feeling he's making some kind of deal with Jedmont and we're being strung along."

"Which is why he got Louis away to Brighton." I shook my head. "Frankly, it's beyond me. Puzzles within puzzles, just for the sake of puzzling. And why should Gledmill make fools of us?

Surely it's carrying verisimilitude a bit too far? He could have said the whole thing was over and saved money."

"It's all one elaborate double or treble cross," he said. "Still, you're going to play along?"

We let it drop while we got on with the meal. When coffee came I thought of something else.

"Drew and Wingram House," I said. "He swore blind that Jedmont went in but didn't come out. Either we've been wrong all the time and Jedmont's had nothing to do with it, or else there're more than two ways out."

"Easy enough to check," he told me. "What's to stop us going along to see?"

So we went. We found the emergency stairs on the top floor and followed them down to the basement. Steps led up to the outside of the building, a smallish L-shaped piece of ground laid out as a lawn with a central flower bed. There was no way out except round to the front by a concrete path.

"Wait here a minute," I told Hallows. "It might be a good idea to see what Jedmont's looking like."

I walked up to the first floor and pushed the bell at the side of Jedmont's door. I waited, then pushed the bell again, and I could hear the ring inside. I rapped on the door and waited again, then I went down to Hallows.

"No one there," I told him. "His wife should have been there even if he wasn't."

At Leicester Square we took a Liverpool Street bus by way of a change. Also I wanted to do some talking and the Underground's too noisy for me. What I did was talk over that matter of a confederate, and whether it could be Jedmont's wife. Hallows had never seen her but he thought it the kind of thing Jedmont might do. With a confederate he could give himself an alibi. A confederate other than his wife might talk.

There was no need for early stirring, except for Drew. He was to repeat the previous day's assignment and note the time of Jedmont's departure for his office. Hallows would pick him up there and, if Gay hadn't accompanied her husband, Drew would wait for her there. If Gay didn't leave the apartment with her husband, Drew would wait till she did. If she hadn't left by half-past nine, he was to ascertain if she was still in the apartment. If she were or weren't, he was to leave at ten o'clock.

At five minutes to ten French and I were in position: he on the pavement that overlooked the seats at the Charing Cross end and I at the other. The fog had as good as gone and we saw Gledmill clearly as he took a seat and stood the suitcase at its end. Those seats must have been wet and only two other people were sitting there, both near my end. Gledmill still had on that comic beard and he was muffled up round his neck as a man might be who was suffering from laryngitis. He sat there for about a minute, then moved off right, towards the near fountain. He peered into the pool, then looked round at the few who were feeding the pigeons. He turned back, quickened his steps and picked up the suitcase. He mounted the steps and the last I saw of him was as he turned left in the direction of the National Portrait Gallery.

I went along to French. "Did you see anything?"

"Nothing," he said. "Nobody went near that case till the gentleman picked it up again."

I was sick to death of the whole affair. We took the Underground at Trafalgar Square and went back to Broad Street. Drew came in just after we got there.

Jedmont, he said, had left the apartment just before half-past nine, and he'd been alone. Drew waited a few minutes and then put through a call. He could hear the telephone ringing and, a couple of minutes later, the apartment exchange told him there was no reply. Just before he was due to leave, he took a chance and went up to the apartment and rang the bell. After a minute he gave it up.

Hallows came in but, before he'd said hardly a word, Gledmill rang. "Isn't it the very devil? Another flop. Wonder what excuse there'll be this time?"

"I'm not interested," I told him bluntly. "Count me out from now on."

"Aren't you quitting at the wrong time? I think he's scared. Probably thinks he's been recognised."

"I don't give a damn what he thinks. I'm quitting from now on. If you want it in writing, I'll have it in your hands in half an hour."

I rang off. I told Bertha that if that caller rang again I was to be out. I was angry and it took a moment or two to realise just how angry I was. It took what Hallows said to calm me just as suddenly down.

"I think you're right. I wouldn't handle that case again, whatever they paid."

"I never should have handled it," I admitted. "I ought to have had the sense to know from the start that there was something fishy about the whole thing."

He gave his dry smile. "All the same, you'd like to know what *is* happening?"

I couldn't help smiling too.

"It's a bit uncanny the way you start reading my thoughts. But you're right. I'd hate not to know. I'd like to see what happens from outside."

"Well, you're in the right position. You know everything that's happened so far."

"Yes," I said, "but not why it happened. By the way, what happened to you this morning?"

"Nothing," he said. "Nothing at all. Jedmont didn't turn up, neither did his wife."

"She must have gone away," I told him. "She didn't leave the apartment yesterday morning, not that Drew saw, and she wasn't there today. Mightn't that mean he's expecting some kind of trouble, and he's keeping her out of it?"

"Could be. It's explicable, which is more than what happened yesterday and today. The two flops."

He was right. That was the fishiest part of the whole unpleasant business. Louis' refusal to give himself up for the mere formality of an enquiry had been disquieting enough. He'd been stubbornly, almost vehemently against a comparatively easy way out of the whole affair. There was his flight to Brighton, with Gledmill the instigator, and another flight intended if things went wrong and Jedmont blabbed after all. Even that, as Hallows agreed, didn't make sense. Why should Louis choose to be on the run for maybe the next few years of his life?

As for Jedmont's two failures to carry out a course of procedure suggested twice by himself, that was even more inexplicable. He wanted ten thousand pounds and there, for all he knew, it was: waiting in the suitcase he himself had suggested all ready to be picked up. And while we were prepared to except Jedmont's own explanation of the first, as given just afterwards to Gledmill, we weren't now prepared to accept it at all. One trial run might be explained away; a second, considering all the circumstances, was absolutely unnecessary. And that made both suspect.

"Almost a pity," Hallows told me, "you let Gledmill know you were dropping the case, otherwise he'd have told you what excuse Jedmont made this time. If Jedmont rings him."

I said I wasn't interested. It was like going to the dentist's. Once you'd made up your mind to go, you had to forget all about the electric drill and go. Hallows did have one last question.

"What Gledmill said about the blackmailer being scared. Anything in it?"

The answer to that was another question: on what exactly was Gledmill basing that opinion. If Jedmont had rung him immediately after that morning's fiasco, then Gledmill would have told us so, and therefore Gledmill's opinion was purely his own. And he had no reason for it. What we had done had been with the utmost precautions and instructions had been carried out exactly as ordered.

"That business of Jedmont's wife being the confederate," Hallows said. "If she were, then Jedmont could have been looking around this morning. He might even have spotted you."

"According to Drew," I pointed out, "she almost certainly didn't even spend the night in the apartment. If she was a confederate, why operate elsewhere? No," I said, "I'm dropping the whole thing. If you don't mind waiting. I'll get Norris to make out the account and write a formal notice of withdrawal."

When I came back it was with an idea. I offered him the envelope.

"Why don't you deliver this personally? It'll give you the chance to hear anything Gledmill's got to say."

He shrugged his shoulders: not too good an attempt to show he wasn't exactly rearing to go.

Bertha got me some sandwiches and made a pot of tea before she went to her lunch. Hallows didn't get back till after two o'clock. Nothing urgent had happened, so he'd also had a scratch lunch.

"You might like this," he said.

It was Gledmill's cheque for the full amount of the bill.

"He said he'd pay it himself and collect later from Marquette."

"Suits me," I said. "What was he like? Had he heard anything from Jedmont?"

"Don't know," he said. "It was all so unexpected. You'd have thought he'd have taken the envelope and told me to get out, but he didn't. He opened the envelope and had a look and asked me if we weren't being in a bit of a hurry, and then he sat down and wrote the cheque. When he gave it to me, he said we might be sorry. When I asked why, he said what had happened this morning had told him a whole lot of things. When I said what things, that was the only time he really flared up. Reckoned it was no damn business now of mine. Then, as I was going out of the door, he asked me what I'd bet he didn't clear the whole thing up himself."

"What did you say?"

"I said, 'Good luck to you, sir. We'll be only too pleased if you do.'"

"He took it all right?"

"I thought for a moment he wasn't going to, then he just smiled. And that was the lot."

I thought things over.

"He must have been bluffing. Just throwing his weight around. Trying to show it didn't matter whether we got out of things or not. What could he possibly have learned this morning that we didn't learn ourselves, which is damn-all."

"Well, he did pick up that case and leave straight away. It's possible Jedmont was hanging around somewhere and he spotted him."

"A million to one chance," I told him. "Even if he did, it only makes everything more ridiculous. If Jedmont was there, why didn't he collect the suitcase?"

That was the end of that. I took the cheque to Norris and Hallows went in with me to get new orders. After that I felt I wanted to get right away from things, so I put in a couple of hours at the club and went home to the flat.

It was about half-past nine. Bernice and I were looking at a television programme when the telephone went. It was Louis Marquette.

"Good lord!" I said. "I thought you were down at Brighton."

"Just a day or two's holiday. I've only just got back. Look, Mr. Travers, I want you to come round here. You're going to be surprised."

"You mean now?"

"Why not?" he said. "It's early. I'd like you to be here."

There was no point in asking him why. If it was some trouble between him and Frank about our quitting the case, then I wasn't going to be persuaded to get back in. But there was the little matter of curiosity. Louis had sounded almost cheerful, and I didn't see why. At any rate I said I'd be along.

It's no distance, as I've said. There was visibility of about fifty yards and I was there in ten minutes. Doris was at the stand giving me a smile as I came up, but I shook my head and went past her to the office. When I rapped at the door, it was Louis who called a "Come in".

He came forward, hand outstretched. Frank was sprawled out in his chair, back to the desk, and was giving me an enigmatical sort of grin. The side table had been brought to the centre of the room and on it was what looked like a champagne bottle in a bucket of ice. There were three glasses. Louis began helping me off with my overcoat.

"Looks like some sort of celebration," I said. "Anyone going to tell me why?"

Frank got to his feet. He moved towards the bottle as if he was going to uncork it. He still had that self-satisfied smile.

"Everything's over," he told me. "Louis has got his photographs and prints and he hasn't had to pay a damn cent."

I just couldn't believe it. My face must have showed it.

"Make yourself comfortable," he told me. "It's quite a story."

"It's true, Louis?" I said. "You've really got them?"

"I did have," he said. "I burnt them about ten minutes ago. They were the right ones."

There was the pop of a champagne cork. Frank began filling the glasses. He handed me mine.

"Well, here's to the Broad Street Detective Agency," he said, and raised his own glass. "If it hadn't been for you, Travers, we wouldn't be here."

I shook my head incredulously, but I drank. As I managed to say, I rarely was offered the chance to drink to something I hadn't done.

"But you did," Frank said. "You didn't know it, but you did. The only reason for those two false 'go's' yesterday and today could only mean that he was scared. At least that's the way I figured it out. He must have spotted you or one of your men. Don't ask me how, but that's how I figured things out."

"And then?"

This was his story. He hadn't seen it necessary to mention anything to Hallows, but the blackmailer had rung just before noon. Frank told him as usual to hold the line but all he'd done was to give the impression of someone else taking over. Then he'd spoken in a voice the blackmailer had never before heard.

"I spent two years in America," he told me, "so I spoke out of the corner of my mouth like this: 'Look, mister, we know who you are, see? You do as Louis says or you're in bad trouble. Two of my boys'll be round to carve you up and, mister, they know their job. So just be reasonable and put them prints and negatives in an envelope and drop it through the letter-box. You've got till six o'clock and then we'll come looking for you. Okay?'"

"And he fell for it?"

"He did. I didn't know then because he waited a moment and then rang off. The envelope was slipped in at half-past five when the fog was getting nice and thick."

"You tried to spot him?"

"Good God, no! To tell you the truth I was damn sure it wasn't going to work. No one was more surprised than I was when it did." He smiled. "Mind you, I thought at the time I did that gangster stuff pretty well, but you know how it is. Soon as he'd rung off and I began to think it over, it didn't seem so good. Too melo-dramatic. All I can say is, he must have been a damn sight more scared than I'd thought."

I wouldn't let him fill my glass again. Louis looked hurt but I still said there was a job I'd been finishing for my wife when I'd been rung.

"All the same, it's been a happy and unexpected occasion. That's why I hate to be a wet-blanket by asking one little question."

Frank stared. "What question's that?"

"Well, you got prints and negatives, but are you sure there aren't some more prints?"

Frank laughed. "Never a hope. If he was scared enough to give us what he did. then he's still going to be scared." His eyebrows lifted. "Like a little bet?"

"Oh, no," I said. "My mother warned me never to bet against certainties."

Louis helped me on with my overcoat and shook me warmly by the hand again. Bernice and I were to drop in whenever we liked: everything on the house. I said that was good of him, and I might take him up on it. Frank actually patted me on the back as I went through the door.

I walked home as briskly as I could, just in case Hallows hadn't yet gone to bed. He hadn't. Bernice had turned in, so I used the lounge telephone. As near as I could remember it I told him everything I'd just heard at the Mayland. My American accent wasn't, as the say, all that hot.

"I just can't believe it," he said. "How the devil could we have scared anybody!"

"Don't ask me," I said. "But there are the facts. I'm sure Louis wasn't lying when he said he'd burnt the prints and negatives. Jedmont parted with them, and that's that"

"Yes," he said. "You know one thing? I think it's going to be a longish time tonight before I get to sleep."

"Do what I'm going to do." I told him. "Have a stiff whisky and soda. Where are you tomorrow, by the way?"

He said he was going to Birmingham to interview a man about an undercover factory job. All the same, if he had any ideas about the Louis Marquette job, he'd get in touch. I told him to let sleeping dogs lie. Louis was satisfied. Frank was more than satisfied, we'd got our money, and so what?

"You letting them lie yourself?"

I told him, almost indignantly, that of course I was. Somehow I don't think he believed me.

13
INTO THIN AIR

I WOKE next morning with a feeling of enormous relief. All that Mayland business was over. No more playing cops and robbers: no more travelling back and forth and no more listening to lies. Somehow I hated all three of those liars. Jedmont had lied to me about an inheritance from his aunt. Louis' part in that Resistance affair must have been altogether different from his own version. Frank Gledmill—hard as it was to find facts with which to pin him down—must have been lying all along.

What made my gorge rise was the way he'd tried to divert attention from those lies by ascribing the return of those prints and negatives to the good work of the Agency. I can stand lies but not the buttering up that's used as a garnish. What the truth was I didn't know: only that Gledmill must have employed far different means from the one he'd thought a glass of champagne had induced me to swallow.

One other thing did puzzle me: whether or not Gledmill had fixed on Jedmont as the blackmailer. If he had, all I could think of was that in the first few months of the reopening of the Mayland, Jedmont had made fairly frequent appearances. Then he'd dropped out. Then, four years or so later, he'd appeared again, and his reappearance coincided with the new blackmail attempt on Louis. Frank, looking around for someone to be the watch-dog whom the blackmailer had mentioned, had put two and two together. Frank, even though he'd always been an exhibitionist, had plenty of brains. Also, when I came to think it out, he must have known about Jedmont for quite some time: as far back as when he'd boasted to me that he might do some detecting himself. Not that it made any difference or not about actually knowing Jedmont. After all, he might have always been dealing with only a voice.

The whole business left a nasty taste in the mouth and I was glad to get shut of it. Financially we'd come out reasonably well, but that wasn't the point. What I knew deep down was that I should never have let sympathy for Louis induce me to accept the case at all. Even now, when I knew the whole thing was over, I couldn't help feeling a certain uneasiness: a premonition that it mightn't be over after all.

It was back to the Agency that morning, with other things to occupy my mind. Lunch-time came and went, and it was just after four o'clock when Norris came rather hurriedly, for him, to my room. I was looking out of the window. The weather had changed in the early hours of the morning and the rain was coming steadily down. I was in the act of pulling down the blind.

"Have you seen this?"

He gave me one of the evening papers and indicated the bottom right-hand corner of the front page. I sat down at the desk and had a look.

UNCONSCIOUS WOMAN IDENTIFIED
NOW IN METROPOLITAN HOSPITAL

The woman, reported in our earlier editions as having been found lying unconscious in the car park at the back of a Knightsbridge block of flats, has now been identified as Mrs. Gay Jedland who, with her husband, occupies one of the flats. Mrs. Jedland, who was found last night at about a quarter to nine by the night porter at Hepworth House, is now in the Metropolitan Hospital, where her condition is stated to be serious. She is suffering from exposure and shock.

"What d'you make of it?"

I couldn't make anything.

"We'd assumed she was away on holiday," I told Norris. "She definitely wasn't in the flat yesterday morning."

"You think it's anything to do with that job we did?"

"Don't know," I said. "All I know is, I don't like it. It doesn't seem, though, as anything more than what it says. The paper isn't making anything like a splash."

He said he'd thought I'd be interested, and I was. When he'd gone I couldn't help thinking about Gay Jedmont and the last time I'd seen her: how pretty she was and gay like her name, and very much in love. When a few minutes later Bertha brought in the usual cup of tea, I asked her to get the hospital. It was a woman who came on the line. I gave her my name and private address and had to spell them out.

"I'm enquiring about a patient of yours," I said. "A Mrs. Jedland. I'm a friend of hers and I'm anxious to know how she is."

I was told to hold the line. I held it for so long that, if there hadn't been background noises, I'd have thought it was dead. The voice that ultimately spoke was a man's.

"You're Mr. Travers—Mr. Ludovic Travers?"

"Yes," I said.

"And you're enquiring about a Mrs. Jedland?"

"I am."

"You're a friend of hers?"

"That's right."

He waited for a moment and I was beginning to wonder what it was all about.

"How did you know she was here, Mr. Travers?"

"I don't know what this inquisition is about," I told him, "but I've just this moment read about her in the evening paper."

"I see," he said. Then, "Well, Mr. Travers, all I can tell you is that Mrs. Jedland is a very sick woman. I'm afraid there's no more news."

He rang off. I held the receiver for quite a few seconds before I replaced it, and again I was feeling a curious uneasiness. A minute or two later I saw Norris. I wanted to know what he made of it.

"I'd say there's more to it than they've let on," he said. "There's probably a detective sitting alongside her bed in case she's able to talk."

"You mean the police don't think it was only a fainting fit or some sort of accident?"

He shrugged his shoulders. "That's what it looks like to me. Why they wanted to be sure exactly who you were was because they're interested in anything they can get hold of."

I didn't like it. I didn't like it at all. A few minutes later I was convincing myself that Norris had been giving only his personal opinion, and that all that had happened had been the usual procedure. When I got home I mentioned it to Bernice. She used to be on the board of governors of our local hospital and still does quite a lot of hospital work. She couldn't give me an answer. Hospitals varied in their procedure. In any case, she said, they didn't give out information to all and sundry, especially in serious cases. It was only natural they should make sure who the caller was.

I decided to use a private acid test. If the police rang me that night, then Norris was right. But nobody rang. Bernice had been right, and I'd been alarmed about nothing at all.

I was just setting off for Broad Street the next morning, debating whether to put on an overcoat or a waterproof, when the telephone went. It was Superintendent Jewle, and I think I froze almost stiff when I recognised his voice.

"Haven't seen you for quite a time," he said. "How are you both?"

"Fine," I said. "No colds, no nothing. How're you keeping?"

"Can't grumble," he said. "It's about time we got together. You busy this morning?"

"Not too busy."

"Then why not drop in here round about ten. That be all right?"

As soon as I'd said I'd be looking forward to it, he rang off. That left me with quite a hole in my insides and it was a minute or two before optimism took over. Maybe it was to be just a friendly visit. At the worst, he might want my opinion on something far removed from Gay Jedmont. And suppose it *was* Gay Jedmont about whom he wanted to talk? What was wrong about a friend ringing a hospital to inquire about a sick inmate?

It was an almost jaunty Travers who shook hands that morning with Superintendent Jewle. He took my waterproof and hat, said how nice it was to see me again, and asked if I'd like coffee.

"A bit early," I said. "All the same, a cup wouldn't do any harm."

He drew in a chair for me.

"Not early for me," he said. "I've been here since half-past six this morning. Got rather a puzzling case on my hands. Which reminds me. I believe it concerns a friend of yours."

"Here it comes," I told myself, and gave him a quizzical sort of look.

"Yes," he said. "A Mrs. Jedland. I believe you rang the hospital about her. As a friend of hers."

"Good lord! How on earth did you know that?"

"Well," he told me casually, "we're trying to get all the information we can. Just how well did you know her?"

The coffee arrived. He remembered I liked it only just white with two lumps of sugar.

"What was I asking?" he said. "Oh yes, how long you'd known her."

"It isn't a question of how long," I said. "It's what impressions I had about her. What I thought of her. If you want to know that, I thought she was a very nice person indeed. Cheerful, friendly, most attractive. Frankly, I thought she was far too good for Brian Jedmont. That's his name, as you probably know. The Monty Jedland's just a showcase name."

"How long since you saw her?"

"A week or so. Did I ever show you an eighteenth-century miniature I'd picked up? In an oval, ebony frame?"

"Don't know. You may have done."

"Well, we thought we'd like it photographed in colour, so I asked Jedmont if he'd do the job."

"What's he like?" he said. "I gather you know him pretty well."

I told him everything I knew, from personal experience and hearsay. He looked almost startled when I mentioned that job we'd done for him at Sandford.

"That was years ago," he said. "Didn't you ring me about it? I remember: you were going to send me a picture and prints of a con-man operating at Sandford, only he skipped before you got down there. What was his name now?"

"Courtney. Hubert Courtney."

"Ah, yes," he said. "We did a lot of co-ordinated work on that racket. There's quite a file here somewhere. But getting back to Jedmont. He seems to be a tricky sort of customer." He gave me a queer sort of look. "Makes me wonder why you went to him to do that miniature job for you. You didn't by chance have any other reason, did you?"

"You're mixing two people up," I told him. "Jedmont's a nasty specimen but a damn fine photographer. You don't patronise a particular butcher, do you, because he happens to belong to the Salvation Army?"

He laughed. "I see you haven't lost your touch."

"Never mind my touch," I said. "Suppose we let this talk be a little less one-sided. What're you trying to find out?" He hesitated only for a moment. "Very well, then. Strictly between ourselves, what we'd like to know is why she was found where she was, when she was and how she was. You can't contribute?"

I said that all I knew had been gathered from a paragraph in an evening paper and neither of my morning papers had even mentioned the matter. He said there was no reason why they should. Picking up an unconscious woman, unless she had publicity value, didn't make news.

"Also, we're keeping the whole thing buttoned up," he said. "Keep it to yourself, but I'll tell you why. This is the picture we've got so far."

At about nine o'clock that night there was a call to the block of flats where the Jedmonts lived—I'm telling it, by the way, as Jewle told it to me—and this call said that a drunken woman was lying in the car-park. It wasn't really a car-park; just a longish, single line of reserved space between the flats and Monument Road. The porter on duty went to investigate, and he not only found the woman but identified her as well. Since she was a resident, the management played the whole thing down. The Press would never have heard a thing but for a leakage, probably by the porter.

They carried her into the main vestibule and tried to get Jedmont but he wasn't in. There was no smell of drink about her and she was in such a state of collapse that they called the hospital. Jedmont came in a few minutes after she'd been taken there. He seemed staggered by the news and at once went off to the hospital himself. There they let him see his wife, and no more.

"And that's where we came in," Jewle said. "There was an immediate examination and it was found she was under the influence of drugs. There were several needle pricks. And there was a bruise on the back of her head that couldn't have been caused when she fell in the car-park. It was at least a couple of days old. I went along yesterday morning and spent most of the day on the job. So far the whole thing doesn't make sense. That's why, when it was reported you'd rung the hospital, I thought you might be able to help."

I said I only wished I could.

There was what looked like a small dossier on the desk.

I thought he was going to hand it to me but he changed his mind.

"That's all the evidence so far," he said. "I thought of asking you to read it but I think I've got a better idea. If you're not too busy."

I said my time was my own.

"It's this," he said. "You seem to know Jedmont remarkably well. By the way, could he have any idea that you've ever been associated in any way here?"

"He couldn't have," I said. "He's the last person I'd ever discuss anything with."

"Right," he said. "He's been given permission to go to his office as usual, so he should be there now. We'll pay him a call and you'll hear everything he says. What I'd like you to judge is whether he's telling the truth."

He rang for his car, put the file of statements in his brief case and we were off.

On the way he told me just what attitude to adopt. He also said I was probably going to be surprised. I could have surprised him, too, if I'd told him all I knew about Jedmont.

It was a short enough trip from the Yard. Jewle led the way from the lift to the door. Almost at once Jedmont was opening it. He just looked enquiringly at Jewle but, when he caught sight of me, the look turned to bewilderment. Jewle was making his way in and I followed him.

"Sorry you're being troubled again, Mr. Jedmont, but do you know this man?"

Jedmont could hardly believe his ears. "You mean Mr. Travers?"

"You do know him?"

Jedmont, still bewildered, said he'd known me for years. Only a few days ago he'd done a job for me.

"He rang the hospital asking about your wife," Jewle said. "We had to know just how well he knew her. Sorry to have inconvenienced you, Mr. Travers, but you know how things are. Would you mind taking a seat over there? If Mr. Jedmont can spare the time there're a few things I'd like to clear up."

I took a seat not far from the other door but still within earshot. Jewle drew up a chair for Jedmont and one for himself. He took the file from his briefcase and ran an eye over it.

"Mr. Jedmont, do you know what you're going to say to me? You're going to say that everything's being gone over twice. You've told it all before. If you do, I'm going to tell you that I haven't heard all of it myself and I'd like to hear everything just once more. Understood?"

He'd been smiling. Jedmont actually smiled. A bit feebly, but he smiled. When Jewle spoke again, the tone was far more business-like.

"First of all, tell me just what happened that night your wife disappeared?"

Jedmont moistened his lips. I thought he was looking pretty ghastly. He never had had a lot of colour but now he was looking as if he'd just crawled out after a few years under a stone.

"Well. Gay went home at her usual time, about half-past five but I stayed on because I had a business appointment at the Dorchester at half-past six."

"Ah, yes," Jewle said. "The business appointment. Tell me about that first."

The editor of a Canadian photographic magazine had made the appointment at about four that late afternoon. Jedmont found a recent copy of the magazine—*The Photographic World*—and showed it, and the editor's name, to Jewle: a John H. Hengrove. Hengrove said he was just about to take a plane from Birmingham, so he'd be at the Dorchester easily by six-thirty. What was to be discussed was an arrangement for a regular supply of Jedmont's work to the magazine. Jedmont arrived on time. A reservation had been made that day for Mr. Hengrove but he didn't arrive. Jedmont waited till nine o'clock, then gave it up. The next morning Hengrove rang him. The flight had been delayed on account of the fog and then cancelled. Hengrove had rung Jedmont's office but there'd been no one there, so he stayed the night in Birmingham and then his plans had had to be changed. Jedmont was now to send full particulars and specimens of his work to Montreal.

"All that's been checked," Jewle said. "You were at the hotel and waited and then you went home. What happened then?"

"My wife wasn't there. I couldn't understand it. There wasn't a note or anything. Then I thought her aunt might have called her and she'd left in a hurry to catch a train."

Jewle told me about the aunt as we drove back later. She was Gay's only relative, and living in Lincoln. Jedmont had first met Gay four years ago when he'd applied to an agency for a model, but a year later the aunt had been taken ill and Gay had gone to look after her. She came back to London in the spring of 1960 and had made Jedmont's acquaintance again. She accepted a full-time job as secretary-model and later they were married.

"And then?" Jewle said.

"Well, I waited till the morning and then I rang Gay's aunt in Lincoln, and she hadn't seen her or heard a thing."

"And then?"

"Well, all the time I knew she'd ring me and tell me where she was. Tell me about it. I expected her to walk through the door there. I just didn't know what to do. I was worried nearly to death."

"But even the next day you didn't go to the police. Or start ringing up the hospitals to see if she'd had an accident."

"I was worried. I didn't know what to do."

"And so you did nothing. You were in love with your wife?"

"I'd have cut off my right arm rather than this should have happened to her."

"No quarrels?"

Jedmont gave a helpless shake of the head.

"No monetary troubles? This office and the apartment must have been costing you a lot of money."

"I make a lot of money," Jedmont said with a quick show of pride. "If you like, you can see my books."

Jewle smiled. "Save that for the Inspector of Taxes. I'll take your word for it But let's move on to the night when your wife was found. You weren't in your apartment, so where were you?"

"I don't know. Just walking about. I was nearly crazy."

Jewle stood up. "Well, I'm much obliged to you, Mr. Jedmont. Just one last question. As far as you've been able to tell us, your wife didn't take even a small case with her, or any clothes except what she was wearing, or even her toilet things. She did take her handbag and it was found with her, and nothing, as far as you could tell, had been removed. The position's this: she disappeared mysteriously from the apartment She was seen going along the downstair corridor towards the car-park and, after best part of three days of absence, that's exactly where she was found. It may sound fantastic, but she might have gone to the car-park and never left it. Can you throw any light on that? Any possible explanation?"

Jedmont couldn't even speak. Jewle took the silence for an answer and held out his hand.

"Thank you for your help. I hope when you ring the hospital again you'll have much better news of your wife. Sorry you've had to wait like this, Mr. Travers. Is there anywhere I can take you?"

I said curtly that the nearest Tube station would be as good a place as any. We went through the door. I could almost feel Jedmont's eyes trying to catch mine, but I kept my head averted.

"Sorry about your wife."

That was all I said and then Jewle was closing the door.

Jewle dropped me in Northumberland Avenue, just round the corner from Trafalgar Square. I hadn't had a lot to tell him, even if the little did seem to him important. When he asked me if at any time I'd thought Jedmont had been lying, I said there was one occasion when I thought he was and one when I was sure he was.

He might have been lying when he said that on the night of his wife's disappearance, he'd relied on her having gone to her aunt. Since no note had been left—and how long would it have taken to scribble a note—then it wasn't natural to wait till the next morning before contacting Lincoln.

When in my opinion he was definitely lying was when he gave worry as his excuse for not going to the police or ringing the hospitals. Either, both in fact, were the obvious things to do.

"That's roughly what I thought myself," Jewle said. "Sure you won't have lunch with me?"

I said I ought to be getting back. I hadn't warned Norris where I was and he might be going to the police or ringing the hospitals. Jewle laughed. I don't know why. In view of everything, it was a macabre sort of joke. But he did tell me that he'd keep me informed.

14
ALARUMS AND EXCURSIONS

I DIDN'T take the Underground at Trafalgar Square as I'd hinted to Jewle. I walked on instead to Charing Cross Station and the bookstall. I asked for a copy of *The Photographic World*.

"Afraid we don't keep it in stock," I was told. "You mean the Canadian magazine?"

"That's the one," I said. "I'm told it's one of the best."

The assistant said it was. He also told me where I'd be pretty sure of finding a copy—at a bookshop just off Leicester Square.

I didn't go there. I didn't even want a copy. All I'd wanted was to know if that magazine was obtainable by the casual English purchaser. Apparently it was.

I thought of crossing to Duncannon Street and taking a bus but it was a dry, cold morning with a bitter north wind and I took the Underground instead. I wanted to think, but somehow I couldn't find sufficient clarity of thought. There were too many things to think about; all of them unpleasant and some which I hated to face in too open a light. That was why I went straight to Norris's room instead of my own.

When I told him about that morning, he wasn't happy either. It wasn't hard to see that that absence of Gay Jedmont and its tragic aftermath must be connected with that job we'd only just concluded for Louis Marquette.

"Naturally you didn't give Jewle the slightest hint," Norris said. "That might be bad. I mean if things get worse."

As I told him, I'd done everything that Jewle had asked me. What I'd told Jewle was the absolute truth and I could always claim that I hadn't told him more because I hadn't at the time seen that more might be needed. If he in some way unearthed a connection between Gay Jedmont and that blackmail business, then I'd look very much of a fool in admitting I hadn't been able to see beyond my nose end. Not that I minded that. What we had to fear was getting in bad odour with the police. What I had personally to fear was that Jewle should think I valued friendship so little as to risk a double-crossing for private ends. The old plea of protecting a client wouldn't hold good once Jewle knew I'd been up to the ears in that sordid blackmail case.

Finally I took Norris's advice. If things did get worse—if Gay Jedmont should unfortunately die—then there'd have to be some quick reconsideration. I was thinking about that when I went back to my room, and before I'd had time to hang up my overcoat Bertha was buzzing through to say that Jewle was on the line.

"Glad I caught you," he said. "I feared you might have gone to lunch. Just some news I thought you might like to have. That magazine editor, Hengrove: he hasn't been away from Montreal for weeks. You see the implications?"

"I think so," I said. "Our other photographic friend was sent to the Dorchester on a wild goose chase. What about the wife? Was she sent on one too?"

"Probably. We know she had a telephone call at about half-past six. Can't be traced, of course. The exchange there only keeps a record of outgoing calls."

"And the patient," I said. "Any more news?"

"Still just holding her own. Pneumonia's a tricky thing when you're still in the state she was. Oh, and just one other thing. It may sound trivial after that other business, but there's something you just might help us about. Remember I told you this morning that after that widow-racket business five years ago we had a bit of a conference and pooled our knowledge and so on?"

"I remember, you said you had a file you'd like to show me some time."

"That's right." He paused for a moment. "You been to lunch yet?"

"Just thinking of it. Why?"

"Change your mind and have lunch with me. I'll bring the file along."

I did change my mind, but not because of that file. What I'd thought was that a half-hour or so with Jewle himself might help me to a decision about disclosing the Marquette case.

It was latish—almost half-past one—when I got to the little restaurant near Westminster Bridge. Jewle, being who he was, had been able to reserve a table, and he was there when I arrived. He and I often had a meal there. It wasn't cheap unless you took into account the fact that the food was always good.

We began talking about the Jedmont business and who had lured him away to the Dorchester. As Jewle said, the whole thing had been most meticulously planned. The pseudo-Hengrove had left nothing to chance, either at the Dorchester or when dealing with Jedmont himself. The only risk he took was to do with that air flight from Birmingham, and even that had turned out lucky. Just before the call to Jedmont had been made, flights had already been cancelled at London Airport on account of the fog.

"You got any theories?" I asked him.

"I did have one at the very beginning," he told me. "I thought she'd been playing around with some man or other but I discarded it almost at once. Nothing fitted in. It was all too elaborate for just a day or two in a love nest. And, of course, she'd have had ultimately to come back. What I'm working on now is that Jedmont himself must have been tied up with some shady business or other and someone had the idea that she knew too much. It took all the time she was away for whoever it was to find out she didn't."

I kept my eyes on my plate. Even then I had the feeling that he must be reading my thoughts.

"Could be," I said.

"Then a funny thing happened," he went on. "You must have wondered when I rang you why I brought in that widow-racket file. I'll tell you. After you left me I began thinking about Jedmont and where the money came from to set him up in that place of his. so I rang him. I told him we had information that a few months before he went to Wingram House he'd only been scraping a living. He tried to argue the point, but you'd told me too much, so he said his aunt had left him the money. That's what made me remember that file. And I wondered if you happened to know when the aunt died. It might be worth checking up on."

I thought I saw an opening. It wouldn't be currying favour: just giving an immediate co-operation that might later stand me in good stead.

"That's extraordinary." I said. "When I saw Jedmont about photographing that miniature, I had the same idea. I don't care two hoots about insulting Jedmont, as you've probably guessed, as I asked him the same question—where the money came from, and he gave me the same answer. I thought he was lying. You know what a curious chap I am, so I thought I'd do a bit of private checking."

I told him all about that visit to the Quinton Hotel, Cove Bay.

"You taxed him with it?"

"Why should I?" I said. "I'd proved that what I'd guessed was right. No point in telling him what I'd done."

"Of course not," he said. "All the same, you've told me something that might be very important. I think I'll get along there straight away myself. I can kill two birds with one stone."

He caught my enquiring look. "I forgot. Something I hadn't told you."

He finished his coffee, pushed back the cup to clear a space and took that file from the briefcase.

"This is the result of about three months' co-ordinated effort. Every Chief Constable has a copy, and it deals with the activities of just one man. There were other cases, of course, but everything was thoroughly sifted according to methods employed and what descriptions we had of the swindlers. Most were smallish fry and carried on operations only for a few months. This particular one made it a profession. I'm not boring you with all this?"

"Just the opposite."

"Well, one very curious thing was that this particular man ceased operating practically from the very moment when he left that hotel five years ago, just before you got there, and he hasn't been involved since. Then, about three months ago, we had a stroke of luck. During the course of the enquiries, we'd naturally had to make confidential calls on people like bank managers and solicitors and it was a solicitor who got in touch with us. A client of his who'd been a victim had died and, when her papers were being gone through, a photograph was discovered. It had been taken by one of those beach photographers at the time the swindle was being operated, and three other victims have identified it as the man concerned."

He showed me his copy of the photograph. The man looked in the middle forties: tallish, well-dressed, somewhat distinguished-looking and wearing a clipped moustache not unlike my own.

"Curious," I said, "but I've a feeling I've seen him before. Something about the eyes."

For the life of me I couldn't place him. I said if I did remember anything I'd let him know at once.

"I'll let you have a spare copy," he said. "Perhaps that'll bring it back. What I shall do, of course, is make my own report as to where Jedmont did or didn't get his money from. I can't very well say the information came from you. Also I'll ask the lady to identify the photograph as Hubert Courtney."

That was only one of his names. What his real name was had never been discovered.

"What was his modus operandi?"

"He was an expert," Jewle said. "As far as we've been able to trace, he did only five jobs in the five years he operated. The sixth would have been the one you were involved in. The amounts varied from three thousand to as much as nine thousand, all worked through the old line of patter about oil wells, uranium mines and what have you, according to the victim. We think that after he made a killing, he used to lie low for a time, principally in the summer when hotels have mostly the holiday trade. Then he'd put in short reconnoitring stays at hotels till he found the likely victim. After that he could enjoy himself till funds were getting low: then the whole thing would start all over again."

He beckoned to the waiter. "Think I'll be getting along. Plenty of trains to Cove Bay so I ought to be back pretty early. You'd like me to give you a ring?"

He rang me at about eight o'clock. There were no surprises. Harriet Coome, as I knew, hadn't financed her nephew but she'd identified the man of the photograph as Hubert Courtney. What surprise there was, was for him.

"I think I've unearthed something else," I said. "I'd like to talk it over with you. Bernice is in but we can talk in my room."

"It's as important as that?"

"It may be," I said. "It'll be for you to judge. I think you ought to hear it."

A quarter of an hour later he turned up. A few words with Bernice and we adjourned to my den. While I opened two cans of beer, he was admiring the copies of the miniature.

"This is what I thought you ought to know," I said, as soon as we'd settled down. "I shall probably be a bit long-winded but you'll see the point before too long. The point, that is, why I thought you might be interested. Just a fifty-fifty chance, but here goes."

What had set me thinking had been the modus operandi of Hubert Courtney, to give him one of his names: particularly that bit about operating only in the non-holiday months. It had made me remember another man who used to have quite a lot of spare time in the summer, but who was away for various spells in the other months. It was a man whose photograph I'd never seen but whom I'd come very much to know at the time. I mean Harry Wale. Hubert Courtney had gone out of business five years ago and had not been heard of since. Harry had left his wife at the same approximate time, and had also vanished into thin air.

Mind you, I didn't tell Jewle why we'd undertaken the assignment to find Wale: tell him, that is, about the mysterious Charles Ashman. I merely said that a client had asked us to find Wale, and I so manipulated things that Jewle had to think the client had probably been Wale's wife.

"It fits in remarkably well," he said. "Making himself out to be a secret-service agent to account for those exploratory trips to various hotels. You think that was his real name?"

"It was the name he was married under. It was the name he was prepared to sign in order to get possession of her house."

"Yes, that," he said. "Funds were low. He'd had to lose the probable killing from Harriet Coome and he had to finance a new venture. That's the vital thing—what that venture was. It wasn't anything in the nature of his usual racket, so what was it? And what made him think it profitable enough to make him lose money that was as good as in his pocket. And could it somehow tie in with what we're engaged on now?" He leaned forward.

"Jedmont could have double-crossed you. He knew Wale. He could have tipped him off. And have managed to blackmail Wale into letting him in on that new venture. That may have been where the Wingram House money came from." One thing he said he'd do as soon as he got back to the Yard: check if the files had anything whatever on a Harry Wale.

"He's a real enough person," I said. "As I told you, I traced him right back to his boyhood. Right up to the time his father died and he disappeared again. One thing I wish you wouldn't do, though. Don't go questioning his wife. I told you the sort of woman she is and I'm sure you couldn't find anything new. If she'd heard anything about him she'd have kept her promise to let me know. She's that kind of woman."

"No necessity at all," he told me as he got up to go. "What we may have to be dealing with couldn't possibly concern her."

"You mean?"

He looked surprised that I didn't know. "Well, finding out if Jedmont was mixed up in some shady business with Wale. Whether Wale's now a member of some gang or other and they thought Jedmont was about to squeal about something or other, or had talked to his wife. That theory I told you I was working on."

"Let's hope it fits in," I said. "Jedmont might be a hard man to get to talk."

He had a word with Bernice and left. I went down with him to the lift. Since it might be as late as eleven before I went to bed, he said he'd let me know if he found Wale in any of the files.

He rang me soon after ten. The Yard had nothing, but the outgoing *Police Gazette* would stimulate enquiries. Interpol would also have a photograph and all that was known about Wale. A man as fluent as he in languages might very well be known abroad. Jewle also thanked me most warmly for what I'd told him earlier.

That night I slept the sleep of the just. Before Jewle rang I'd been feeling much as Blondin must have felt when first making his way along a tightrope stretched across Niagara Falls. Now, for a time at least I was safely across on the other side.

The morning did bring another quick qualm when Jewle rang me up at the Agency.

"Just a trivial matter." he said. "Something I wanted to clear up, but do you recall asking me to get you some information not so long ago about a Harry Wale and the intelligence services? Was that in connection with the same enquiry?"

"The same. The one I told you about last night."

"Just wanted to make sure." he said. "Soon as you mentioned the name I knew I'd heard it before, but I only just now had an idea where."

"Any more news?"

"Too early yet. I might be seeing Mr. J. in the course of the morning. It ought to be interesting watching his reactions when he hears the glad news that his aunt's alive."

"Any chance of my being there?"

He thought for a moment. "It might be all to the good. About eleven? Outside Wingram House?"

That memory of Jewle's, I told myself ruefully, might one day land me in considerable trouble, not that I wasn't already far too near it. The previous night's sleep had come in a rosy-hued haze, but you see things more clearly when it's a cold November morning. It had been foolish, I was telling myself, to suggest that I should go with him to see Jedmont. Sooner or later he'd begin wondering why it was I was clinging to his coat-tails.

The real trouble would come if he was ever able to put two and two together and discover that I must have known, almost since it occurred, just what had happened to Gay Jedmont. You yourself must have at least guessed at it quite some time ago. You were in possession of everything that preceded it, and the moment Jewle arrived at only some of those facts, he'd be asking some mighty awkward questions.

You, as I've said, may be sure: I still had a few reservations, not that they really mattered. What I did actually know had both logic and a right sequence. And there was something else. Heaven knows I didn't want Gay Jedmont dead, but, at that very moment, one of Jewle's men would be sitting by her bed, ready to record the first words she spoke.

Then, with a cold shiver, I thought of something else. Maybe she'd already spoken. There'd almost certainly been the usual delirium, and every word she'd uttered must have been taken down. And then again, in almost the same moment. I knew I was being ridiculous. Delirium was delirium: it could never stand up as evidence. Unless, of course, she'd mentioned the name of either Louis Marquette or Frank Gledmill, and that would be enough to send Jewle hot-foot to the Mayland.

It must have been instinctively that I called Bertha. She was lucky. Jewle was in his room.

"Travers here," I said. "Sorry to bother you, but I neglected to ask you something when we were talking earlier. Any news of the patient?"

"She's just about at the crisis," he told me. "They're hopeful, but not much more."

"Was she delirious? Did she do any talking?"

"Not a word. Just occasional mutterings and couldn't be identified, so to speak."

I thanked him, said I'd be seeing him and rang off.

You may not believe me but I'd still have given a lot to have Gay Jedmont live: in fact it was the thought of her dying that made me busy myself with the job I was doing for Norris. Then I had my coffee earlier than usual and set off for Wingram House. I saw Jewle's car drive up just as I was about to cross the road.

"I'd like to play it this way," he told me while we waited for the lift. "You were told his aunt was dead and that's supporting evidence for him telling me the same thing. Just in case he denies it."

The solitary passenger got out of the automatic lift and we went up. Jewle pushed the bell and listened. He gave me a look and rang again. Nothing happened. He waited for a moment and let his thumb stay quite a few seconds on the bell-push.

"Can't make it out," he said. "I rang him about an hour ago. Said I was coming and would he be in."

A similarly frosted glass door across the wide landing gave the name of a firm of toy manufacturers. Jewle went over, rang, was admitted and disappeared inside. I guessed he'd asked to use the telephone and I was right.

"He isn't at the apartment," he said. "Wonder where he's gone?"

"He couldn't have bolted?"

"Why should he? He's never been led to suppose he's any kind of a suspect."

He frowned. "Wait a minute. I think I'll use their telephone again."

This time there was quite a long wait. When he joined me again I could see that something was wrong.

"He's at the hospital," he told me quietly. "They rang him. Must have been just before we arrived."

"His wife?"

"Yes," he said. "She's dead. Died about an hour ago."

My eyes must have screwed up in pain.

"I know," he said. "It seems all wrong. Everything to live for and then this had to happen."

We were at the head of the stairs so we didn't turn back to the lift. "What now?" I asked him.

"Don't know," he said. "I can't go asking that poor devil questions with things as they are. He was pretty fond of his wife. Maybe the only good thing about him."

I asked him to drop me at Leicester Square. When he drove on I still hadn't made up my mind what to do. People like Jewle are used enough to most of the forms of death but even he had felt a kind of hurt. As for me, I'd never grown callous or indifferent, and I couldn't get Gay Jedmont out of my mind. I didn't feel like going back to the Agency. I didn't feel like going anywhere, and what I finally did was to walk to the flat. I rang Norris and gave him the news. It was then well on the way to lunch-time so I had something sent up. Bernice was out: I'd forgotten where.

After lunch I thought I might as well go back to the Agency. I was wishing that Hallows was there but he was on that Birmingham job and not due back till at least another day. Still, I found a job to do and the afternoon went reasonably quickly by. Just before five I went home. Bernice was in and we had tea together. Just before six o'clock we turned on the television and listened to the news. What followed it was one of those "Look" programmes that she likes so much, and it was nearing its end when the telephone went.

I took it.

"That you, Mr. Travers? This is Inspector Matthews. The Old Man wants you to come along to the Mayland and to make it quick. You know where it is?"

"I know it," I said. "What's happening?"

"Just get along," he told me, and rang off.

Matthews I'd known for years. He'd always been Jewle's sidekick. The Old Man was Jewle, and Jewle was at the Mayland. I wondered why, but somehow I was suddenly unable to think. I must have been in quite a mental daze as I grabbed my hat and overcoat, had a quick word with Bernice and made for the lift.

THERE was a misty drizzle and the light was poor in the narrow Soho street. A policeman was keeping back a gathering crowd and another was diverting traffic at the Waggon Lane end. Until I caught sight of the ambulance and the police cars I might have thought some celebrity—crooner, maybe, or rock-and-roller—was visiting the Mayland. A third policeman was at the door.

As he let me through, a well-dressed couple brushed hastily past me. It was early for the Mayland but a few tables should have been occupied: as it was, not a soul was in the place except a couple of waiters talking quietly in the far corner by the service hatch. Then I caught sight of Matthews over by the hat-check stand where Doris should have been. As I threaded my way through the tables he moved a few yards to meet me.

"What's going on?" I said. "Why's the whole place deserted."

The quietness everywhere made my voice unnaturally loud.

"There's been a bit of trouble. The Old Man's closed the place down for the night."

"But why send for me?"

"He'll explain," he said. "Everyone's in the office. You'll soon know."

He waved me on down the short corridor. He reached forward at the office door and opened it.

Except for the murmur of a couple of voices, that office had a deathly quiet. Inside the door something made me stop where I was. Something covered with a sheet lay stretched out on the floor by the desk. Behind it stood Maximilien, the head-waiter, and Doris. Doris had been crying.

Just to their left was Jedmont, handcuffed and looking stolidly down at the floor. A plain-clothes man had him by the arm. Further to the left, where Louis used to sit, something else was on the floor. Doc Anders was masking my view and Jewle was there too, down on one knee. It was their voices I'd heard as I stepped in. Two stretcher men were standing ready.

Old Doc. Anders got to his feet, and began dusting his knees. He caught sight of me and grinned. "Well, if it isn't the undertaker! Haven't seen you for months."

Jewle's quick smile seemed a bit reserved. "All right," he said. "Take him away. We'll arrange to move the other one later."

Doris began sobbing quietly. I could see now that the man being placed on the stretcher was Louis. As I drew well back from the door I could see that his face and neck were smeared with blood.

"You can go now," Jewle told Doris. "Soon as you feel like it we'll take an official statement. You too, Maximilien."

Matthews followed them out.

"Take him out too," Jewle told the plain-clothes man. "Better keep in the corridor. By the stairs."

The door closed on Jedmont. He didn't even look at me as he went through. Jewle let out a breath.

"What a night! Haven't had such a mess for years."

I pointed down. "Is that Frank Gledmill?"

He drew back the sheet. Gledmill looked as if he were asleep.

"Must have been a lucky shot," Jewle said. "Jedmont's no marksman. Got him first time. He had to have three goes at Marquette. One miss, one through the top of the lung here and one clean through both cheeks. Just missed the base of the brain."

"But Jedmont: why'd he do it?"

"Because they killed his wife."

I stared. It seemed incredible that Jewle could have discovered so much already.

"That's what he says," Jewle went on. "That's the only thing he did say."

I hoped he didn't see my look of relief.

"And because it was Jedmont you wanted me here?"

"Well, not exactly." He gave me one of his shrewder looks. "It was something Marquette said, just before he collapsed. As a matter of fact he mentioned your name. Just as if he wanted to tell you something."

The time for shilly-shallying had gone. I had to make a quick decision. Even then I don't know why I acted as I did. There ought to have been something of a panic, but there wasn't.

"So that was it," I said. "The hundred to one shot was right."

Jewle was doing the staring.

"I don't know what you're talking about. What hundred to one shot?"

"You tell me all you know about this evening," I said, "and I may be able to explain. A whole lot of things have got to fit in."

What I was doing was asking for time: time to fit my own story snugly into what Jewle might tell me.

"What happened tonight," he said reflectively. "Very well. Let's take it easy and I'll tell you."

I took off my overcoat. Frank Gledmill's chair had been moved across the room and I took it. Jewle was in Louis' old chair.

"What happened seems pretty clear," he told me. "Just after the doors were opened Jedmont came in. He went straight across to the hat-check recess where the woman, Doris Finkel, was. She thought he was depositing his hat and coat but he went past her towards here. She says she called to him, 'Where're you going? You can't go in there!' Something like that. At any rate, Max Bristow, that's Maximilien's real name, heard her and came to investigate. He didn't hear anything except the shots. Neither did Doris. She was scared and ran back into the restaurant. Then she had sense enough to rush out for a policeman.

"After the shots, by the time Max got here, Jedmont bolted out. Max was scared of the gun but he jumped Jedmont when he made for the stairs. A couple of other waiters had come running and, as far as I can make out, there was the devil of a struggle. Jedmont kept hollering that they'd killed his wife. The gun had dropped and one of the waiters hit him on the head with it and knocked him out. Then the constable arrived while Max was dialling 999. And that's about all. To show you how quickly it happened, I was here myself only about a quarter of an hour after Jedmont first walked in."

"And Louis later mentioned my name?"

"That's right. Anders got here about five minutes after I did and it was while he was looking at him that Louis Marquette suddenly mentioned your name. He couldn't speak very well because of the blood, but there wasn't any doubt about it. He was trying to get up. We had to hold him down. It was as if he had to tell you something urgent. Then he collapsed."

"Yes," I said slowly. "I'm beginning to see."

I looked up. "Do you think Jedmont would talk to me? It might save a lot of time."

"I doubt it," he said. "No harm in trying."

He brought Jedmont in. He waved his hand as much as to say he was now all mine.

"Hallo, Jedmont," I said. "They tell me you've got the idea Louis Marquette and Frank Gledmill were responsible for what happened to your wife."

He gave me just the one quick look.

"What made you think that, Jedmont?"

I might have been talking to a dummy at Madame Tussaud's.

"Listen," I said. "Get everything off your mind. No use harbouring things. That's the way to go mad. Just tell me quietly what made you do it. I can't help you if you don't."

Jewle was patient. He waited through five minutes of that one-sided questioning before he lost patience.

"It's no use. He'll talk when the time comes."

He took him out. I heard him telling the detective to take him away. You may think me callous in questioning Jedmont at all, but that wasn't the way I saw it. I'd known he wouldn't talk. I knew Brian Jedmont, and my guess was that he too wanted time to tell a story. How could he talk when what he said would incriminate him in that blackmail business?

Jewle came back and with him a waiter with a couple of drinks—stiff whiskies with not much soda.

"Don't know about you but I feel I want this. It's been a pretty nasty evening, one way and another."

He took half his drink at a gulp, wiped his mouth and sat back in his chair.

"Now let's hear this story of yours."

"Right," I said. "You're in a hurry, or can I tell things my own way?"

He actually smiled. "Who're you trying to kid?"

"Just trying to work things out," I said. "May I have a word with Max? And then with Doris? If they're still here."

"They're here," he said. "Matthews has been getting their statements."

He brought Max in.

"Hallo, Max," I said. "You think you can answer a few more questions?"

"I will if I can, sir."

"Good. They're about Jedmont, the man who did the shooting. Were you aware that when he had a meal here he never paid? He just put his name on the bill?"

"Yes, sir," he said. "We don't do that sort of thing here, but he was an exception. The first time it happened, I was—"

"Just a moment. That was when?"

"Just after we opened, sir."

"Getting on for five years ago. Carry on, Max."

"Well, sir, I was called in by Fred, I think it was, and then the boss—Mr. Marquette—told me Mr. Jedmont was a friend of his and it was all okay."

"Anything else?"

He gave me a queer look. "Now you come to mention it, sir, he told me I wasn't to say a word to Mr. Gledmill. He'd see to it himself."

"And you didn't mention it to Mr. Gledmill?"

He hesitated. "Well, not till a few days ago and then Mr. Gledmill asked me about it. Said it was in confidence and I wasn't to say a word to the boss."

That was all. A rather puzzled Max went out.

"I'd like you to remember that," I told Jewle. "It's a very important bit of evidence."

Doris came in. She'd made up her face but she was still looking pretty scared. There wasn't much heart in her answering smile.

"Now, Doris, I'd like you to help us by telling us just one thing. By the way, we happen to know you had a visit one night recently from a Mr. Hallows and you told him in confidence how you came to get the hat-check concession here. Would you mind telling us?"

Her voice was hardly audible as she told us.

"I see," I said. "Mr. Jedmont said if you applied for the concession, you'd get it, and you did. Later he took a percentage. Then he had other fish to fry and he dropped you. But you and everybody here had been getting along well together and you've been here ever since."

That was all. Jewle told her she could go home. When the restaurant would reopen he didn't know.

"I'm not seeing just now where all this is fitting in," he told me. "Am I just being dense, or what?"

"You'll soon know as much as I do," I said. "Just one last thing to do. I'd like Max to take us round the upper floor." He shrugged his shoulders, but he went out to find Max.

I waited at the foot of the stairs. The three of us stopped at the widish landing. A corridor led off to our left with doors opening into the two bedrooms and the bathroom. To the right was the kitchen. As Max agreed, there was no connection whatever between it and the living quarters.

"Was the kitchen door ever left open?"

He looked surprised. "And let the kitchen smell get all over the place? No, sir. All that was ever opened was that side door when stuff for the kitchen came up by the lift."

I told Max that was all we wanted. A crate or two and some boxes stood against the wall near that service lift. It was a simple affair, worked by ropes. The cage was hardly big enough for both of us to squeeze tightly in.

On the ground floor it was pitch dark. We flashed our lighters and crossed the couple of yards to the door. The key was inside and we stepped into that loading space off Vickery Street. You could see and no more. I gave the door key to Jewle.

"When you come here in broad daylight, you'll get a better idea of things," I told him as I gave him the key.

"Anything else to do?"

"Nothing," I said. "You've seen and heard everything for yourself. Quite enough to understand what I'm going to tell you."

Once more we made ourselves comfortable in the office. I took a long time over my story in order to place the right emphases. That, for instance, I'd been approached almost casually and certainly unexpectedly by Louis that night when we'd dined and danced there. That I'd disliked the idea of helping him and that I'd told him to go to the police.

"You believed his story?"

"Yes and no," I said. "I believed it up to the time I'd received assurances from the French Embassy that an enquiry in his case would be very much of a formality. When he wouldn't take that easy and obvious way out, then I knew he'd done a lot of lying. He wasn't an innocent victim. He was a collaborator."

"Yes," Jewle said. "And if that was so, we can find out."

"I'm pretty sure now of two other things," I went on. "It was only because I hadn't any real heart in the case that I didn't do something about it. It was those two fiascos when the money should have been handed over that made me drop the whole thing. In any case I was working only on suspicions."

"What were the two things?"

"That he'd known all along who the blackmailer was, and that his real name wasn't Louis Marquette. And possibly that the events he related hadn't taken place in Toulouse at all. His name couldn't have been Louis Marquette, otherwise he'd have been traced when he opened a hotel in Paris."

"You didn't think it was about time you came to see us?"

I looked astounded.

"Not like you to mess about with a whole lot of monkey business," he said. "Still, you'd dropped out of things. Maybe what you did was right. But what about when things happened to Jedmont's wife? You and I talked about it and discussed it. Don't you realise that if you'd told me only what you suspected, what happened here tonight mightn't have happened at all?"

"That's hind-sight," I told him. "How could I know the facts about Gay Jedmont? I discovered them only tonight. Could I—could you for that matter?—have come here and started making enquiries?"

"No need to get all het-up," he said patiently. "Just what did you discover tonight?"

"A whole lot of things. Let's take them in some sort of order. That Gledmill discovered who the blackmailer was. He was sure. I'd only suspected. And he thought up the simplest way out of all: kidnap Gay Jedmont so that the pictures and prints would be handed over in return. He rang her that night. She thought she was going to join her husband. It was very foggy and she wouldn't see where his car was taking her, and when they got to that unloading passage he knocked her out. He'd induced Louis to go to Brighton and he probably kept her under sedation in Louis' room. He had to bring her back under sedation and dump her in that car-park just before he'd told Louis he could come back from Brighton. Whether or not she'd seen anything to remember later, didn't matter. Jedmont couldn't afford to let her tell anything to the police. Also Gledmill might have been wearing that disguise of his."

"Those fiascos at St. Paul's and Trafalgar Square were only eyewash?"

"Must have been. Gledmill was already holding Gay Jedmont."

"Yes," he said slowly. "It certainly seems to fit in. And that original blackmail money was what set Jedmont up in business."

"There's something else I haven't told you," I said. "Something that made me decide to have nothing more to do with the whole fishy business. Jedmont never served abroad in the last war. He was exempt, and from doing his national service."

"You mean he must have got those negatives from a third party?"

"How else?"

He leaned back in his chair, eyes wrinkled as if in pain.

"No—o—o! Don't tell me we've got to go looking for some-one else?"

"Well, that'll be up to you," I said. "At any rate, you'll appre-ciate now why I got out of things the very moment the contract allowed. I never ought to have handled it in the first place."

"It isn't your fault it turned out as it did. You got caught up in something that got out of control."

He looked at his watch and got to his feet.

"What's beginning to worry me is the one from whom Jedmont got the photographs. He may be up to the neck in all this too. And how could Jedmont know the photographs had any value? It pre-supposes that he knew all the circumstances and just what use they'd be for blackmailing Marquette."

He chuckled ironically. "And me thinking this business tonight, and what you've told me, had the whole thing as good as cleared up."

There was a rap at the door. A couple of Jewle's men had come to collect Gledmill's body. Before they replaced the sheet I saw his face again. Even in the better light, it still looked as if he was asleep. And he'd go on sleeping soundly where they were taking him. You don't worry about hard beds in a morgue.

"Well, there goes someone I wish was alive," Jewle said quietly. "One thing I will say for him. He did have pluck. Everything shows he went straight for Jedmont as soon as he produced the gun."

"Did you ever see him fight?"

"No." he said. "He was one of the few I've missed. They tell me he was good."

I was making for the door. He asked if his driver might take me back to the flat. He himself was staying on to arrange about closing down the place temporarily.

"Just a minute," I said. "Do you have the key of the safe?"

"I've got all the keys. I'll have to go through the safe to look at any papers."

"Remember I told you that Louis showed me a photograph? He had it in that safe."

He went back at once. It was an old-fashioned safe and he only had to turn the key. He got down on one knee and began taking things out: various documents, some correspondence, old ledgers. It took us a good ten minutes to go methodically through the whole lot but there wasn't a photograph there. Jewle smiled ruefully.

"Damn silly, I suppose, to expect to find it. When he burnt everything that Jedmont handed over, he'd have burnt that one too."

At the door he said he might want to get into touch with me in the morning. I turned back for a last look at that room, and in those few seconds I thought of a whole lot of things: Louis almost cringing as he refused to give himself up: Frank Gledmill at the desk, and that half-smile, half-sneer. Depressing things, most of them, so that even the cold drizzle of Vickery Street had a queer something that made life suddenly better.

Jewle rang just after I got to the agency the next morning. He was at the Mayland, trying to clear various matters up.

"I've seen everything in daylight now," he said, "and what you told me seems a hundred per cent right. Thought you'd like to know."

I asked him how Louis was. He said he'd never had more than a fifty-fifty chance. At the best, he couldn't be interviewed for quite a time.

"About that third party," I said. "The one from whom Jedmont got the negatives. I've got an idea. Could you bring a kind of gentle pressure to bear? Say about having him released under surveillance to attend his wife's funeral? If so, mightn't he decide to talk?"

He said it might be worth thinking over. Matthews had reported that Jedmont was still refusing to say even a word.

"Look," I said. "Take this in the right way, but mightn't he talk to me rather than you people? He hasn't the faintest idea I've been working on the case, so mightn't he regard me as a friend?"

"Might be worth thinking over," he told me. "I'm up to the ears at the moment but I'll let you know."

He didn't ring till five o'clock that afternoon. He'd seen the Mayland solicitors and neither of the partners had made a will.

The partnership deed showed that Gledmill had a third interest and there was no clause about the survivor taking all. Just the standard kind of deed with either partner able to withdraw at six months' notice. Max would be temporarily in charge till Louis recovered.

"If he does recover," Jewle said. "I didn't say so, but there'll have to be certain things to clear up with the French authorities even if he does. One other thing. We got into touch with Gledmill's father and he'll be seeing us in the morning. There's no need to tell him everything we know. Matthews'll be meeting him."

I asked if he'd thought any more about my private talk with Jedmont. He said that was what he'd really rung up about. If ten o'clock next morning would suit me, he'd have him at his room at the Yard.

16
FIRST DAYLIGHT

Jewle brought Jedmont in. I stood up.

"Hallo, Jedmont. Sorry to see you like this."

He shot a quick look at me, and I think he gave me a nod.

"I oughtn't to be doing this, Jedmont," Jewle told him. "It might land me in trouble, but Mr. Travers thought he could help you if he had a private talk with you. A quarter of an hour. I can't give you more, Mr. Travers. The buzzer's just there if you should want anything."

He went out. I got Jedmont seated. I offered him a cigarette but he shook his head. I lighted my pipe to make things more homely.

"I know a whole lot of things I didn't know last night," I began. "Even if it was wrong to take the law into your own hands, you can't be too much blamed for settling up with the two who killed your wife. That's what I thought till I learned about the blackmail."

That shook him. It was something, he'd been sure, that no one but Louis and Frank had known.

"Never underestimate the police," I said. "That's why you were so silly to tell me and them that your aunt had left you the money to branch out at Wingram House, when all the time she was alive and hadn't given you a penny. That money came from Louis Marquette, and they know it. Louis had owned up to everything not long before you shot him. Not that he had a hand, mind you, in kidnapping your wife. Gledmill did that. You see what I'm getting at?"

He was beginning to see it. He was looking at me and not away.

"You'll face two charges," I said. "One for murder and one for extortion. Killing Gledmill might have some justification. Killing Louis hadn't."

"He's dead?"

It was the first word he'd spoken since the murder night. "Only a question of time," I said. "What the police want to do is compare his story with yours. If you don't help them, I can't help you. All I want you to do is tell me how you came into possession of those negatives."

He looked away. I knew I'd have to begin all over again. "This is Louis' story," I said, "and I'll make it short. You probably know it in any case. He was in Toulouse during the war and working with the French Resistance. He was taken prisoner and forced to collaborate. The proof of collaboration was some pictures taken surreptitiously by the Resistance. After the war he bolted to Paris, changed his name and later came over here and opened the Mayland. You came into possession of the negatives and threatened to hand him over to the French authorities if he didn't pay. He did, to the tune of five thousand pounds. But all you let him have were prints. You kept the negatives. Not long ago you put the squeeze on him again."

A curious thing had been happening. It was as if he were out with his camera and had suddenly seen something—a puddle of water, maybe, under some trees—and had as suddenly realised that in it was a picture. The camera had slowly begun to focus, just as his eyes had slowly focused on my face.

"What we want to know is where and how you got those Resistance negatives," I said. "Only a simple thing to ask. You couldn't possibly have taken them yourself. And if the man you got them from is as much up to the neck in all this as you are, why should he go scot-free? Or did you just buy them outright, and he didn't know what he was selling?"

He shook his head. A moment and he changed his mind. "I just bought them."

"When?"

"A long time ago. About six years."

"Then how did you know they were valuable? Six years ago you couldn't even have heard about Marquette."

He clammed up again. A moment and again he changed his mind.

"All right. I'll tell you. It was about five years ago. Frank Gledmill asked me to develop them."

I don't think I showed it but it staggered me.

"You mean he and you cooked up the blackmail plot?"

"Yes, if you want to call it that"

"I see. So he must have told you a whole lot of things. How, for instance, they came into his possession."

"No," he said quickly. "He never told me that. Only about him being what you said. A collaborator."

Jewle came in. One of his men was with him.

"Sorry we can't spare you any more time, Mr. Travers. I hope he's decided to help us."

"He already has."

"That's fine," he said. "Take him away. Better keep him handy in case I should want to see him myself."

Jedmont went out. Jewle sat down at the desk, took some time in lighting his pipe, then looked up. "Well?"

"A fantastic story," I said. "He got those negatives from Gledmill. They worked the racket together."

Jewle's mouth had gaped. "Would you mind saying that again?"

I said it. I embellished it. Jewle was still looking as if he couldn't believe his ears.

"You believe all that?"

I shrugged my shoulders. "That's almost word for word what he told me."

"I see."

He realised his pipe was already out. He gave it a look and laid it in the ash-tray.

"Then where did Gledmill get the negatives from? And why should he have to blackmail Louis to get the partnership money? I've seen his bank manager and his estate'll probably total up to twenty thousand pounds. And why should Gledmill hook up with a cheap crook like Jedmont? And another thing. Why should Gledmill have to kidnap Gay Jedmont to get back what he already had?"

"Maybe Jedmont had double-crossed him somehow. He'd got possession of the negatives."

He frowned. When he looked up he had that ironic little smile.

"You know what's the deciding factor in all this?"

I shook my head.

"This," he said. "Jedmont knows Gledmill is dead. He was there, remember? Dead men don't talk."

After that there was no more to say. Jewle did admit there might be some little something in what Jedmont had told me, but now I knew he threw that in as a kind of palliative: just his way of saying what I'd done had really been some help.

Matthews came in. Gledmill's father had just arrived.

"Right," Jewle said. "Mr. Travers is just going, so you can bring him in straight away."

I left at once. A deflated Travers took a bus at Westminster Bridge and even the longish ride to the City didn't do much raising of spirits. After I'd had some belated coffee in my room, I began telling myself that the morning hadn't been altogether wasted. At least I'd induced Jedmont to talk.

If I were ever asked to say a thing or so in favour of myself, I think I'd come up with two: that I hate snobbery and I'm always aware of my own limitations. Why then did I begin trying to find some vestige of truth in what Jedmont had told me? I don't know.

Most likely it was because I hated to admit, even to myself, that anyone like Jedmont could hoodwink me. That's why I went over everything that had been said in Jewle's room. Jewle's final piece of logic had been like a blow with a sledge-hammer: now I'd recovered I was hoping to find in Jedmont's story at least a substratum of truth.

I like working by questions and answers, so I reached for the note-pad. The method is to write down a question and worry it till you come up with an answer: then you go on from there. Not more than three minutes later I was laying the pencil down. What I'd discovered was pretty shattering. In the urgency to induce Jedmont to talk, I'd gone about things in the worst of all ways. I'd done the talking: I'd envisaged the situations: in other words, I'd as good as put words into Jedmont's mouth. I'd almost forced him to shift and merely share the blame. And who a more likely fall-guy than the dead Gledmill?

Then and there I decided to keep far, far away from that case. Only if Jewle most urgently asked, would I give it another second of time, and to show my resolution I went to lunch. When I came out I hesitated a moment, then went by the newspaper seller. What Jewle had given out to the Press was no concern of mine. There was nothing much for me to do at the Agency but I managed to find enough to occupy me for an hour and then I went to my club. Just before six o'clock I went home. Bernice induced me to take part in a double-handed game of patience and we'd nicely settled down to it when the telephone went. It was Jewle.

"Sorry to bother you but I'd like your help. It's a long while ago but didn't you see Wale's wife? You remember—Harry Wale. I'd like to get into touch with her myself."

"I thought we'd agreed she needn't be seen again?"

"This is different," he said, "Altogether different, so have you got her address?"

I asked him to wait while I found my old notebooks and it didn't take too long to find what he wanted.

"She's taken her maiden name," I told Jewle. "She's a Carol Nevett, or was. The address at which I saw her was: 38 Horburn Avenue, Kingsdale. The telephone number was Kingsdale 7723."

He thanked me and rang off. What it was all about I didn't know. What I wondered was why, with so much now on his hands, he was busying himself with anything so comparatively trifling as that old widow-racket affair. I didn't even bother to ring up Enquiries to find out if Carol Nevett was still at her former address.

By the time we'd finished our game I was feeling ready for a meal. We weren't going out, so Bernice had one sent up. I'd just got back from taking the crockery on the trolley to the lift when the telephone went again. Once more it was Jewle. He was far too polite.

"So sorry to keep disturbing you like this, but could you see me in the morning? At about ten?"

I hedged. "I think I may be a bit busy. Anything important, is it?"

"I think so," he said. "One thing I'm sure of: you won't be wasting your time."

I said I'd try and make it I hadn't a clue to what it was all about, but this time I settled one thing by myself: I ascertained from Enquiries that Miss C. Nevett had the same number and address.

There was quite a surprise for me when I entered Jewle's room in the morning. It shouldn't have been: after all. I'd been warned.

"Ah, Miss Nevett," Jewle said. "I think you know Mr. Travers."

"It isn't all that long since we saw each other," I said as I held out my hand. "Nice to see you again. Miss Nevett"

In spite of her smile I thought she was looking a bit on edge.

"Miss Nevett has very kindly come to help us identify someone," Jewle explained. "The person happens to be a patient in a hospital." He smiled. "Not a mental hospital."

"You ought to feel quite at home," I said to her. "You're still doing voluntary work at your local hospital?"

She mightn't have heard the question. "This person you want me to identify. It isn't my husband?"

"Frankly, I don't know," Jewle told her soberly. "He might be. He might be any one of a thousand people. All I'll say is I think he may be someone with whom you've come into contact. Also it's highly important to us to know who he is, or isn't. That's why I'm glad you're willing to help us."

I think she might have hesitated if he hadn't stood up. He gave me a quick nod and almost at once we were on the move. Carol Nevett and I sat in the back of the car and what small talk I could muster seemed to be putting her more at her ease. Not that she was openly nervous. She wasn't that kind of woman.

As soon as we walked into the hospital, it was clear that we were expected. Up we went to a waiting room where Jewle left us. When he came back, a sister was with him. There were introductions: plenty of smiles and a minimum of sedateness.

"Shall we be going?" Sister said. "It's only just along the corridor. The patient is sleeping now, so we must all be very quiet. A doctor will be there, but please don't be in any way alarmed."

She looked into the room before opening the door to let us through. It was quite a small room, the bed only a few feet away. A youngish doctor was standing at the head on the far side, and he nodded to Jewle as we came in. The man in the bed had his head towards us and you could just see the bed-clothes move as he breathed. What little I could see of his face had a transparent pallor. He was a stranger—till I saw the reddish wound on his cheek.

There was a sound. Carol Nevett was beginning to sob quietly as the sister led her slowly away. I caught Jewle's eye and we moved away too. When we reached the corridor, the two women had disappeared.

"You recognised him?"

"Louis Marquette," I said. "He had me puzzled till I realised they'd have had to shave him to treat those cheek wounds."

"You didn't notice anything else?"

I thought for a moment.

"Should I?"

"What about that photograph I showed you of Hubert Courtney?"

"Good lord, yes!"

Then the full implications struck me.

"It was Harry Wale, calling himself Louis Marquette?" I shook my head ruefully. "I remember now. When you showed me Wale's photograph I told you the eyes reminded me of someone. It was Louis Marquette."

"Listen now," he said. "Carol Wale will be back in a moment and I'll have to stay to see her on her way home in the car. Then I'd like a talk with you. Where do you suggest?"

I suggested that old haunt of ours near Westminster Bridge. We'd both be car-less and it'd be easy to get to by bus.

There was only a five-minute wait. I ordered coffee as soon as I saw him come in.

"Any scenes?" I asked him.

"None at all," he said. "As a matter of fact I think she was more composed than she'd been the whole morning. And don't make too much of those tears." He snapped his fingers. "She hasn't got that much affection for Wale. She didn't even wilt when I told her he was a crook."

The coffee came and we got down to a reappraisal. As far as we could see at first, things weren't very much changed. Wale had definitely served in the forces and it was conceivable that he'd been guilty of something which made him open to blackmail. Maybe he'd been a deserter. Or absconded with company or regimental funds. We didn't know, but one thing we did know. All that story of collaborating had been nothing but lies to cover up something else.

"Let's trace his fairly recent history," Jewle said. "He gave up the chance of making a packet out of Harriet Coome in order to work some racket that would be more profitable. We agreed on that before we had any idea he was Louis Marquette. We don't know what that racket was but he must have made the devil of a lot of money out of it because he was able to acquire the Mayland. It also explains something else that was worrying us—how Jedmont came to be in a position to blackmail him. Jedmont knew him pretty well and he saw through that Marquette disguise."

He asked me what was worrying me. Wasn't it reasonably plain?

"The pictures," I said. "If Jedmont had facts, why did he need pictures?"

"Yes," he said slowly. "You've got me there. But tell me something. You saw the picture Louis had in the safe. Just what was it like?"

"Two men obviously just parting after a meeting. I know now that Wale was definitely the one on the left and he was giving a sort of parting wave to the other. He was an older man. Bearded. Foreign looking. The only background was just the side of a door. It was supposed to be a picture taken by the Resistance of Louis and a high-up German civilian connected with the Gestapo."

Jewle frowned.

"I'd give the devil of a lot to have that photograph now. You think it still might be somewhere around?"

"Wait a minute," I said. "Seeing Carol Wale this morning reminds me of something else."

I told him about the day she came unexpectedly home from the hospital and saw Wale with a stranger. He also was a foreign-looking, foreign-speaking man with a beard. Wale had said afterwards he was a colleague at Intelligence.

"It fits in," he said. "It wasn't long after Wale disappeared from Sandford. Might have been someone concerned with the new racket. He and Wale were making plans."

The coffee had gone and he signalled to the waiter to bring two more cups. That was when I remembered something else.

"I think it was when we were here last and you'd showed me that Wale photograph that I told you about a client I'd had. Or was it when you came to see me at the flat? It doesn't matter. I told you I'd taken on an assignment to find Harry Wale and I felt at the time I needn't disclose who the client was. But tell me. Did you get the impression that the client was Carol Wale herself?"

"I think I did. Why?"

"Then you got the wrong person. Settle well down in your seat because I'm going to tell you about one of the most extraordinary clients I ever had in my life."

I began at that early November morning and the first sight of Charles Ashman, and how Hallows and I had given him a lift back to town. I told him how Hallows had been suspicious of Ashman, and why and how I'd thought those suspicions could be explained away. That was why, when Ashman called later at Broad Street, I'd believed his account of the reasons for finding Wale. He'd also been able to give me a clue—Wale's address when, five years earlier, the American relatives had last heard from him.

"That led me to Carol Wale, as I told you. Nothing emerged from it and then later I heard from Ashman again, this time from New York. The aunt had died and he was her executor, and among her papers he'd found another clue. That led me to Wale's birthplace, as I also told you. Nothing came out of it either. In the bank at the moment, credited to Charles Ashman, is the balance due to him."

"Extraordinary," he said. "Anything else?"

"Only this," I said. "I'd got suspicions for various reasons so I spent some money—his money—in checking up. Know what I found? A Charles Ashman wasn't known at the addresses he gave, and there wasn't any aunt in Butte, Montana. Hallows had been right about him all along."

"You don't say!" He shook his head. "And he hasn't tried to get into touch with you since?"

"Never. Not that I'm worrying. What is worrying me is precisely why he was so anxious to find Wale. And conducting the whole business in such a surreptitious way."

"Yes," Jewle said. "He couldn't have been a relative of one of Wale's victims or he wouldn't have needed all that funny business. Or would he? Mightn't he have wanted to avoid scandal?"

I thought it a hundred to one against.

"You know who I now think Ashman was? There's only one snag. The man I saw was clean-shaven and definitely had an

American accent, but isn't it just possible he could have been the man Carol Wale saw that morning with her husband?"

"Could have been," he said. "A beard's nothing. Neither is a phony accent. If you're right, he and Wale pulled off some job or other together."

I pointed out that, judging what Wale made of it, it must have been quite a job.

"Then why does Ashman want Wale again?" he wanted to know. "You think he had another big job nice and handy and only Wale could help pull it off?"

"Don't know," I said. "But there might be just a faint chance of finding out."

"You mean through Wale himself?" He shook his head again. "He's on the mend but he won't be able to talk for some days. Even then he'll probably tell us another pack of lies."

"Not through Wale. Through Ashman himself."

He gave me a quick look. "How d'you mean?"

"Well, I've a queer feeling that Ashman's still in town. The more I think about it, the more I'm convinced he wanted Wale uncommonly badly, and here's the most likely place to find him."

"Just a minute," he said. "Oughtn't Ashman to have known where Wale was? Assuming they'd been confederates?"

"Not necessarily. After pulling off that job, they'd almost certainly have had to split up. An elementary precaution: at least that's the way we have to look at it if we're going to find Ashman. We've got to assume Ashman's still in town and just as eager to find Wale. If that's so, then there's just a chance we might lay our hands on him. And within twenty-four hours."

"You really mean it?"

Two big cups of coffee had made me pretty uncomfortable. I said I'd adjourn for repairs and tell him about Ashman on the way to the Yard.

17

MEET MR. ASHMAN

THERE was only a short distance to walk, even allowing for stops, and we were actually outside the Yard for most of what I was telling him. He wanted me to come up to his room but I said I'd have to be getting back to Broad Street. Hallows was due and I wanted to see him.

"This is the idea," I said, as soon as we'd left the restaurant. "It'll need your co-operation and the hospital's. You get in touch with the Press at once and give them the whole of the new slant on the Mayland shooting. Get them to give prominence to the fact that it's been established that Louis Marquette was really Harry Wale. Make it a sensation. You can divulge, if you like, his former activities. Anything to get his name in as near banner headlines as makes no difference."

"I'm beginning to see. But go on."

"What has to be done is to make sure every paper runs the story, and runs it big. It's got to be something that Ashman, if he's still in town, just can't miss."

"I see. And you think he'll call up at the hospital to make enquiries?"

"On certain conditions. You'll have to fix things with the hospital. Take them into your confidence. Get them to understand just what you want done and why. Why, for instance, you want to have printed that the patient's now on the mend and likely to be transferred very soon to a prison hospital. If that doesn't bring Ashman running, what will?"

"And then?"

"Again you'll have everything fixed with the hospital. You and I'll be there and I'll be able to identify him as soon as he steps up to the enquiry desk. All we'll need is somewhere handy, so as to have him under observation soon as he walks inside. Any other arrangements are up to you."

"Well, any port in a storm," he told me. "It's worth trying. I may have to have a word with the Higher-Ups. I'll ring you when everything's fixed."

As it turned out, I was to be the one who rang him. Hallows was waiting for me when I reached Broad Street. We adjourned to my room for a word or two before he went home.

"Norris was telling me you did pretty well at Birmingham,"

I told him. "Don't take that the wrong way. Don't start talking about a raise."

He laughed.

"I may do so yet. Wait till you hear what I've got to tell you. You remember after we'd first seen that man Ashman, that I thought I'd seen him before? Well, it was when I was driving back this morning I suddenly remembered where. At Sandford, when we were doing that job for Jedmont. The man Manning. The one we saw leaving the morning after we got there."

"Manning." I said. "Wale had been hobnobbing with him suddenly during that weekend. But wait a minute. Manning was a much older man, surely. He had a game leg and walked with a stick."

He smiled. "I could powder my hair and have a game leg. Easiest thing in the world."

He was right. I asked Bertha to get Jewle. A minute and she was telling me he was engaged. He mightn't be free for another half-hour. I told her to leave a message that he was to ring me.

"You're wondering what all this is about." I told Hallows. "Since you were here, there've been quite a few developments in the Jedmont blackmail case."

"More than there was in the papers?"

I brought him bang up to date, including what might be happening the next morning. I'd just finished when Jewle rang.

"Sorry I was engaged," he said. "You had some more ideas, or what?"

I told him about Manning. Manning. Hallows would be prepared to swear, was Ashman. If so, he and Wale had probably cooked up their scheme during that weekend at Sandford. Jewle said he'd bear it in mind.

"We've had a bit of good luck here too," he said. "Matthews didn't know anything about that missing photograph, but he now remembers that when he was checking Gledmill's personal belongings and handing them over to his father, there was a photograph, like the one we want, in his wallet. We got on the telephone to him and he found it. He's putting it in the post and it ought to be here at the latest by the morning."

It was nine o'clock before anything else happened. Jewle then rang to say everything had been arranged. I thought we should run no risks and be there at the earliest moment. We settled for eight o'clock.

I had breakfast early that morning and I took a packet of sandwiches and a Thermos of coffee with me in case we had a long wait. Jewle was arriving by car. At that hour of the morning there'd be plenty of parking space behind the hospital. I took a bus and went in by the Romney Street entrance. He was waiting for me just inside.

Across from the enquiry desk the small room that had once housed the cleaners' buckets and mops had been cleared and a couple of chairs had been brought in. The upper half of its door was glazed and we had a perfect view. A special arrangement had been made at the desk. If any caller whatever enquired about a Louis Marquette or a Harry Wale, whoever was on duty would stand up.

The room was far from warm. Jewle had brought his own coffee, so we had an early tot and settled ourselves in.

"My newspapers hadn't arrived when I left," I said. "They made a good job of it?"

"Pretty good," he said. "The bait's good enough. Now it depends on the fish."

It was slow work. You watched, you interchanged a few words and watched again. There was plenty of movement at even that early hour: staff comings mostly, but it meant you couldn't relax.

Then things got a bit easier after nine o'clock. Jewle suddenly felt in his pocket and gave me something. It was that photograph.

"Came by the last post yesterday," he told me. "You were right about Wale being the one on the left. Do you see how it's been cut down?"

I thought I'd mentioned it some days before.

"We think it was heavily trimmed so as to conceal the background." he said. "As it is, it might be anywhere. Luckily we happen to know the exact locality." He smiled. "And it isn't in France."

"Who did the trimming? Jedmont?"

We had a little argument then about names. To avoid getting muddled, Louis would still be Louis and not Wale. "It was Louis," Jewle said, "who'd done the cutting down. If he hadn't, the photograph would have revealed that the yarn he'd spun me was an obvious lie."

"And the other man. You've identified him?"

He chuckled. "Didn't take much doing. I was the one who hauled him in."

He caught my look of surprise.

"His name's Hensell: George Hensell. I looked up the whole case again last night."

He began filling his pipe. There wasn't any need for a leading question. I knew he wasn't going to leave things there.

"George Hensell." he said. "One of the cleverest crooks in the game. Con-man, thief, international swindler."

He got the pipe going.

"I almost got to like him," he told me. "One thing about him, he was a sportsman. And no strong-arm stuff. The only thing he ever used was his brain. Never let a confederate down. The only ones he ever double-crossed were the victims."

"Sounds interesting," I said. "Tell me about him. How you came to pick him up, and so on."

"I'll give you the whole story," he told me. "Keep your eyes out there in case I should be looking away."

The pipe had gone out but he got it going again.

"George Hensell," he said. "The cleverest crook I ever ran across. Unique. That's the only thing you could call him—unique. And you'll see why."

He looked up as if to marshall his facts.

"He was one of those absolutely bi-lingual French Canadians. Born at a little place not far from Montreal, called la Messière. Why we know that is because he started off his career on the wrong foot. Did one job in the American North-west and then tried another far too close. That got him two years. It also taught him that if he was to go on being a crook, he'd have to use his brains. And he did.

"He pulled off a big coup in Florida a couple of years later. Three years after that he did another job in the Argentine. Some time later he did another on the French Riviera, and it takes brains to do a job there. They tell me the crooks are so thick, they have to queue up. The last he did was in Cairo. No, not the last. That was the one he did over here."

"How was it known it was he who did those jobs?"

"Correlation of technique. When he did a job it had always been planned down to the very last detail, even the getaway. Also he never pulled off anything but the real big stuff. And with diamonds. Always with diamonds. It's reckoned he's got a young fortune salted away in various banks all over the world. The job he actually pulled over here will show what I mean. I'll tell you just what he did. A lot of this, by the way, never came out at his trial. Pleading Not Guilty was just a formality. He was hooked and he knew it.

"What he did was to live for a year at various London hotels while he looked round. The last was the Golden Vine in Carswell Street. Then he had all the preliminaries in his mind. The victims he chose were Elwin and Vine, of Old Bond Street. You know them?"

I shook my head.

"Nothing much to look at from outside. The surviving partner was a Robert Vine, a man of about seventy. A tall, well-groomed, military-looking sort of man. Reckoned to be the best judge of a stone in London. He was the man Hensell had to deal with.

"First he went to Amsterdam and bought a single diamond from a well-known firm called Dirkssen. It cost him just over five thousand pounds. Then he hired a smart Daimler: a Rolls might have looked a bit too impressive. His confederate, Wale, was the private chauffeur. Then he called on Robert Vine at Old Bond Street.

"He was executing, he said, a commission for a friend: a wealthy Texas oil-man. He produced the diamond. Money was no great object with the friend. What he wanted was not less than six reasonably matching stones to be made up into a sort of necklace-pendant for his daughter on her twenty-first birthday. Vine thought he could find the stones. To show good faith, Hensell left his diamond, merely taking a receipt: ostensibly so that Vine could be better able to do the matching up. He also mentioned where he'd bought that stone. I should tell you that Vine wasn't the fool he afterwards appeared. He did check up on that stone.

"Hensell said he was only in England for a fortnight all told. He was going to Manchester and then on to Edinburgh where he had relations. He'd be back in five days, and he wanted to bring with him an old friend, a German named Pieter Lander, who'd spent some years in South Africa and who was an authority on stones. Vine naturally agreed. Lander, of course, was Wale.

"On the eve of the final visit, Hensell rang Vine from Edinburgh and learned that there'd be stones ready for inspection. Hensell said he'd get into touch at once with Lander and have him fly over. I didn't tell you the date. It was April the 20th, four-and-a-half years ago.

"The appointment was fixed for five o'clock the next day. At half-past, Vine was getting anxious. Then Hensell rang, ostensibly from London Airport. Lander's plane had been delayed and he'd only just arrived. The two would get to Old Bond Street just as quickly as the car could make it.

"The shop was closed at six o'clock as usual but Vine asked his head assistant, a man named Yalden, to stay on. Hensell and Lander arrived at a quarter-past. They'd been further delayed, Hensell said, through looking for a parking place. The car, I should say, was now non-existent. It had been returned to the hire company the day before.

"At any rate, the four men got down to business. Lander's English wasn't all that good and Vine had no German, but they got on well enough. The stones were produced and then Lander produced a gun. It was a dummy, but Vine didn't have time to investigate. Hensell had cord and gags in his briefcase and before you could say Bob's your uncle, he and Yalden were trussed up. Lander got the keys from Vine's pocket, the safe was opened and that was that. The total haul was worth about eighty thousand pounds."

He chuckled. "You see the beauty of it? That original stone never cost Hensell a cent."

"All the same, it took nerve," I said. "What if something had slipped up?"

"It wouldn't," he said. "Hensell knew it wouldn't. If he'd had any suspicions when Yalden let him into that shop, he'd have gone through the business in the orthodox way and then asked for one more day in order to make up his mind."

"Wait a minute," I said. "Something must have slipped up. You arrested him."

"I know," he said. "That's something I've never quite fathomed. Within an hour of that job being pulled, we had an anonymous call telling us about the robbery and where Hensell could be picked up. He was drunk, or so I thought, when I entered the room, and later that night Vine identified him. There wasn't a trace of the loot, or of Lander. Hensell never revealed a thing, and all we could think was that Lander had double-crossed his partner. Lander was never caught up with. No one knew a thing about him. Hensell got five years."

So there it was. Practically everything, as I told Jewle, was crystal clear. Hensell and my Ashman had to be the same person. And no wonder Ashman wanted so badly to find Wale!

"It couldn't fit in better," I told Jewle, and that was all I said. He was suddenly gripping my arm. My eyes had momentarily left the area I should have been watching and now I saw the man who was approaching the desk: a tall man wearing a dark overcoat and a black Homburg. A tightly rolled umbrella hung over his arm. A dark, trimmed beard neatly encircled his chin.

"Follow my leads," Jewle told me, "and don't be surprised at anything you hear."

We moved out of the room while the caller waited patiently at the desk. The duty sister looked up and he raised his hat and leaned forward. A moment and the sister was standing. She was probably telling him she'd have to consult a doctor. Jewle and I were practically at the desk when she sat down again. She was asking a question. Jewle coughed loudly and the man looked round. Jewle's face beamed.

"Well, if it isn't an old friend! How are you, Hensell?"

Hensell smiled. He caught sight of me.

"How are you, Mr. Ashman?" I said. "Glad I caught up with you. I owe you best part of a couple of hundred dollars."

He wasn't abashed. He was still smiling gently as he held out his hand. It might really have been a meeting of two old friends.

"Nice to see you again, Mr. Travers. You are a friend of the Superintendent here?"

"You might say that," I said as Jewle began shepherding him away from the desk.

"And you two boys cooked this up?"

Jewle took his arm. "Something like that. But what about a nice quiet chat? There's a little private room just over there."

Ashman—let me call him that—stopped in his tracks. He brushed off Jewle's arm. The smile left his face and I was suddenly wondering just what he'd have done if he'd ever caught up with Wale.

"Why a chat?" he said. "You've nothing more on me. I served my time."

"You've got me all wrong," Jewle told him placatingly. "I'm asking you to do us a favour. Just one or two things I'd like to hear straight from the horse's mouth, so to speak. Things I've never understood. Just a friendly chat. And I give you my word you can walk out of that room whenever you like. No one on your tail. Everything strictly confidential."

Ashman shrugged his shoulders. He looked at me but I'd nothing to add. A moment and he was moving forward.

It must have been the most extraordinary interview that Jewle had ever taken part in, and I'd known some queer ones in my time. I said I'd get another cup if Ashman would like some coffee. He hesitated, then he smiled for the first time since entering that room.

"Just so long as it's only coffee."

"No dope this time," Jewle told him.

I found an orderly and brought back a cup. Jewle lifted his own plastic container.

"Happy days, Hensell. May we all keep our noses clean."

Ashman drank. He said it wasn't bad for English coffee.

"Where're you staying now?" Jewle asked him. "The Ritz or the new Hilton?"

"Just staying," Ashman told him gently. "But, just between ourselves, I'm thinking of retiring. When you two boys can trick me, I'm losing my grip. By the way, what was it you wanted to ask me?"

"I'll give you some information first," Jewle told him. "You've read the papers, so you know that Wale set himself up in the restaurant business under the name of Louis Marquette. He had a partner: chap called Gledmill. Gledmill was shot dead the same time Wale was badly wounded. He'll get a pretty long stretch if he recovers, so just leave him alone. When you've retired to Honolulu or Miami or whatever it is you're thinking of, you'll be able to think of him, sweating it out in jail. But tell us. How'd you ever come to get tied up with a slippery customer like that?"

"May I put in a question?" I said. "Wasn't it at the Farina Hotel in Sandford? When you were a certain Mr. Manning?"

He looked surprised. "How'd you know?"

"A little bird told him," Jewle said. "But seriously, how'd you let yourself get suckered like that?"

Ashman shrugged his shoulders.

"Because I wanted someone and he fitted in. I had that Bond Street job lined up and I'd been looking for someone. I'd been watching him working on that dame and I liked his technique. Smooth. Economical. I told him he was wasting his talents. Working for peanuts. Then I found out he spoke a couple of languages. His French wasn't all that hot but I saw a use for his German, so I gave him the chance to cut in."

"And later you saw him at Ilmoor?" I suggested. "Must have been a surprise when his wife walked in."

He smiled a bit grimly. "You sure did get around."

"Just another little bird," Jewle told him. "But tell me something else. I've often wondered exactly what happened that night when I picked you up."

Ashman thought for a moment.

"Well, you must have been played for a sucker in your time, so there's no harm in telling you. We split up outside that shop and I had the stuff in my pockets and we were to meet at my hotel. When we got there we did a quick appraisal of the stuff so as to work out his cut, then I got out the cash ready to pay him off. While I was doing that he suggested a couple of drinks to celebrate. He handled it When you walked in that night I was only just beginning to wake up."

"Tough luck," Jewle told him. "And when Mr. Travers met you that morning at that country pub, I take it they just turned you loose?"

"That's right," he said. "Dansbury Jail. Not too bad a place as things go. All I was doing was avoiding anyone who might be having any ideas. You know, that I might have stashed the stuff."

"Tell me," I said, "why all that hocus-pocus about Butte, Montana? Why there?"

"I can tell you that," Jewle said. "He operated in the North-west when he first set up in business. A long, long time ago. He made his first slip in Butte and it cost him two years in Deer Lodge. But here's something that might interest you. Take a good look at it."

It was that photograph. Ashman looked at it. He looked at Jewle and he looked at it again.

"You can keep it if you like," Jewle told him. "Something to look at when you're in Miami. Taken, as you see, just as you and

Wale split up outside that shop. Someone saw you two together that early evening and he knew you both. He used to go down to the Farina to see his aunt: the one that Wale was working on. So he kept you two in sight. He was a very skilled photographer. For all I know, he may have used a long-distance lens, or whatever they call it. A chap called Jedmont. You've read about him. The one who shot Wale and his partner. But what you don't know is that he certainly followed one of you to that hotel and when Wale came out he followed him too. The next morning he read about that robbery and after that he stuck to Wale closer than a brother. Later he blackmailed him to the extent of five thousand pounds. Then he waited till your sentence, with remissions, was over, and put the screws on again. If Wale didn't pay. he was going to hand him over to you. He didn't know where you were, but it was good enough to terrorise Wale."

Ashman shook his head. His jaws clamped together.

"Another dirty bastard."

"Yes," Jewle said. "But let's get things in the right perspective. You thought you'd pull a neat little job over here, and you did: only it just didn't end there. One man got killed. Another may die. Also a woman got killed. Jedmont's wife. They had to kidnap her to get the negatives back. A young woman, Hensell. Just twenty-six and the whole of her life in front of her. And all that because you decided to do a neat little job."

"No, no; you're getting it wrong. Let me tell you how I see it—"

"No!" The word was like an explosion. "You'll tell me nothing. I'll do the telling and I'm telling you this. You'll be out of this country in twenty-four hours. If you ever set foot here again, by God I'll get you! I'll get you if I have to pin a rap on you."

The voice was shaking with anger. He let out a breath. He waved a hand.

"Now get out of here. Go where you damn well please, but get out!"

He went. We stood at the door and watched him go. He stopped for a mere moment at the swing doors and just lifted his hand as if in ironic salute, then he went through.

Jewle let out another breath. "Five years ago there were times when I almost liked him. But not today. You know what I mean?"

It was easy enough to know. I was rather thoughtful myself as we collected our belongings.

Then I thought of something: just one of those queer things one remembers at queer times.

"I should have known about him just coming out of that jail. We'd passed it on our way and later on Hallows began suggesting various odd things about him. And there was at the pub. Something he said. He said it almost vehemently. About the only thing for a man was God's fresh air."

"Oh, no," Jewle said. "Far too long a shot. Where'd you like me to drop you? At Broad Street?"

"The case is over," I said, "so doesn't that entitle us to a little celebrating ourselves? Look, I'll stand you a lunch. I'd love to. What about the club?"

During that meal we did a lot of talking and I propounded my theory of the three-ring puzzle. Here it is by way of epilogue. Straight from the brain of the old philosopher himself: Ludovic Travers, the poor man's Bertrand Russell. Or should it be Benjamin Franklin?

As I tried to point out to Jewle, the whole of that case had been a three-ring puzzle, and I explained just what that puzzle was. The three rings aren't intact. They're cut through and then pressed inwards so that the cut ends overlap. That's the great thing about it. It seems so easy to slip a ring through the gap. But you're not allowed to use force. You have to get two rings in one special position and then—hey presto!—they're joined up. After that, getting the third ring on the other two is only a matter of form, except that the two rings tend to clutter things up.

You could draw all sorts of analogies. After all, a puzzle is a puzzle, whether it be to discover the correct manipulation of three pieces of stainless-steel wire or to discover what lies behind the manipulations of certain men for their own special ends. Our three rings were Ashman, Wale and Jedmont, and it took a very long time to know they were rings at all. It took till that very morning to fit them snugly together. The whole thing had been cluttered up with lies: not that that was a matter for grumbling. A puzzle wouldn't be a puzzle if it had no false trails.

There's just one other thing I should add. In a little Soho shop that deals largely in the apparatus of practical jokes—fake cigars, rubber-tipped matches, exploding golf balls and the like—I actually found the other day one of those three-ring puzzles. When I asked the proprietor how it worked, his quick look had in it a touch of superiority. After he'd worked on it for three or four minutes, he said, too offhandedly, that he must have forgotten. In any case I didn't want it for myself. I'm sending it to Jewle for Christmas.

THE END

CPSIA information can be obtained
at www.ICGtesting.com
Printed in the USA
LVHW050538180322
713725LV00004B/57

9 781915 014702